A Certain Woman

A Certain Woman

Hala El Badry

Translated by
Farouk Abdel Wahab

The American University in Cairo Press
Cairo   New York

English translation copyright © 2003 by
The American University in Cairo Press
113 Sharia Kasr el Aini, Cairo, Egypt
420 Fifth Avenue, New York 10018
www.aucpress.com

First published in Arabic in 2001 as *Imra'atun ma*
Copyright © 2001 by Hala El Badry
Protected under the Berne Convention

First paperback edition 2006

Dar el Kutub No. 8081/06

Dar el Kutub Cataloging-in-Publication Data

El Badry, Hala
      A Certain Woman / Hala El Badry.—Cairo: The American
  University in Cairo Press, 2006
      224p.   23cm.
      ISBN 977-416-028-2
      1. Arabic Fiction
      813

Designed by Joanne Cunningham/AUC Press Design Center
Printed in Egypt

Translator's Note

In consultation with the author, I have edited and condensed parts of "Unplanned Communities" in Part Four and "Land Mines" in Part Five. I take sole and full responsibility for these revisions. The controversy depicted in "Pursuit" in Part Six is an almost factual description of the furor created by the re-publication in Egypt, by an agency of the Egyptian Ministry of Culture, of Syrian author Haydar Haydar's novel, *A Banquet for Seaweed.* Deemed blasphemous and denounced as such by vocal Islamists, it caused riots by students of al-Azhar, Egypt's oldest Islamic university, and started a heated, sometimes quite violent discussion about censorship, art, and freedom of expression, a discussion that is still going on. I would like to thank the following friends for help with various aspects of the translation: Dina Rabadi and Katherine Strange (University of Chicago) and Neil Hewison and Kelly Zaug (The American University in Cairo Press).

A Maze

She turned off the headlights of her car and sneaked through the gate of the garden into the house now bathed in a quiet semidarkness. A strong fragrance wafted from the white lilies she had picked in the early morning and put in the crystal vases in different rooms. The flowers shed smooth yellow pollen that looked like a light powder throughout the ground floor of the villa, creating a pervasive presence akin to lavender. Most of the sunflowers had drooped, except those that were close to the pale light escaping from the yellow chandeliers casting variegated shadows through the brass, which was cut in shapes suggestive of branches and leaves. Everything in the place suggested a delicate, soft taste; jarring it, though, was a mess of rolls of paper, drawings, and maps stacked under a statue of Alexander the Great, above which a constant light burned. At the other end of the long corridor, she moved quietly, anxious not to be heard, and stood under the clothes tree, her shadow reflected on the glass table that rested on a porcelain nymph. She tried hard to avoid disturbing the creatures she loved—the plants, the dogs, and the cats—by her physical presence.

She reached for a light cotton nightgown and a pair of slippers, then carefully unbuttoned her blouse as she followed the movements of a cricket that kept chirping more loudly than her own heartbeats, which she thought were thundering. She threw all her clothes on the chair and a statue of Venus on the nearby bookshelf almost toppled. She dashed to catch it before it hit the floor. She swallowed hard and breathed deeply. When finally she found herself safely inside her nightgown, she grew bolder and turned on the television only to find that it was toward the end of the programs for the day—the late news. She turned on the radio, turning the dial to "The Music Program." She didn't know, as she opened the big window overlooking the garden on the north side, that she did this every day at the same time and that she took deep breaths thousands of times, as if she were trembling, for fear of making any sound—as if she were penetrating invisible barriers.

When she pushed the door, which made its usual squeaking sound, she turned toward it, placing one hand on her mouth and the other on the door to prevent the screen door from slamming back hard, but it did anyway. It was as if she were hearing it for the first time. She stepped into the garden and her dog Rocky came and rubbed against her feet. She patted his head thinking, "He's the first to sense my presence. He always comes to me cheerfully." She had taught Rocky not to make a sound when he welcomed her so she wouldn't be found out. He would just sit next to her as she read, as if the two of them had been created sitting like that from the beginning of time. She patted the head of a statue of the famous Greek horse which was rearing on its hind legs, opening its wings halfway as it got ready to fly. It represented her recurring dream that she is unable to realize, unable to free her feet which are planted deep into the ground. "O Pegasus, Pegasus!" a sigh that often reverberated in the midst of the plants and the flowers. Her eyes surveyed the garden and she reassured herself of the calm, which she described as "the condition that allows beings other than us to possess the universe on their own, regardless of us." A male frog called his mate and a disquieting thought occurred to her: "Is Mustafa really asleep or just pretending, or avoiding me? I know he wakes up when I enter the house. Many times I think he knows everything."

She picked up the last chapter of Omar's new novel *A Maze* as her shadow grew longer on the garden wall and extended so much that her hand seemed to reach their neighbor's first floor apartment. She began to read the murder scene. "Omar describes my house so precisely, as if he has lived in it even though he hasn't visited me here even once. Maybe because of the many details he's heard from me." She continued to devour the words with loving, proud eyes under a lamp that focused the light on the pages of the book alone.

"His comments," she thought, "do not come from just thin air. Does it make sense that he has resigned himself to our situation? Living a double life together, one half of it public, preserving the social status, and the other half secret? Why does he accept it when he's always turning his back on the past? Is it just to hold on to what he owns? Is it a question of pride? This is an oversimplification! Why do I feel that my senses are so worked up, as if things around me were throbbing inside my own nerves?" She shuddered as she felt unable to concentrate on her fear of sounds getting louder, or the lights dancing, or the heat permeating her body, or the suspense that Omar was creating around his heroine, who represented her. She read on:

"Everything around me is tied to a wire wound around my guts. There's something mysterious, some debris that I keep trying in vain to climb out of, as if seeing a cloud darkening the sky the whole time. It is seldom cloudy during the summer here. Is the sky telling me something that I fail to grasp?"

A long black tail. It must be that of a cat, for rats don't have such big tails. How come I didn't see it when it went by me to reach the bamboo chair on this side? It's a cat, no doubt about it. A second set of eyes shining on the other side means they are getting together for one reason or another.

"Omar," she thought to herself, "wrote this ending without being convinced of it, just to be contrary to my opinion. I told him, 'Let him kill her.' But he said, 'I don't want to give in. It would mean that the novel is condemning her. This would satisfy society, which is leading two con-tradictory lives itself.'"

She was startled when a gray cat suddenly appeared in front of the black cat. She made a gesture as if she was going to throw something at it and the two cats ran towards the trees. Their shadows that a short while ago looked like a wedding of ghosts, scattered. She clasped her hands together as she stretched on the chair, resting her feet on the opposite chair, exactly like the scene she is reading:

When he made out the car's lights and sensed her sneaking into the house, he stood in the midst of the plants in the balcony, quietly blending in with the prevailing calm until the atmosphere got accustomed to his body heat. He thought to himself, "How come she doesn't feel this heat near her when she uses instinct to know the world around her exactly like wary wild creatures? Does the daily physical caution and her focus on not waking me up make her fail to realize that I am actually here? Perhaps she thinks I am unaware of how she is leading her life. She has eliminated me from her life as if she has the ability to do that. We'll know now who can eliminate whom."

He had spent the afternoon rearranging the plant pots. He replaced large pots with smaller ones placed on the shelf above where she always sits to read after midnight. He placed a thin piece of wood between the steel shelf and the pot so it wouldn't slip prematurely. When he was totally sure that he could pull the piece of wood causing the pot to slide down, he carefully put it there, making sure the piece of wood kept it in place. He replaced two other pots using the same method. The sky above the garden was now full of perils.

She noticed her shadow elongated in front of her on the wall as she turned the page. She wondered to herself, "Who put the chair for me with such precision as if preparing it for me?"

She smiled as she raised her head towards the sky. Her eyes caught a huge plant pot hurtling down from the edge of the balcony on the floor above. Behind it she discerned a deep gleam in Mustafa's eyes as they narrowed with an intense hate that she hadn't seen in him before. The sudden panic was mixed with an ironic understanding of the story, so she smiled broadly without moving from where she was.

Meeting

I watched him take the cigar out of its cellophane wrapper and calmly put it in his mouth in silence, and as he lit it, he gave himself totally to it, puffing it with a smoothness that reminded me of the sun setting in October, then exhaling as if saying goodbye to a close friend. His sharp eyes were alert the whole time, yet if one watched closely, one would observe that he was totally absorbed in the moment at hand, in a single thought that was in sole control of his mind. It was as if his eyes were a vigilant sentinel watching the outside and leaving his full attention to the depths of his world.

I decided to attract his attention. I chose a seat opposite his, awaiting an opportunity to have a direct conversation with him. The group was discussing censorship of books. I described my own experience of shipping my library after finishing my studies in Paris, and how I was a strict censor to make sure only certain books reached Egypt. I sorted out the books meticulously, sacrificing everything that was published abroad— books about the Camp David agreement signed by Sadat and Begin, things about the July Revolution, and the memoirs of General Shazli on the October War. He took note and participated in the discussion, which lasted a long time. His answers came as I had expected them, reflecting a broad culture, of one who was comfortable with himself, one who, at least, knew what he wanted. Thus, I scored a goal and waited.

Where do you get the feeling that you know where a certain point initiated by another will end? How can you be sure that you are in agreement about pivotal subjects that have not even been broached, or about the very basic foundations of life? Is it experience? Intuition, feeling, or equations by which the mind can solve the riddle of the person in front of it and classify him? Is this classification any good at knowing the qualities of the person you fall in love with, such as being broadminded, highly cultured, kind, precise, brave, self-confident, firm, polite, and handsome, to say that he is the awaited one? Why does someone attract attention before uttering a single word and we count them in the group? Are certain qualities sufficient as a reason for love, or is the reason something mysterious that touches a need that is invisible and perhaps hidden from oneself, something that the person knocking on the soul's door has? It was the course of a wave that I allowed to travel freely from me to him and which I received without wariness upon its return, warm and redolent.

O God! Where did I get this certainty that I knew everything about him, everything he thought of or worried about? I didn't wait for any explanation or information. His deep and melodious voice was enough for me. Does a deep voice offer reassurance or intimate knowledge? I still don't know the details of his features but I feel them in their harmony. When I listened to him the first time, I noticed the perfect harmony between his voice and his being, and that it was inevitable that his voice sounded as it did. The voice did not make his features complete, but rather emanated from them. I didn't know the shape of his eyes or their color but I knew what the iris reflected. What happened to the constant chatter I usually hid behind? And why did I content myself with a nod or a small gesture or an understanding glance? I almost touched his hand to let him know I understood what he meant, but I stopped short of that, content with what remained available to me after I lost my words, retaining only "yes" and "I understand," as I followed what he was saying. The title of one book or another would be mentioned and one of us would start talking while the other would be all ears. We conspired against words, sacrificing their meanings for what was behind them, for the continuity of the moment, for that which was flowing between us without prior planning, exuding warmth, covering us unawares within a circle that kept getting tighter, bringing us close together and abolishing the distance between us. For a few moments I felt the heat of his body across the table separating us.

I nodded this time to myself, reassuring, without a sound, "I understand." My eyes clouded for a short journey during which I rested my head on his shoulder and I felt its heat, and that he was coming away with me even though my eyes were still staring at his face as he kept talking. We defied our apparent apartness as our friends engaged in the conversation enthusiastically. We dug a secret passage to which we had a key and through which we were able to escape, away from the noise and the crowd of friends. It was enough for one of us to turn our head for the other to understand that one is looking for the other and for the silent dialogue to begin.

When I told him that I had organized my world in a manner satisfactory to me, that I knew what I wanted out of life, I was telling him the truth. I described my family to him, my job, my present and future goals, and placed them all together in a small, tiny bundle in his hands. I was telling the truth because, at that moment, I was not introducing myself at the deep levels but rather at the level I dealt with inside me, away from the accesses that were totally closed. I had accustomed myself to accept what I planned for within what was available, and to spare my hidden secret a battle for control of the rest of my world. I contented myself by leaving for that secret a shadow of grief that I couldn't control, one that could be discerned only by a very attentive person who could undo the many veils of mirth that covered my every movement. But the shadow would cover the whole area once I fell silent. That was why I was always boisterous, my smile filling the void of my soul, not permitting the hole to get wider, letting out the big question that Omar might pose: "This is what you've accomplished?" So hearing it one day would be like someone shot by a blank cartridge, not deadly, but forcing them to look at the only place they don't want to see.

I didn't ask, as I got closer, *Why get closer, considering the details of our lives?* I got closer because I was aware I needed him, I was comfortable with him, because a channel between us had opened up. So why should I go looking for a name for it? I was accustomed over the years, with every man who attracted my attention or stirred a question inside me, to counter curiosity with knowledge, to take real delight in his entering my life as a friend. So the private between us became public. I would tell him in a loud voice that he is close, in other words, I would divulge the secret. Thus, I took part in self-deception and did not have to resort to little tricks to continue talking throughout the trip and when we sat together for hours on the way back, talking non-stop, we noticed two prying eyes whose owner said, "Wow!"

We got off the train. I bid him farewell and left, clutching my bag in my arms like a teenager. I wanted to walk alone for a long time before a car took me home. My movements were those of a young coquette, joyous and feminine, to whom a big, wide world was beckoning. I silently hummed Laila Murad's song, "Love is Beautiful." Was I happy that I was about to fall in love? The question brushed against me tentatively. I dismissed it as I smiled, with the consciousness of a yearning woman and let Omar steal into my veins. And in a moment of resistance to the giant that stood before my forbidden desire, I told myself that he would never find out my feelings. They will be my secret and mine alone. I am capable of putting on masks of imperviousness that will repel any attempt to break the barriers between us. And what if he found out: What are you going to do? He will not find out. I will jam his radar. I have my hands full already with that which is stealing me away from myself. I will let him into my secret garden and close all doors and I'll never give its address to anyone. How about *his* desire? Have you thought about what *he* wants? Don't you at least want to know how *he* feels? I know. His feelings reach me or I give myself the illusion that they do. It doesn't make any difference. I'll enjoy whatever reaches me of his feelings, and that will be enough. I know that I've touched him and I think he'll appreciate my wish to stop at this point and he'll understand. Aren't these questions premature? I don't know!

A few days later I had a change of attitude and kept murmuring to myself, "I'll stop all that's taking place between us. What does this Omar want from me?"

I went out of al-Hanager Hall chewing my words, stung by the cold of a March night after midnight. I made a decisive resolution to remove everything that had to do with him from my life: I've lived all these years capable of protecting myself, not allowing anyone to hurt me. So how come I am such a wimp all of a sudden? Omar had come up to me in a whispering voice to give him a ride at the end of the evening because his car had broken down. I smiled. I had seen his car in the parking lot before entering the Hall. "I'll leave it till the morning and come back with a mechanic," he said.

I was pleased with this unexpected turn of events. I agreed perfunctorily and got lost in thought. A point of light fell into my heart and carried me like a burning meteor to his world, settling there, while leaving part of my mind to tend to my friends. It was a part that, strangely enough, made it possible for me to talk and be merry and to move from one boisterous mood to another, even more boisterous. Oh my God! How was I able to run all these distances without touching the inside? How was I able to be one, then another, then a third, without getting lost? Who said you didn't get lost and that what's left of you is really you? I know who I am. Stop it.

I look around and find that he is silent as usual. An aspiring singer comes in carrying a lute. He sits in the middle singing an old song. I clap rhythmically, accompanying him, and Omar opens one of his curtains and joins in the singing. He comes closer and closes the door to his world on the two of us alone. Am I just imagining this? I run in the corridor between us and meet him in the middle. We become one. Turning back is no longer possible. The hours evaporate. It is time for me to go. There is a meaning in his eyes that I don't understand. I signal to him but he doesn't get it. At the urging of our friend Shaza, the group decides to stay up until the morning and find a place where they serve beer or go to her place. I hesitate to ask him whether he will come with me. I awkwardly extend my hand to shake their hands. Our friend Mahmud says, "Stay with us. We want to spend some time with you before you travel. We'll miss you."

"That's why I want to leave early. I haven't packed yet."

"We will need your car, together with Omar's."

I didn't hear him telling them that his car had broken down. Shaza pulled me by the hand and I sat in anguish for a few minutes. Omar turned towards me, "To Greece? Did you know that Maggie's half Greek, half Italian?"

"Yes."

"I refused to let Sharif, my son, speak anything but Arabic as a child. I wanted him to be pure Egyptian."

"You are right."

The silence in his eyes surprised me. I got up suddenly, waving to them as I stammered, "See you later."

I gripped the steering wheel in anger. I drove my car to an open road that bypasses the city. The air was quite redolent with the early blossoms of March and the fields were showing off their resplendent colors, enticing me to capture them, but I resisted. I am going to stop all that's happening between him and me. I will stop it. Am I holding him responsible for my illusions? All this persistence, then he backs off just because Shaza wants to stay up! He knew her wish before he talked to me. He treats her in a special way. So what does he want from me? I've noticed that from the beginning and I've come to the conclusion that if they had a real thing going, then he wouldn't need me. Why couldn't his interest in her be more than I estimate it to be? Could it be that he is torn between the two of us? That he is still attached there and cannot quite come over to my side completely without stumbling? She is giving him what I cannot. She stays up till the morning with him, that nightly escape which he needs. I don't know why. Am I chasing illusions? A man in love does not look at another woman unless his relationship with the first woman is dying or unless it is just a whim. Yes, I shouldn't expect special treatment. Am I the same woman who said only a few days ago that she will never allow him to find out how she feels about him, that she will treat him like a friend? My passion for him will not torment me and I will not weaken. My passion? Has it come to passion already? Tomorrow I'll be in Greece and I will be busy with my other world. So make the passage with your crackling fires, in fear.

Why did I take his book with me and what was I looking for? The smoke of anger dissipated like lines erased by the wind. When I voraciously began to read between the lines, knowing how he thought helped me figure out what he gave of himself to his characters. I know that an author gives each hero a little bit of their soul, making the characters and their contradictions, and their wavering between good and evil, a little more human. I may be mistaken about that, but I like to believe the idea. I got hold of a thread and stayed with it: the protagonist of his novel suffers in silence and displays bitter sarcasm and great self-esteem, very much like the author. I set up a trap of details that I knew about him and kept closing it on the minutiae of a world that I took to be his world. The more certain I became of my reading, the more deeply I was involved with him. I listened to the cells of his soul in the rhythm of the unspoken, in the words of the book, and I discovered that in his absence he was present at the very heart of my heart. I began to open the curtains in the secret pathways that we paved every time we met and dispersed the dark till he appeared before me. I see him. I am one with him.

Several times I started to dial his number and hung up before I finished dialing, then I grew bolder and finished the dialing and heard his telephone ringing normally as if I were dialing from Egypt, but I hung up before he picked it up. I kept calling him at the times I knew he was not there just to assure myself that he was nearby, then would go back to my world. I caught myself calling him at the newspaper at three a.m. after I finished reading the book, even though I knew that his office was closed and that there was nobody there but the night shift. But I liked the fact that it was possible to try.

I hugged the book as I lay on my bed facing the sea, resting in its dark expanse in the night. The sentences and paragraphs flew to the sky of the room and turned into butterflies that I tried to catch to no avail. They kept coming closer then moving away, beckoning to me, "I am he. I am he." They kept glowing then disappearing in the dark. I called out to them and they quivered and bowed down. They summed up his absence in four letters that they formed in the sky of the room: OMAR. I appealed to them for help. They dispersed and landed everywhere except on my body. They awoke my senses with a flame that broke the spell of an old amulet that had held my soul in thrall, kindling in me a desire to fly to them. And when they rose, I began to shake as I called to them, "Come, come to me." They landed lightly on my hand, then my arm, then my body and my face until they covered me completely. I let my hair down and they climbed in it and disappeared in it as I lay hugging the book whose words I now knew by heart. The butterflies kept going and coming, passing through my body to the pages of the book, the rustling of their wings touching my soul very gently, and leading me to a sleep which was interrupted each time one of them folded its wings. As my eyes open, I see as if through a mist, the resplendent colors of a tender creature, and in my half-awake–half-asleep state, I see the sun lighting its forehead, and in the place of the rustling of the wings whose tunes accompanied me to sleep, I hear its reverberating voice in the expanse, its call to me echoing in my head. I fall asleep only to wake to the movement of a bird with the soft down of a duckling, clearing a spot to lie down in my chest. My heart disappears into depths that I cannot reach, as if I have fallen from a rock onto a precipice. I fall asleep and I hear the whisperings of the water in a lake filled with swans, which call out faintly then clamor. A light coming from wisps of dreams floats before my eyes and a gentle breeze caresses my face. I discover that another night has departed, that the morning has visited me through the window opened by the wind and that the sea has begun its day by bellowing its efforts to escape its confines.

His voice came over the telephone just one day after my return. I had forgotten that I had told him how long I'd be gone. Although I had extended my stay, he thought I had returned a week ago, and was giving me some time to rest, as he told me a month later. Then in a slip of the tongue, which came in the course of a story about a friend of his who was mad at his sweetheart, Omar said, "Sometimes I was dying to speak to her and I sat by the telephone, reading, in the hope that she would call me!"

It hadn't occurred to me that we were acting according to a plan. I thought what was happening between us was spontaneous. I wondered, but I got over it. There is a lot I still don't know about him.

Seduction

Are you the same woman who, when I asked her one day to adjust the folds of my shirt sleeve, gave me a long reproachful look and bowed her head in embarrassment? And when I asked her to hold on to me to catch the bus that had started to move without us, said, "Where?" For whom I suppressed a roaring laugh as a joke occurred to me and I realized that she would be shocked if I said it?

I had begun to form a tentative picture of her, a picture, however, that I couldn't believe. How can a woman approaching forty be so naïve, in spite of her job that forces her to travel, go on excavations, stay in hotels and tents, and deal with workers and engineers of different nationalities? How does she meet all these different people without gaining more experience and knowledge? Is it conceivable that she has not met one man or another on one of her trips that managed to break down the barriers that she hides behind? How has this open world not changed her simple experience with men? How is it possible when she's a married woman?

Sometimes I believe what she offers me consciously or unconsciously, and sometimes I refuse to believe. Why am I so patient with her, giving her more time, feeling my way to her? Have my feelings gone beyond my reach? Have I fallen in love with her, or is she like many other women who crossed paths with me, held my interest for some time, then went on their way? Why does she keep vacillating? Is she in love with me? I feel her gestures taking hold of me, breaking down my dams without meeting any resistance, leaving one of her fingernails inside scratching the wall of my soul. Until when will she refrain from pushing me to take a positive step toward her? And why doesn't she move toward me?

Usually, I let women take the initiative with me. I don't impose myself on them. I make absolutely certain that there is no ambiguity about my understanding of what they want, for I hate nothing more than the attempt of some men to impose themselves boorishly and for no reason on women. So why this silence when it comes to our feelings? We talk on the telephone, we meet among friends and sometimes alone, and we talk about things that interest us, but we don't break the silence. True, she reads my books, and she surprises me with long comments that show not just culture, but also an interest that has not been shown except by my fellow writers. I don't know why or when she began to read books on theory and literary criticism and whether it was before or after we met. No, I remember now. I think I was the reason. She told me once, "True, I am a voracious reader of literature, but I want to read your novels at a level higher than ordinary readers. I want to be able to give you well thought-out opinions that might help you. I also want to place your works among other works, not just in Egypt or the Arab world, but throughout the world. I think you are one of our best writers. Something inside you has not come out yet. I don't know when it will come to the surface, but I can assure you that what you've written, despite all this success, has just barely touched the surface of what you have. Believe me, in a few years, you will be the number one writer in the world." I admit, her words intoxicated me and I hid a tear that almost defeated me, not because she addressed my vanity, but because she touched a dear dream that I secretly revisited from time to time.

I remembered Maggie right away, her always devastating opinions of my books, and the day I asked her not to read any of my work before it was published. I never imagined when I fell in love with her, and not until some time into our marriage, that the day would come when I would fear for myself and for my writing. I thought she would be the biggest motive for my coming success. Now I know she just wants the results of that success, the celebrity and the social status, and the pride she felt when she responded to her family's allegations of alienating herself from them. She would tell them, "I've chosen the right place and the right man." But I never imagined that she would madly delve into the world I create on paper, to take me to task for my thoughts, accusing me of selling my relationship with her in writing, accusing me of prostitution, of revealing the secrets of an intimate relationship. She told me once that the hero's divulging his relations with his woman, like a scandal, has killed her. And she kept searching my thoughts, looking for the secrets that she accused me of disclosing on paper. The night we celebrated the publication of my novel *Cities*, she screamed hysterically as she turned the pages, "I am not this woman! You are presenting me to society as a horrible woman! How will I meet your friends and people? What will they say about me? Socrates' wife?"

We spent an arduous night, during which I tried to explain to her that she was not that woman, and I asked her, "Why can't you be the other woman? Why did you choose this particular type?"

"I know what you instill in the character to make it my likeness, but it's an awful likeness. Didn't you hear the critic in the panel discussion at the Atelier describing your relations with women in your writings as the relationship of a defeated man and that women in your work represent all the evils of the world?"

"That is *her* view, which is not necessarily correct, and you know how some women that criticize are not impartial, and how fanatic about women's issues they can be."

Images of a furious Maggie who turned every celebration of a new work of mine into a fight, after which we stopped talking to each other for months, flashed through my mind. Nahid noticed that I was preoccupied and asked me suddenly, "Did my words upset you? I know you're a daring writer, but you haven't tapped the most precious thing you have: your humanity. I didn't mean that I didn't like what you wrote. Quite the contrary. But I also see what is coming."

I needed to embrace her, to crush her in my arms but I couldn't. I saw her blushing as if she knew my desire, as I haven't seen a fourteen-year-old girl struggling to hide her eyes, turning her face away from me as if she feared being caught in the act of understanding, or finding herself forced to reciprocate the desire with the expected step.

I couldn't sleep that night. I stayed up as usual writing until the sun of the most beautiful morning rose. I was about to dial her number at six o'clock in the morning, but I suppressed my longing patiently, noting how terribly slowly time went. Then I dialed the number and she answered it in a comfortable voice and didn't ask me about the reason for the relatively early time I called. Rather, she welcomed me instantly into her world. Out of the blue I said to her, "I didn't sleep a single minute. How could you sleep?"

I didn't hear her reply. She laughed and asked me if I had spent the night counting the stars. I said, "Yes, someone had caused me to stay up and robbed me of my world."

"You know . . . last year . . ."

I didn't listen to the other words, which took me to an abstract level. I am not used to pleading with women or talking to them about my feelings. I had stayed up preparing my line and she simply swept it aside, not realizing how difficult it was for a man like me.

Where is she taking me? And why am I paying this price when I am so careful to avoid all wounds? I even decided not to bother her again, for I was at least at a stage when I could still control my feelings. She is in a different world. I don't know anything about her marriage and she doesn't talk about private matters. All she talks about is out in the open, which means she says nothing at all. How have I fallen so far despite being so careful? But it doesn't make sense: why does she spend so much time with me if she doesn't think I am somebody special? Why does she show me such playfulness and tenderness that dispels the image of the schoolmarm, which is how I described her when I first saw her? Why does she show me alone this unspoken affection? People love her, yes, but for different reasons; perhaps she takes an active interest in them and declares her sympathy with them, or because of her gaiety or gentleness. It's a picture in which the feminine is missing. I am not going on like this anymore.

I received her first telephone call cautiously and the second less cautiously, and the next time I invited her to dinner.

The familiarity with which we went upstairs to my office did not portend that the course of our lives would change forever. We met by chance at a traffic light. I wasn't paying attention, my mind was still dwelling on a quarrel I had had with the managing editor that morning, when I heard a finger tapping on the car window. I turned and saw her as the light was turning green. I said, "Get in, quick."

She jumped into the seat next to me, asking me as she laughed, "Where to? You will take me out of my way and I have an important appointment."

"Cancel it. I must go to the apartment I use as my office. I have an appointment with some workers. The company will run some tests today to change the plumbing system. If I don't go today, the tenants will be mad at me. And later, we'll see."

"I didn't know you had an outside office."

"Every writer needs a place to write and I am also preparing it to publish a newspaper, and trying to get a license from Cyprus."

When we arrived, I left her to do what she pleased and went to tend to the plumbing. She immediately headed for the books. When I came back she said, "Would you believe that whole shelves are almost an exact copy of my library?"

"I believe."

"Why?"

"Because we haven't met just a short time ago!"

"Is this a poet's or a novelist's imagination?"

"The difference is not that great."

"Tired?"

"Very."

She picked up a little cushion and held it like a baby, rocking it gently and playfully without making a sound. We both burst out laughing and I said to her, "Come and sit by my side." She continued to rock the cushion and blushed. I extended my hand to her and she got up to sit next to me. I stroked her hair and she bowed her head. When I bent over to kiss her, she withdrew inside herself and I couldn't tell whether she had desire or was just acquiescent. I hugged her and noticed her hands shaking as they tentatively clasped my waist. I pressed her lips and she moved her palms and felt my back. I felt that that act was the utmost she was capable of. I said to her, "I love you," and she said, "Me too." Then she fell silent and I felt the heat of her face turn into a burning flame against my shoulder.

I received the news of the separation from her husband calmly. Months had passed with us deep in love. Neither one of us could stand to be apart from the other for even a single day and neither one of us dared ask the other about the other person in our lives. She told me much later, "I didn't want to picture you with her. That would have given me pain that I couldn't bear. She, until now, does not exist in my memory, totally erased so I can live."

I didn't know how she managed to maintain that erasure. I watched in silence without intervening. We still have a lot to discover together.

Waiting

Long physical skirmishes that lead nowhere. This is what makes a man so tense. I know. I first had to make the decision that my desire for him was final, that the meeting of the bodies will mean I will not one day go back on the decision to end my relationship, my complex relationship, with Mustafa. Even though I had gone such a long way in separating from him that we no longer had an actual married life.

Despite my dreams of someone dropping in from the sky on a parachute, my being a mother made my desires unrealizable dreams, or made me content to have them as just that—mere dreams. My personal life was lost under the pressure of motherhood. I have never shirked my responsibilities. Can a mother leave her young or deprive them of their father if the father wished to continue? Maybe some other mother. I hadn't realized that children stayed children even after they grew up and that there was no hope for reciprocity after they moved out on their own. My ability to adjust made the status quo palatable, acceptable to all. Mustafa's relative calm and his love for me softened the bitterness of my anger and threw it into the well accustomed to catching grief. Our mutual respect for each other's feelings in the minutest daily details was reflected in both our relationship and outside in the society at large. So we were envied and cited as perfect models of happiness in marriage. We organized our lives in routines that each of us knew very clearly, and made sure they provided for the other's needs. Each of us was able to make decisions that accommodated the other, even if we had not consulted one another about it. Strict discipline and sound child rearing principles gave the children real care. We were able to overcome the bumps and detours on the road of life and we had friendships that I made sure were not very intimate.

I dealt with myself the way a political prisoner dealt with his mind in solitary confinement. I once listened to the experience of a communist who described how he protected his mind from breakdown, using his education and the experiences of other prisoners of dictatorial regimes that tortured them brutally. I never imagined that one day I would need his method to keep my psychological balance and protect my mind from collapse. He said, "I divided my day into hours, each of which was devoted to recalling specific pieces of information or special memories in a time schedule that ended with my release from prison. When that program neared completion I added other topics, some of which were problems that had faced me in the past, and I would correct decisions that I had made or courses that I had taken. Loneliness helped clarify my thinking. A large chain made up of endless small circles each always leading to the next. The dream is about to become reality. Tomorrow will bring the revolution."

This is exactly what I did with myself: "Tomorrow will bring the solution to the problem," and a series of little goals which I pursued, postponing the big dream to the following year, then the one after. Thus, I immersed myself in my daily tasks, teaching my children, being creative in my work, and following my job from one project to another. Can this success be accomplished without a whip flogging my back? Nothing gave me full satisfaction, nothing blocked the path of this runner, because if I stopped, even once, to think about the use of the path I had taken, I would never go back to it.

Therefore, I had to change the course of my whole life if I allowed Omar to touch me. I couldn't imagine leading a double life with two men. I faced inner stirrings urging me to live it up a little, a little bit of craziness brings an unbearable life some renewal, makes it bearable at least. The answer was decisive. I can't. This might be possible with other psychological make-ups, not because I am rigid, moving on railroad tracks, as someone once told me, looking neither to the right nor to the left, or because I am a strict traditionalist, but because, inside, I am most uncontrollable, and getting off the tracks once means getting off forever, and any craziness would get out of hand, and it would be hard to predict where it might lead. I am the one who knows what the active volcano inside me is like, despite the quiet face. That is why I insist on keeping the lid on firmly so that its eruption will not destroy the people closest to me. Yes, I made my chains myself and tightened them and left my mind and heart dreaming: tomorrow the revolution.

I loved Omar in his waiting for me to calm down and reach a decision. From the first moment I knew him, I figured he would understand my situation. The days, so far, have proved me right. I said to him, "We were separated before I met you. As if fate was preparing for me an opportunity for happiness larger than my ability to dream. I had built a stout wall around my desires, and as time passed the wall grew stouter and I moved in life as a colorless shadow, even its black is pale. Can you tell the colors of shadows? Lead is too green and blue won't do. The shadow is gray, perhaps, I don't know, the color of sad neutrality.

"Yes, it is the answer to the question you didn't ask; the fact that the house has two stories and is big has helped keep the children and the family in the dark about us. Many unfortunate circumstances, now is not the time to talk about them, led to that. We did not agree to have a divorce. There was just silence and isolation. I don't know whether I am free or not and until when. Perhaps this is the source of my torment. To you, I say that my conscience is clear about him. I exhausted all ways and means to repair our relationship, to no avail. I couldn't declare my love to you without taking care of old business. It's a difficult phase that I will get over. Help me.

"I knew all my life that I would come across real emotions and I believe I deserve them. And it has happened. I need your holding on to me for I am like mercury, which cannot be still. Whenever a man came near me I slipped between his fingers."

Symmetry

The mistress of contradictions. I didn't imagine her to be so simple and direct, as if she had been living outside the world, in the innocence capable of launching the paradox, as if she hadn't married, hadn't given birth, hadn't lived a full life. The solitude, which she created for herself or which was imposed on her, gave her the time to craft the masks that hide her intricacies and her longings, so that no one would see them; masks made of ideas and mental images of what she should be like to others, and to herself. She made these masks so carefully and precisely over many years that they have become a part of her; she can take them off only with great difficulty and pain, as if tearing out an intimate part of her body.

She waits. She never takes the initiative. And she desires, but she will not reach out or take a single step, as if, in that stronghold of hers, she invites *you* to reach out and to take the step and to take her. When you do, if she is desirous, you will find her ready for you in every way.

Her beauty is quiet, not the loud type that attracts attention to itself, the ordinary, beautiful beauty that does not arouse lust or desire, one that does not provoke. It's a beauty which, if you examine closely, will give you a sense of serenity and tranquility, as if you have known her for a thousand years. Her voice imparts such mercy and compassion she can relieve you of a lifetime's load of worries, simply washing them away. And you can ask: where did she get all this serenity and contentment as if she had never known pain or torment or pangs of any kind, as if she embodied acceptance of past, present and future? No worrying, no shouting, no loudness, no crude features standing out to call attention to themselves. Rather you will be taken by the symmetry and harmony of the black eyes, light brown complexion, jet black hair, and delicate face, and you will fall in love with that symmetry and harmony.

When we first met, I looked at her figure—a firm body without flabbiness, not skinny, rather, somewhat full and quite proportionate to her height. Another time, when we met at the Granada Tea Garden, she was wearing tights. I looked at her thighs, strong and enticing. The third time I looked at her buttocks as she turned her back and strode to the restroom. No one but me could see the light swaying of the hips and I said to myself, "Beautiful."

From a distance, with her prescription glasses, she looked like a schoolmarm. Outside or in the street, her features settled in a certain pose or expression that was appropriate for the outside world, a pose of quiet seriousness hiding any suggestion that behind it was a woman full of femininity and desires. I called her 'schoolmarm' in jest to break that fragile, outward pose, and, as if she expected that from me, she didn't cling to it.

She did not break the masks all at once, but one after another, and between each one and the next there was a lot of struggling and suffering which I sometimes felt and at other times I could see in her resistance and tenacity, until the mask became so fragile it fell on its own.

She had great difficulty telling me about the man she once loved. She told me the story in disjointed words as if she was ashamed of its being associated with her. She didn't tell me the story all at once, but I got it in fragments and snippets over a long time, and I had the arduous task of picking up the shards like a mosaic worker to form the picture in my mind and to resolve some of the contradictions in the details. She would tell it one way at one time, then forget what she said and tell it a different way, or deny it only to offer other details or an altogether new version. She was always running away from the past with its details, unreconciled and finding no peace with it. Her face and her mood would change if the conversation led in that direction. Sometimes I regretted getting into those areas or trying to explore and know them. I would tell her, "You're all mine, all of you, since the day you were born and until now, with your past, your dreams, those that were realized and those that came to naught, with your good and bad situations. Your history is mine and I have to know it to know you. I am not curious and I am not jealous about your past, but I want to know you." But sometimes she is inclined to silence and I content myself with the crumbs that come out from time to time; I gather them and take good care of them.

Abduction

I toss and turn on twinges of fire, each one an awakening. Your image occupies my consciousness as sleep, which I desperately need, flirts with me, pulling me by the feet, lodging in my limbs. I give it my memory and my thoughts. It rocks me and I almost drown in corridors that meander between blue and black as I follow a purple spot of light taking over the upper reaches of my mind. Fiery pinpricks, each one an awakening, burn me. Your image occupies my consciousness and I resist. I shoo it away only to reach out and try to hold on to you. You float above the memory which forms quickly, then disappears. I withdraw to the stillness, unfocused but calm and hopeful, promising myself that I'll see you tomorrow. I go back to sleep only to be awakened by another pinprick, and heat from a place in my body seeps smoothly, wrapping me in a diaphanous cover which I feel radiating around me, touching me and not touching me; I only feel it coming when it gathers, spear-like, then it pierces me like a jagged diamond, dispensing both pain and forgiveness. It is then that I feel that you've come to me. Why does it feel like a shock that passes without my knowing when it started or where it ended?

Four days without being together. The tumult of the night's pinpricks rises. Each twinge plays itself out in a harmony of longing that softly drains me, bores into my body which wrestles with sleep. With these twinges, neither promises nor attempts at being calm do any good. They do not lead me to sleep. My heart is elated with hopes for tomorrow, then toward dawn it surrenders to the whisper that you are near.

I hurry toward you. I am no longer ashamed to be a woman who longs for her man. Before crossing the street, I see my neighbor Salwa trying to hail a taxi, moving with difficulty because of her pregnancy.

I help her in my car. Throughout the ride we laugh happily, oblivious to our usual worries. My attention is drawn to her effervescent femininity, the roundness of her full face, her broad lips, the wild sparkle in her eyes, the naughtiness of her breasts, and her joyful complexion. Salwa has never been like this before. I have known her since she was a little girl, as a wife, and as a first-time mother. What happened to her this time? The question preoccupies me even as she leaves me to tend to her business. The answer comes easily: she has ripened. There is a forwardness about her. Why forwardness? It is I who have started to notice nature's work and play. There is a lust for life in her face and a consciousness of and pleasure in her femininity. I've never been like her. Yes, this is true. I became conscious of feelings of motherliness, but not those of femininity. Was she conscious of these feelings at the beginning of her marriage, during her first pregnancy? That consciousness might even have preceded pregnancy and marriage. Perhaps it is I who think it is synonymous with femininity and not she. Everything that had to do with her proceeded naturally: she ripened, learned the arts of living and relationship with a man, step by step. As for me, I am learning all of that at once.

You smell my happiness even before I enter the room. You raise your eyes from the book and you see me leaping towards you. I land between your fingers. I wrestle with a blend of tenderness and roughness. Which will win? I want all of it; I want that mixture and I don't fear it. Yes, I no longer fear my contradictions and I won't trim away any of them. I will let them out of the bottle in their primal freshness. I won't allow my wounds to interfere and I won't hold anything back with you.

I don't know why my mind disappears and hides at the moment of our union, as if it has come to realize that it's been tired for a long time, that it is time to rest and to give me over, free and whole, to you. I become intoxicated and all parts of my body play melodies they have known for hundreds of years, before I was born. I realize that this music has been destined for you and for you alone. Who taught me that? Who set me free? Who liberated my cells from their cocoon to dance with you without any rules, with insufficient instinct, moving from one sensation to another, and one path to another? We light the dark corners together and bring life to them. And when the dancing gets furious, I don't know where the sound of the flute comes from or how the piano chords enter me and I can no longer tell them apart. I hear the chorale rising in a boisterous symphony, feeling its tremors in my body as you and I come together as one, rising and rising until a bird flies away from my chest, not leaving it empty, but filled by another being which I cannot name.

Is it satisfaction, maybe, or a greater hunger? I don't know.

And when I become aware of the depth of our absorption and consciousness once again tickles the cells exhausted by our passionate union, and our human ability, which we discover that moment to be fragile, forces us to move apart, I feel I am being snatched from my mother's womb, and that I want nothing but to cling to you. I cry, calling you: "Don't go away." You caress my body tenderly, "Don't be afraid." I hug you with the strength of my longing and long deprivation, as sleep beckons to me, flirting with me. Today, unlike all other days with you, I won't resist it. Just as I am used to staying awake so I won't miss a moment of your presence, I will give in to it. You sense my struggle and you tell me that our time is up and that we have to go back. I remember the street and people and America and Kosovo and Palestine and the petty battles at work. I remember the doorman who waits for us with questions in his eyes, and fate and the short time allowed us, and the death that takes place when I am taken away from you. I feel a wound cleaving my chest as I see you move away until you disappear and I go on my way trying in the few remaining minutes to regain my balance and accept all that has left me, painting a faint smile to meet the world as the question forces itself upon me: "Until when?"

Writing

Two eyes are spoiling the joy of the free flow of writing. Two apprehensive eyes are looking for the real in the imagined, in the written, looking for the hidden feelings deep in the unconscious. Maggie is getting more tense everyday as I work to develop my novels; she is suspicious of every character I construct and every opinion expressed by one of these characters. When I began writing my new novel *A Maze*, she accused me of writing my autobiography even though I had explained to her that it was just a narrative device that writers use. And even though I don't have to explain or justify what I am doing, I am not unsympathetic to her apprehensions. I tell her, "Writing has its own nature and laws, even when it depends on a real event, because that event will be filtered by the imagination. It makes its way as it wishes and not necessarily as I wish." She replies, "Its way is different from that in your conscious mind but it conforms with what your unconscious wishes because it is the result of your interactions. And, as you know, writing is not innocent."

She calms down after a long discussion and, after she agrees to restrain her relentless curiosity about the drafts of my work in progress, she resumes her secret monitoring during the day of what I work on all night long. I notice the signs of conflict on her face before she utters a word and I realize that she has compared what I have written with our daily life and suspected every woman in my novel, which has begun to give shape to a splendid beloved whom the hero desires immensely. At the beginning, she contents herself with watching from afar, waiting to jump into a fabricated fight that I do my utmost to avoid as if I were skirting a patch of quicksand. When I feel it coming, I try to keep my awareness of it from influencing what I am actually doing. For years, I have been trying to prevent her from affecting my creativity by discussing ideas and concepts that have not yet been fully developed, that are still sorting things out on paper, interacting to create a coherent or paradoxical texture that is impossible to grasp during the creative process or even after it is completed. I refuse to take my work elsewhere and insist on doing it here where I live, or living where my work is. What good is my being here without it?

She resumes her secret monitoring of what I write. I find this out from the way the papers are arranged. For despite the care she takes in returning them exactly the way they were, one slip-up or another is bound to happen. What she does not realize are the secret, palpable ties between me and the paper, that daily accumulation of familiarity which makes it reveal to me any changes in it as soon I liberate it from the drawer. Her scent reaches me through the paper, a fingerprint on the penciled script, the turned down corners of the pages—a lifelong habit she has not been able to kick when she reads. I try to decipher what she may have found out by comparing the details of our life she knows with what she has read. I feel her anguish and I resent writing, postponing it for a few minutes during which I try to regain my nervous equilibrium.

I am exhausted today by her hovering around me and clinging to me even though she knows from her close monitoring of my work that I am writing a climax that has been tormenting me, one that I have rewritten dozens of times, each one differently. It is as if she fears my decision on paper. I realize from her increasing tension that she is making a connection between my decision to stay with her and the decision of the hero and the heroine of the novel to separate from their spouses and to lead a normal life together. She deliberately turns up the television volume until I ask her to turn it down, then she turns it up again after a few minutes. I close the door and put on some music and shut the world off but she brings me the telephone even though I had kept it away from my desk and she says, "So and so wants to talk to you." Sharif intervenes and says, "Daddy said not to disturb him." She yells at him. I pick up the telephone and conclude the conversation quickly. She brings a pile of newspapers and magazines and sits in the chair next to my desk and asks me a question about what she is reading every five minutes. I re-read the page I am writing from the top and when the writing begins to flow freely she asks another question. I ask her gently to leave me because I am busy now and she says, derisively, as she leaves the room, "When are you ever not busy?"

She closes the door behind her after she manages to let loose unbridled horses in my head that impede my ability to put my thoughts into focus, nothing but horses galloping, destroying under their hooves any illusions that I might be able to pick up where I had left off. One sentence comes to my mind: "Leave me the hell alone!" I hear her yelling at Sharif about I don't know what, but something that, of course, does not require any yelling. I get up and away from my writing possessed with one desire— to throw her out of the window. She feels my anger, and, having reached the pinnacle of her wish to provoke me, she lets loose a barrage of accusations. I explode after falling into the trap she has so skillfully set up for me; she has succeeded in keeping me from writing. I don't know when Nahid will make her decision to commit to me. I have postponed my important projects until we are living in one house. I cannot separate from Maggie before Nahid has officially separated from Mustafa. How will we face moving to our apartment without arousing society's suspicions about her visiting me but not living with me? When, Nahid, when?

Collapse

Despite the passage of all these months, Mustafa was not quite certain of my insistence on a separation. His experience with me indicates that I am unable to anger him or deny him any wish, that I am content with his needs. He hasn't understood the difference between my loving him because I've known him all my life and his now standing in the way of my respect for myself and my feelings. Yes, I have been a woman deferred for a long time. I postponed making a decision but the confrontation has taken place and going back was no longer possible, for it would mean that I despise myself.

When he got close to me that night, showing true feelings, he wounded me, placed me between the blades of two knives, one in his hand and the other in mine. I kept watching him in alarm and trying in vain to get away. He's always been able to pick up signals of my inability, but this time he deliberately ignored them and I found myself in his arms. His kisses started fires of rejection and did not arouse any desire. I tried to free myself but he had immobilized all parts of my body, every last one of them. I was aware of them one by one: this is my head, this is the torso, and this is a leg. My heartbeats raced at triple the usual rate; I could hear them in great alarm between my breasts as my breathing almost stopped. I asked him to move his chest away from my lungs but he was having a good time. I pushed him away hard and he came to in shock as I kicked, and my arms flailed in all directions. I screamed, choking on my voice, which traveled only a few centimeters, muffled by traditions and the family asleep in the next room, but my loud breathing and an involuntary rattling in the throat managed to convey the message to him to take me to the hospital because I was dying. After I fainted, I awoke only to start crying silently. When I arrived at the hospital and gave myself over to the hands that were reaching to me, I was busy patting him: I didn't want him to be alarmed; I still feared for his feelings. I didn't want him to suffer. I wanted to apologize, to surrender, to surrender to sleep. O God!

My going to the hospital forced me to tell Omar what happened. I didn't tell him the rest of the story, and the reasons for any word about that would be one of Mustafa's secrets, which I saw no reason to divulge. I had evaded talking about my life in the past. I told him succinctly, "I haven't and won't live with two men." He held me in his arms and the question in his eyes caused me to lose sleep.

Accusation

Nahid left today for al-Wadi al-Jadid, where we met for the first time, as a member of a team of experts investigating the theft of antiquities in which for the first time, local, educated people—a doctor, a teacher, and a young woman—were implicated. She called me and said, "It's time to be together again where we first met and noticed each other. Take the first flight to cover the investigation. We need you to start a big campaign in the paper to save the situation here. For despite the wadi's vast area—more than half the size of all of Egypt—and the fact that it has more than two thousand archaeological sites, most of which are pristine, antiquities are guarded by only forty guards, who are almost illiterate to boot. The Antiquities Department owns one Land Rover with a very meager gasoline allowance. There's not a single Tourist Police outpost. The French archaeological teams working here have yet to find anything, but they are on the verge of unearthing one of the missing links of ancient history."

I was tempted by the case and by the detailed information that Nahid provided, so I decided to join her, promising myself to spend a long time with my beloved outside the capital and away from our problems. I arrived at Kharga airport in the early morning as the robust sun made its presence felt in the region, which is warm during the day, but bitter cold during the night. I was surrounded by representatives of the Ministry of Culture, the governorate, and the Antiquities Department, all displaying the warmth I have experienced firsthand on my previous visits to the oases. A car took me to the governor's office and then to the Antiquities Department offices. We passed by the museum, which was supposed to have been opened some time ago, housing all the antiquities of the wadi. I asked the public relations director why it was still empty and he said that security measures had not been taken into consideration, and that was why the Ministry was reluctant to move the warehoused antiquities to it.

I remembered that I had noticed during one of my previous visits to the wadi that the women who worked at the guesthouse where I was staying laughed when I left the room. One morning, one of them approached me and asked why I locked my room. I knew then that I had offended them with my city ways, without meaning to, so I left my room unlocked afterward. So how did this happen to a society that was so safe that there wasn't a single theft throughout its history? And why this uproar? Was it such a big crime?

Ibrahim al-Khalil from the Ministry of Culture told me that the latest crime was beyond anything they imagined: forty-six antiquities were found in a citizen's garden. They had been collected in preparation for selling them outside the governorate. He also told me that the last few months had witnessed several cases of theft of antiquities, some involving unauthorized digging, and some transporting antiquities.

I went to the police station to look at the police report. I noticed that a number of the accused had come from the village of al-Munira, which had the dubious fame of being home to the Mahariq prison, in which intellectuals—Muslim Brothers as well as leftists—had been detained after the revolution. Now it has become famous for theft of antiquities.

Finally I met Nahid and the Kharga antiquities inspectors. She introduced them to me. I had met some of them before. I realized that they had discussed at length what a large scale newspaper campaign might do to confront the problem. I talked with the archaeologist Adil Hussein who, together with some colleagues, was credited with unearthing many antiquities in the Dush region a few years earlier, and also in the al-Labkha region. He said that, first of all, many guards needed to be hired because right now there were only forty-two guards entrusted with guarding an area the size of half of all Egypt. And although they have four warehouses where movable antiquities are housed, six temples with writings and inscriptions, and two tombs with very important reliefs hewn in the rock, the guards have had to concentrate on the temples and tombs. He said there was an area in the Kharga Oasis that was about ninety kilometers long and between thirty and forty kilometers wide without any guards at all, even though it has numerous important archaeological sites such as al-Labkha, Deir al-Munira, al-Gibb, and al-Samira, as well as several other places that needed more guards. As for Farafra, it did not have a single guard.

Hussein said, "We archaeologists try to cover part of the distance between Kharga and Dakhla and so do chief guards and other officials, by periodically traveling among the different sites in the three oases despite the vast distances. We work in an area that's eight hundred kilometers long and between thirty and fifty kilometers wide in addition to the distances between inhabited and uninhabited areas in the desert."

In the evening, I met the accused young woman at her house. She held small wooden statues of birds, and she said she had made them at home and that she was innocent of the horrendous crime. When we left her house, the friend who had accompanied me said angrily, "At first the people didn't believe that a young woman would be involved in such a crime, but her family ties made it appear logical; her brother and her fiancé were apprehended in earlier smuggling cases."

The following day I met a member of the municipal council in the governorate and asked him about the case and the phenomenon which had suddenly spread and he said, "The problem is, who is inciting them to steal? Antiquities here are not in fixed places. They should be clearly demarcated so everybody will know that they shouldn't trespass. I cannot prevent anyone from walking up or down the mountain just because of suspicion. The kids who steal antiquities and take them to foreign countries do not consider it a crime because they are buried in their land. We need to educate the youth."

I asked one of the young men who works at the al-Wadi radio station about his ideas why educated young people steal antiquities. He said bitterly, "I go to school all my life, my family spends all it has on my education, then I finish college only to find no job and no money to get married. Now these antiquities are buried under my house, my own grandfathers put them there. Why aren't they mine?"

I felt the anger of his words and I knew that he didn't need any 'education' about the importance of these antiquities, but rather needed to solve his problems in finding a job and getting married. I asked Nahid how much an antiquities inspector like her made per month and I found out it was only a hundred and fifty pounds. I decided to write a series of fiery features reflecting the anger raging inside me. I sent the first one right away. Then I returned with Nahid on the same plane. I couldn't let her put her head on my shoulder in the midst of the clouds or even hold her hand. We were careful even though the plane was full of foreigners. We were content and happy to be so near each other.

A few days later, the head of the Antiquities Department called to tell me that they had solved the problems of the car, increased security, and were setting up a Tourist Police station. As for the helicopter that I demanded for the workers, he wasn't able to secure one. He also promised more solutions in the future.

Explosion

I love the river. I run away to it whenever I feel down. I drive my car along the bank, leaving Cairo behind and slowly get rid of my frustrations. I love it at night. I hadn't expected the road repair work to leave the pavement rutted before making it smooth again. Where did that dog suddenly come from? Thank God the car miraculously stopped. I know those eyes and the evil quivering nose and those canine teeth.

In my memory, despite my fear and the short distance between us, I wanted to pat it on the head, maybe it would calm down. I hadn't seen a wolf before, but I figured out, though I was only nine, that it wasn't a dog and it didn't have the puffed up furry tail of a fox like those hanging on the walls of our house in the village. It looked dismal in the midst of the roses as the sun was casting its mild late afternoon rays. Its appearance and the deathly quiet of the tombs behind the guava orchard spread the paralyzing terror throughout me, such as one might see in the eyes of a snake's prey as it gives in.

I had gone ahead of my friends, climbing over the garden fence to beat them to the roses as they were delayed by negotiating the doors. I wanted to scream, but the glint in its eyes and its quivering nose paralyzed me. I found myself up in the shaky guava tree and the wolf underneath it snarling, baring its canines and small incisors and dark mouth, a picture that stayed with me, especially when anyone frowned at me for no reason.

I held on to the higher branches as it held the hem of my nylon dress which I heard ripping as my feet flew into the air, trying to latch on to another branch and kicking up my legs. I lost a shoe and screamed. I had gotten over the illusion of being at peace with the wolf and admitted that I needed help—something that I never asked for after that. I wish I'd learned to ask others for help. If only I had.

The roses and the wolf and a young girl riding a galloping horse across the fields in the dark or fearlessly cleaving the wide river: was that courage or ignorance? Neither, because once I became aware of the possible danger, I became genuinely frightened so I went faster, and harder, egged on by the urgency of fear until I made it to safety. I never saw the genie of the water to fear it or the siesta demons that the elders tried to scare me with, so I would take a nap after lunch. But how could I sleep when delicious mulberries were easiest to pick when it was hot outside, when the tree yielded its treasures as the sun poured its rays in straight lines? There was always a fruit, any fruit, high up in the furthest branches of the tree, waiting for me, waiting to be mine.

I love this succession of scenes in front of the windshield of the car: the expansive fields and the open air with the occasional tree standing sentinel over water and crops, protecting the body of Osiris. Why has this van driver turned on his high beams? The road is narrow and the light in blinding me. Oh my God!

"The retina is quite healthy. Physically, there's nothing wrong with you."

"The light is burning my eyes. Please move it away a little, doctor."

"Come and have a look, Doctor Faruq. I've examined her. See for yourself."

"But I can't see either of you. I can only see the large spotlight. My neck hurts as if I am tied to a hook pulling me backwards."

"Calm down, Nahid. This is a temporary condition that will go away as soon as you get some rest."

Now I knew that I needed to escape, to get rid of my eyesight so I wouldn't see how far I'd fallen. I don't know why I remembered van Gogh when he stood for the first time in Paris in front of Rembrandt's paintings and those of his own contemporary, Gauguin, and saw the lines of light radiating from them, how he bemoaned his dark paintings and those of the more somber schools of art. I know now, that the light did not come from the paintings alone, but from the inner moment of recognition which made him define his way and capture what he wanted.

I had a need to be among people. Mustafa hadn't realized how much I needed people. He called the symptoms of loneliness 'the fever of closed rooms.' He wanted me for himself alone, and at the time, he didn't know that he was killing me. I swear I tried, but it was a lazy, petty, frustrated society. Prison is not just four walls; prison is when your words come back to you without connecting; it is when you can't communicate ideas, get enthused, or interact with others.

I had a need to hear new opinions, new ideas. I needed a larger world, a more profound outlook on life, not this narrow circle of people who lived in a trench of petty ambitions, even though they lived on the coast of a sea with an open horizon. Even spatially, they didn't grasp it. I had not prepared myself to play the role of a housewife in a small provincial town whose interests were limited to the details of daily life and whose life revolved around one thing—her husband.

That day, when I lost my sight and refused to see what was around me, things were happening as usual, without any inkling of a sudden collapse. I had been busy throughout the previous two days preparing dinner for Mustafa's colleagues. I felt happy as I made a multi-story cake whose architecture I had designed myself, using aluminum cans of powdered milk, and covered it with chocolate foils, with a large heart bearing three small hearts on top of it. Mustafa couldn't believe the effort I'd put into it and when I was done he said, "Why didn't you tell me? We could've started a catering business instead of looking for metal ores in the mountain."

I was hoping to enjoy that party, to get a charge of vitality that would enable me to cope with my wasted time and to think of doing some work to continue what I avidly did all my life. I knew that Mustafa's colleagues and their wives were different from my colleagues and friends in Cairo. Our interests could not all be similar, but I'd hoped to find affection among them.

The party began as I had expected. At the beginning, I was very busy as a hostess tending to their needs. But it didn't take us long to split into two groups: the men in one side of the garden and the women in another. The wife of the police prefect asked me, turning her head slowly to affect a careless attitude to her question, though her eyes told me she impatiently awaited the answer, "Why didn't you invite the new doctor's wife? They say she's young and beautiful, about your age."

Before I could answer, Engineer Muhammad's wife beat me to it, "She declined because she hasn't tidied up her house yet and because she's exhausted after the long trip." Then she turned to the prefect's wife abruptly and said, "And who says she is beautiful?"

"She's got a nice figure."

"Not as nice as Nahid's. The doctor's wife has the legs of a goat."

"Just give her time until she gets pregnant and gives birth. As they say, 'A woman's figure comes into its own only after pregnancy and nursing.' I heard she's vain and arrogant."

I didn't hear much beyond that. I felt nauseated and out of place as they went on about fashion and babies' diseases and the colors of their stools, which I must pay attention to after I delivered my baby. I tried to hide my disappointment as I saw them off, but Mustafa sensed it when we closed the door.

I couldn't complain or ask for help or think of leaving. This is where Mustafa works. A wife belongs where her husband is. But questions had started to knock around hard in my head as I waited for Mustafa for long, empty hours. I began to ask myself about the meaning of my existence, then gradually another question about the meaning of love began to insinuate itself into my mind: is it our appetite for sex? The body has its needs and we satisfy each other's need? Do we really? And is the physical need everything? Why then do we have an increased emotional hunger after our lovemaking, and after the desire, which has enveloped us for a few moments, subsides? Why does my mind go back to work so fast, as if it has gotten rid of something, and gone back to normal?

Then the questions no longer posed themselves in his absence, but came on more strongly when he was there, after the voices in the house died down and the singing stopped and complaints vanished. In the silence, nothing was heard anymore but the sound of regular footsteps to prepare food or to carry empty dishes. There descended on the house a sticky silence similar to that emanating from stagnant swamps under the burning glow of the sun. Even the attempts to seize an opportunity for sheer survival, such as going out or going for a walk on the beach on a Friday, ceased.

In the morning, with the first breeze, as Mustafa was getting in the car, I asked myself, "What will I do all day long until he comes back in the afternoon?" I picked up a book but I soon found it boring. I looked through the old and new newspapers but I already knew all their content. I felt pain in my back so I got up to lean against the wall. I placed my head on it then left it for the opposite wall. I leaned against it, then once again I dragged my feet into the hall where I stood looking at the emptiness through the window. But I couldn't stay like that for a long time, so I ran out to the garden and watered the plants that were fighting to survive. Then I went back to the house, feeling the walls close in on me. I resisted, but felt them encircling my head. I kept unconsciously going around in circles, then I held my forehead to protect it from falling down and went back outside. I didn't find the garden or the street or the houses. I found a clear sky and birds flying away meekly. The pain in my neck pulled me backwards, nearly causing me to fall. I resisted but I couldn't help facing the sky. I tried in vain to move my face and I hit a plant pot near the door. I used my memory: this is the corridor, after that the street, and, a few steps to the right is the neighbor's house.

I heard a child welcoming me, "Hello, auntie."

"Where's your mom?"

"What's wrong?"

"Take me quickly to the hospital, please."

Did I need dynamite to break my silence, to moan and admit that that society sickened me? I woke up to Mustafa's voice thanking my next-door neighbor Samira and bidding her farewell. My body was quite relaxed and my husband came to pat me on the head. I tried to speak but he stopped me with a gesture of his hand and without a word he propped me up at the small food table. Then he began to talk and was uncharacteristically effusive and merry and gentle. But something prevented me from being on the same wavelength with him. I now know that it was our realization of the curtain gathering up and coming down between us—he was immersed totally in his world and I was waiting. When he returned, his presence did not change my world. A few minutes later, my eyes once again began looking at the sky and nothing else. I stretched out on the couch and cried. The doctor and his wife came. He examined me and laughing, asked me what I did in Cairo. I told him about my studying archaeology and my university activities. I kept talking and we both discovered that we had gone to the same university at the same time. My eyes returned to their normal position and we laughed and soon forgot what he had come for. When we remembered, he got a piece of paper and pen and wrote down, "The sea. The mountain. The sea. The mountain."

"Is my illness too much leisure time?" I said, incredulously, feeling my face and waiting for his lips to move.

"Not exactly. Going out would break the monotony and give you some rest. Change the morning sickness medication—it was too much on your nerves early on in the pregnancy. Besides, you won't have morning sickness again. Take my wife to the beach, she's suffering just like you."

It's as if this happened yesterday. What doesn't kill you makes you stronger. Losing sight for a few moments made me determined to take matters into my own hands. I got my books and papers back and my professors in Cairo helped me register for an M.A. I surveyed the region and acquainted myself with its Greco-Roman relics. Then I developed an interest in ancient Egyptian women. Something drove me to try to find out the features of my grandmothers and fill in the scientific lacunae of what we knew about them. I began to collect data and reference books and considered my being there as an apprenticeship in a lab, enabling me to further my education, preparing me to become, I thought, a unique scholar. That and taking care of my daughter kept me from confronting the many questions seething inside me about the huge transparent wall that had risen between me and Mustafa, between me and the intricate structure of a man who worked too much and who chose to fence himself in solitude, keeping out those closest to him.

I hadn't realized, as I left Safaga going back to Cairo, that the earth was forcibly rearranging its elements, melting us to make a new world. How can we be saved when we've agreed to be at the epicenter of change? I had imagined that I could keep the fire away from my family by consciously, deliberately choosing a precise course for our lives. But that didn't happen when Mustafa decided to change the course of his life, to work in the family business under the eldest brother. Admittedly, it was a legitimate business, but it made our house and each individual a mere helpless cog in a huge machine of interests that would crush you if you fell out of line. I was aware of what was happening around me, but all I could do was talk to prevent Mustafa from acquiescing to the requirements that others laid out. I was unsuccessful and they got our house and left us to face the unknown.

Many a time have I swallowed bitter tears of pain and choked on them without making a sound. It was as if a knife was stabbing me in the back despite the comfortable cotton kilim covering the car seat. It was the life-long fingerprint left by the demonstrations of 1973. The superficial pain was gone, but inside there was a wound that I felt as if it were lashing the skin with an electric current every time I felt anger. I adjust the way I sit, knowing that there's no use doing anything about it.

"Watch out, Nahid. Come here."

I leaned my whole body against him as he pulled me to the entrance of an apartment building.

"Thanks. The belting I got almost stripped the skin off my back. That soldier was rushing after me like a blind bull."

"Are you injured?"

"No, it's just a little pain that'll go away soon."

"This apartment building is a godsend. We'll rest for a few minutes then catch up with everybody in Tahrir Square."

"I know the streets of Doqqi very well. But what are we going to do about the bridges? We'll be caught at University Bridge and even if we crossed Gezira at Galaa Bridge, we'll still have Qasr al-Nil Bridge."

"Let's get out of here first. It's a good plan. We've managed to provoke them and our message has reached the people."

"Would they dare to shoot us, as it happened at Abbas Bridge?"

"No, Egypt was occupied at the time."

"What's the difference? At least then they were fighting an enemy they knew. Now who are we fighting?"

"The goal is clear. First, a war in which we liberate Sinai, then we'll settle accounts."

"There are so many things that I didn't understand but it seems the tear gas and the belts in the hands of Central Security soldiers have explained some of them to me."

"What happened to you? You used to be so apolitical."

"It seems that each of us needs to take a clear stand so we won't be invisible to the regime which thinks of us as no more than scarecrows at best. Let's get out of here."

"Don't be in such a hurry. We've still got time and we'll all meet up, God willing."

"I don't hear anything going on outside."

"Wait. Stay here. I'll see what's happening outside and come back."

Just crossing a threshold cut me off two worlds: the stage and the auditorium. He crossed it and I stood in the dark, waiting. Now I know that I have stood at thresholds, never having the ability to cross. Where did that seed that lived inside me all my life come from? When was it created? Was it born at that moment or has it been slowly pushing its way inside for years? Did change play a role in this? Or did fate leave the decision up to me and I couldn't make it?'

Yasir went to the melée outside. He was gone for a long time. I got tired of standing so I sat on the staircase, enveloped by a cold loneliness which I tried to dispel by hugging my knapsack. Fears assailed me with questions which I started to answer in defense of myself and the demonstrations: all we are asking for is our right to kick the enemy out. Why are they surprised by our demands? They sent Alexandria University Engineering students to the front and that was the last we heard of them. In a dramatic tone, as if we were a bunch of reckless kids, they said, "You want war? Quit school and join the army."

The young men couldn't back out. There was an uneven confrontation and then a deathly silence, as if we were the enemy. They planted their spies everywhere around us. We no longer knew with whom we were speaking or eating or attending lectures or singing at picnics. When we have some peace of mind and forget about them and tend to our lives' immediate concerns, looking forward to moments of truth or communication, one of them volunteers, "Nahid, why are you talking to him? Don't you know he's an informer?" Every day one group produces incriminating evidence against another. What's happening today is proof of their failure to divide us, to sow hatred and suspicion among us so we'd reap nothing, so our voices would get lost. Yasir's been gone a long time. Where did he go? Was he hit by the soldier's stones or their clubs? Did he clash with them and get arrested?

Days later I found out that a police car had picked him up as soon as he crossed the threshold. They took him to the jail in Muhammad Ali's Citadel that still reeked of the massacre of the Mamluks, to add his name to the names of prisoners and revolutionaries inscribed on its walls throughout its history. He had wanted to stay a little longer, to make sure it was safe. Did I, in my impatience, push him to go out? It was a question that gave me many a sleepless night for years afterwards, even though there was no trace of it on his face when we met later on.

A spark of defiance grew inside me as I waited, until I found myself possessed of such an immense energy that I dashed out into the sunshine without casting a last glance at the lobby where I hid. I didn't know what it looked like and I never found that building afterwards. I didn't find Yasir in the street, but I found a crowd of students thundering angrily, "War, nothing but war." I also saw white smoke rising in circles in the street, which reminded me of childhood stories of Ummina al-Ghula and her constantly bubbling cauldron in which wayward children were cooked.

I soon found myself in the midst of a wave of marching students swelling flood-like, my fingers clasping with the fingers of a young man I didn't know. When our eyes met I understood. I turned to the person holding my other hand. It was another young man I didn't know. Unconsciously the waves had become one solid block. The soldiers tried everything to break it up, to no avail. In the midst of that block I forgot who I was and learned what it meant to be a mere atom in a large entity. It was a feeling I had looked for all my life but it had been like a mirage, flirting with me from a distance, rising the closer I got to the earth's surface, riding a warm mist and appearing real to me, but when I ran toward it, it disappeared into nothingness. But now the block was rolling forward, our feet beating the ground wildly and rhythmically as if to unseen African drums. Our heads were raised like sunflowers towards the source of strength. It was as if Ra, the god of the sun, was once again sitting on his throne and we marched towards him, anxious not to lose sight of him.

Lodging

We had to go through the heart of the old city, cross its narrow black streets which meandered in the shadow of the big apartment buildings in the poorer neighborhoods to reach the Sayyida Aisha Bridge, and cross it to the Citadel. From there we continued on a long road that went through the Basatin Cemetery on one side and the Muqattam Hill on the other. There in the dusty uninhabited desert we could see buildings whose construction had been halted years earlier and whose colors had faded, with jagged holes where the doors and windows were supposed to be. On the whole they seemed like object lessons of decay and dejection.

We turned on streets on the sides of which were piled old, unused construction material. The watchman opened the gate for us. We crossed the first street over piles of stones and sewer openings and manholes, unfinished and uncovered. The car proceeded awkwardly over potholes until we reached the door of the apartment building where nobody but us and a newlywed couple lived, even though it had no running water and no electricity. We learned from them how to run a wire with a light bulb attached to it from their car battery, which they re-charged daily, and to use a jerry can of clean water for drinking. The bride told Nahid that she went to her parents' house once a week to do her laundry and that they also used a small radio and television hooked up to their car.

We watched how life developed in their house away from the city. There was a cactus on the balcony and a small vine trellis in front of the building door. They ran a water hose from the water main used for the construction to a large water tank near the entrance to the building and filled it during the night or at a water tanker car whenever it ran out of water. Sometimes we would forget to bring the jerry can and we would knock on their door and she'd gladly open the door with a large guard dog, which was used to us, at her side. She'd give us a bottle of water and invite us to tea, but we'd say we're sorry, but we don't have time. They were happy that we went there, infrequently at the beginning then regularly later on. They knew our schedule and without us telling them anything, they figured out that we'd moved our work to the 'office' as we called it. They asked us many times why we didn't move for good to live in this apartment, but we used the pretext of the children's schools and didn't tell them anything beyond that. I was afraid that in the bride's conversations with Nahid something would slip and create problems for us. But she was not overly inquisitive; she was happy that our presence in the huge silent building somehow brought it to life despite our isolation.

Homesickness

Alone on the beach in Manshiya, she looks into the distance. There, where her eyes cannot see across the Mediterranean, her heart flies to Greece, the land of her ancestors. At the same time, she cannot quite turn her back on her beloved Alexandria where she'd grown up; she is torn between her immediate surroundings, the only ones she's ever known, and a longing for her roots. Maria never doubted that the sea would bring her the knight of her destiny, crossing the Mediterranean like a migrating quail to accompany her on her way to another life in a different world. She would make her daily trip from her house in Attarin to the sea, to watch the sun setting over small boats and boulders and anchored sailboats on a calm surface bounded by concrete blocks and rocks. She would move lightly along the sea coast to Tabya or take the streetcar to Bahari with her neighbors to sit on the grass in front of Ras al-Tin palace, and return after experiencing the liberating feeling that the expansive sea provides.

She trained herself to be alone with the sea even among her friends, listening to its whispers that resembled the rustling of chiffon as it flew around her body in the breeze. She imagined that the sea addressed her alone with voices and sounds that had escaped from over there, in which the water tickling the rocks blended with the raucous chords of the *buzuq* and mountain singing and the beat of a proud dance. She took in the smell of the sea mixed with a fragrance that she never actually inhaled but knew intuitively from the stories of her family that had settled in Alexandria for quite some time: a mixture of the smells of raging waters, fresh fish, sea creatures dried in the sun, salted meats hung, rocks under clean water, green moss, curdled goat milk, processed cheeses, boats old and new, a strong sun, smoked chestnuts, and a strong wind twisting tree trunks in the winter.

Who can quite capture the smell of Greece about which they speak? Her mother said to her, "Pay heed to the smell coursing through your blood, you will recognize it and it will make itself clearly and strongly known to you." Her father said, "It's the smell of the mythology and the cruel gods." She recognized it as she took in the wind coming from the sea, extracted it from the smell of rotting wood in the old harbor, mixed with the smell of iodine and remnants of fishing, and felt homesick, living in the space between reality and the legacy of dreams about roots. She inhaled the air deeply into her chest until her eyes closed, filling her lungs to the utmost, and only when she felt that that air had filled her whole body, down to her legs, did she exhale, only to realize the huge void left inside her, a void that only the awaited lover could fill.

She left the keys to her fate and to her soul with the sea and began to look for its answers from the seagulls, the soothsayers, and the fortune tellers, from the strength and weakness of its gales, from the stories of summer and troops passing through, from the ugly face of the city which it showed only to strangers but which girls whispered about in secret. She eagerly followed the lights of the ships waiting in the harbor, and circled around like a bee that had lost its way to its hive if she heard a departing ship's horn. She believed her dream when she saw Paolo, an Italian sailor who swept her off her feet with his vitality and vigor and sincerity. She married him at once, but he decided to stay in Alexandria rather than go back to Italy. She postponed her dream of departure so he would accomplish the desired success. He settled down and opened a large machine shop in the same neighborhood, which soon provided his expanding family with a life of ease. But Maria didn't lose her desire to travel, and continued to sing the tunes of that song to her children, who grew up as real members of a small community on the margins of a civilization they looked down upon. Maggie, her youngest, was an exception though—she grew up emotionally partial to the country of her birth. She was the only one among her siblings without an accent and had it not been for her blue eyes and tender snow-white skin, no one would have doubted that she was a true Alexandrian woman of Anfushi. Among her friends she went by the name Magda Abdallah saying, as she laughed, that Maggie Paolo was just a corruption of the Egyptian name.

Maggie lived in the midst of three cultures, each with a claim on her, and she combined them and mastered their languages. Maria, taking after Greek aristocracy in Athens, insisted on enrolling her in a French school that also taught English among its subjects. Maggie showed an extraordinary talent for languages. At university she added Latin. And despite Maria's emphasis on European culture and other distinctions that were quite legitimate at that time, she could not shake Maggie's sense of belonging to Alexandria and nothing else. She didn't like the fragility of her older brother who, because of their mother's dreams, had opted to float on the surface of society, rather than putting down roots in the soil as Paolo, who tried sincerely to blend in, wanted.

She realized, as she listened to her grandfather's and grandmother's dreams of return, that it was just a story that they used to alleviate the pangs of homesickness. It was just a hope they kept regurgitating without any real intent after they had lost track of their families over there, and after most of them had been dispersed among five continents, and after all they had left of them were childhood memories and pangs of exile which they sang away as remnants of a lost past.

Her grandfather Demetrius told her one day, "I started missing Alexandria the moment my feet touched the Athens harbor, and I counted the days remaining till my return. I missed my house, my job, and the people and its charm. And when I arrived in Alexandria, I began to hold on to a new hope for another trip carrying me to Greece. I lived suspended between the two cities, but I never thought of settling anywhere but Alexandria. Greece lives in me wherever I go. The gramophone brought my island close to my body and wine from a large demijohn narrowed the distances. When the time for dancing came, I left all my grief behind and stomped the ground and sang in the voice of every Greek who left his island and rode in a boat. I know why our voices are gruff: because they answer the wind as it hammers our rocks hard. And before it escapes, we imprison it in our chests and only let it out when longing becomes too much. Each of us, my daughter, has kept the wind inside our body, our wind which resembles us and nobody else."

Maggie remembers her grandfather and tears fill her eyes. She sees him as he is forced to leave his beloved city after the nationalization and 'Egyptianization' decrees. He didn't leave with the first batches, but held out for a long time; ultimately, however, he had to go. She never saw him after that. He died the moment his feet touched the island without hope of return. His eyes absently followed the waves that had taken him away from where he lived and his soul rode those waves back to where he had always dreamed of being buried.

Her father was able to stay in Alexandria for years after the embassy found a steady job for him and granted his family temporary residency. During that time, two of her brothers left for Italy, then they all ultimately joined them.

The family settled down in Naples after her maternal grandmother arrived there. But that didn't give Maggie a new sense of identity, and didn't make her give up her determination to return to the place in which she'd grown up. She studied history and political science with Paolo's encouragement, to be able to join the diplomatic corps. She managed to join a travel agency that had a branch in Cairo. She arrived in her beloved Alexandria with a tour group from Greece's Greek-Egyptian Association and another from Italy's Italian-Egyptian Association. They boarded a large tour bus and sang traditional Alexandrian songs until they were exhausted, and they came into the city boisterously. They got off the bus at the Metropolitan Hotel and decided to drop off their luggage and rest for a while. She looked around the hotel and saw the work of time and the dark creeping in its halls and lobby, but the feeling of unfamiliarity evaporated the moment she heard someone speaking Greek and spontaneously embraced him even though she didn't know who it was.

They dispersed in the streets and alleys, looking for old addresses and the fragrance of memories of childhoods past. She was moved by the faces she saw and the voices she heard. She followed the Alexandrian dialect and was able to tell it apart from the other dialects in the midst of the crowds on Safiya Zaghlul Street. She wanted to kiss everyone she saw, moved by a sense of familiarity and intimacy that she miraculously kept in check, asking herself whether she really knew these persons or was just imagining. "Is my memory failing me? Were they our neighbors? Classmates? Customers? How wonderful the faces! They're Alexandrian," came the decisive answer.

The members of the group poured throughout downtown, tarrying in front of the stores, someone exclaiming, "This is Santa Lucia." Another, "Here's Yanni's grocery store." The cinema was still in the middle of the square, the streets and intersections were where they'd always been. The end of the streetcar line was still at the Raml Station. The city's topography hadn't changed, but old age had done a number on its old neighborhoods, whose buildings had become decrepit, and the cobblestones that had been installed so carefully and evenly were now gapped and uneven and warped as they came close to the decaying sidewalks. The colors which had given the narrow alleys their distinct character were now faded. The once ubiquitous horse-drawn carriages were now gone. Some Indian jasmine trees persevered, but were now hidden in the midst of the huge high-rises.

They split into smaller groups without any planning and dispersed again. One of them had brought a wife and child who were visiting

Alexandria for the first time. Some old friends came together. The October wind, laden with the migrating flocks of quail and the sense of restored dignity after the departure of the hordes of summer tourists, lit fires in their old memories and gave the city a glowing young look tinged with joy and pain.

They stopped in front of the Elite coffee shop, which occupied the area facing Cinema Metro. Its owner, Christine, stood at the door in obvious good health even though she was over sixty, and as handsomely dressed as ever, wearing huge necklaces of semiprecious stones. She gave them a warm welcome, for she knew each and every one of them and their families. They celebrated their return with her and promised many future visits. She asked them to convey her greetings to the community abroad. They washed away the homesickness with tears and recalled many faded memories and remembered people who had passed away. Questions, answers, news, and shouts of surprise at sudden revelations commingled. They asked her for Egyptian meals daily until the end of their visit. Then they went back to the hotel postponing their visits to their respective former addresses until the evening.

Maggie got her room key after making sure that the members of the tour group had been fully accommodated. She sat in the lounge before the glass barrier following the car traffic on Saad Zaghlul Street with delight. She recalled going frequently on summer evenings with her family to the Trianon, and sitting in the open air watching the traffic of cars and people going by. She remembered how she and Yanni and Stavros, holding hands all together, would cross the street to buy popcorn from the street car stop, her father's long evenings at the Calithea Bar on the Corniche, their evenings at the Cecil Hotel cafeteria and their pestering the pistachio and peanut vendors, the movies they went to secretly, and her grandfather's favorite spot here on this very balcony. How I miss you, Grandpa! And how powerful the magic of this city that brought me back to you. She dried her tears and became aware of her heartbeats, slow at first then very fast. "It's as if I am falling in love. Can a man release in me all this happiness, excitement and longing? Or is my love for Alexandria much more ardent than a man's love?" A dark-skinned young man approached her. He had clear Egyptian features: amber-colored eyes, frizzy brown hair, and Akhenaten-like lips. She made out the features of his face before she heard his voice: "Pardon me. I think the receptionist gave you my room key."

She didn't understand, shaking her head as she looked at him, so he repeated, "I am in the room next to yours. You have the key to room number five and not six."

She opened her hand and found his key. She gave it to him, laughing unrestrainedly. She got up and walked with him to the reception desk to retrieve her key. She introduced herself to him and he asked her about her fluency in Arabic despite her Italian name. She told him the story as they waited for the receptionist, who was talking to another guest. She gave him more details on the stairs as they went up together to the first floor. Before going into her room she asked him whether he would go with her to look for her old house.

"I was planning to go for a walk on the Corniche. I love Alexandria in October."

"Until six then."

She moved with familiarity both with him and the city, as if she hadn't left it ten years earlier. Her eyes devoured the changes that had taken place, then digested them and re-established familiarity in a few moments. They crossed Nabi Danyal Street and turned left. They moved quickly though the alleys until they were in front of the Malik al-Hamam restaurant. She pointed out her grandfather's old house. She talked to him about her childhood, her school, her grandpa Demetrius and her grandma Katherine, the neighbors in her alley and her friends at school, her house at Canopus Street extending from Camp Cesar and Ibrahimiya, about Cinema La Gaieté, where she had been introduced to Yul Brynner in his strange roles and the way he walked, and Kirk Douglas in *Spartacus,* which she hadn't forgotten, and *The Vikings,* which introduced her to music that had accompanied her throughout her life and which always returned her to the atmosphere of Alexandria where she had heard it for the first time. She talked to him about Cinema Odeon, to which she was permitted to go to with her brother Yanni alone for the first time, and they considered it an acquired right from that moment on. They didn't make a distinction between its first run movies and the movies of Cinema La Gaieté which showed old movies, usually two at a time, one an Arabic movie starring Abdel Halim Hafiz and Shadia or Farid al-Atrash and Sabah and Abdel Salam al-Nabulsi and Zinat Sidqi. She forgot about him as she talked about her fights with her brother Yanni to get to the top story on the streetcar to sit in front of the glass to watch the city from above. She talked about the distinct smell of the streetcar, which they discovered later on that it was different from that of streetcars in Cairo or Rome, and about the Greek Club in Shatbi and the machine shop in Attarin.

She was visibly shaken when an old Greek woman appeared on a balcony. She exchanged many words in Greek with her and shed many tears before the two of them went up to her apartment. During their conversation he was able to follow a few isolated words and expressions such as yasus, *klakla, molto bene*. He noticed that everything in the apartment belonged to the past: photographs, diplomas, old tablecloths. He felt stifled by the scent of memories. The loud expressions of joy attracted several old women who gathered quickly and surrounded her without paying any attention to him. He noticed their shriveled bodies, their old fashioned clothes, their dyed hair, their short dresses, their bent backs, and crooked legs. He stood there in silence focusing his attention on that effervescent young woman bubbling with love. She suddenly remembered him as an afterthought as she got ready to leave and as he led her by the hand out of the circle. She introduced him saying, "My friend Omar, from Egypt" and them, "Aunt Clea, our neighbor and aunts Stavrolla, Sophie Marcelle, Martina, Irena, our neighbors and relatives, and my Uncle Titus." With difficulty he was able to accompany her to the Corniche, postponing her visit to her home on Canopus Street till the following day. He quickly expressed his desire to see her again the next day. He wanted to get her out of that emotional turmoil and spend some quiet time with her. He was pleased when she simply said yes to his suggestion, despite the importance she attached to these visits to her old haunts. It was as if she was satisfied for the time being with one emotional dose, in the knowledge that she would get another one the following day after she calmed down, and after she made sure that no power on earth could prevent her from reclaiming her city.

They walked for a long time, which gave them a chance to get to know a few things about each other. They went from Silsila to Manshiya then to the fortress in Anfushi. He didn't know that it was the same route her mother had taken so many times as she communed with the sea, asking it to take her far away. She told him the details of her family's life after they left Egypt.

Before each of them went up to their rooms, she had shared with him how she had survived one failed love story when she said, "Sex is a revealing factor in a relationship; it's like a thermometer that I believe at once." He was struck by it as if he were learning about it for the first time in his life. She told him she had fallen in love with a young man from Puerto Rico who studied music with her. "I was not surprised by how easily we'd hit it off together, I was attracted by the third-world traits that we shared, his brown complexion, his customs, and traditions. He was not European and that was the charm that captivated my feelings since my childhood. But when he lived with me in a small studio apartment that we had furnished together, he would leave the bathroom a mess after he washed up; he would let the coffee boil over, messing up the stove. He unconsciously demanded that I always walk behind him. We couldn't go on, even though our relationship lasted a long time. I tried to change his behavior, but he didn't accept equality, despite knowing how much work I had and my need to study and practice long on the piano. We separated and got back together several times. We spent a whole academic year as if we were attached to each other by an invisible thread; whenever one of us moved away, the other pulled him back. We kept going back and forth until I made up my mind by coming to Egypt at the first opportunity, made available to me by a travel agency owned by a Greek-Egyptian friend with whom I had stayed in touch after I left Egypt."

He didn't know why he told her that he didn't have a woman in his life, but that he had a girlfriend, Fayqa to whom he was bound by 'emptiness and need.' He said this in a soft, calm voice and she didn't comment. He was not used to answering anyone's questions or talking about personal matters, but he answered her without hesitation, perhaps because she was so direct and because he didn't want to be less candid. How did the time pass? How did they get from music and operas which she loved, to international issues and battles, to Marx and Freud, to the Arab–Israeli conflict? She told him about the impact of the 1967 defeat on all of them: "It wasn't the death of a dearly beloved individual, but the death of a whole tribe," and how they received news of the victories of the war in October of 1973. "Did you take part?" she asked. He said he hadn't graduated yet.

In her purse were two snapshots, one of her whole family and the other of Gamal Abdel Nasser. After they get to know each other better on the fourth day, he will see a picture of her as a child holding the hand of her grandfather Demetrius. She will tell him that it is the most important souvenir of her life and as tears well up in her eyes, he will take her in his arms with the familiarity of a thousand and one years.

They will walk through the narrow alleys in Camp Cesar and she will hide away from him between the houses in secret passageways that open up to wide streets in another direction. She will run up stone stairs and stand on the top saying, "This is exactly Naples!" He will eat home-cooked meals with her in a Greek restaurant that is no wider than ten meters and she will say, "These are the Greek tavernas." They will walk around aimlessly after watching a movie in Cinema Odeon and receive evening greetings from women sitting in first floor balconies in the houses of the familiar street, and descend a few stairs to a used bookstore:

"Here I bought my first sheet music and my first literature, history, and political books." They will eat ice cream together at Reda's and she will teach him to buy baklava so they can eat it with ice cream, as a Greek-Turkish secret. Together they look for her friends and one evening they are able to track down Mervat, her childhood playmate. The moment he kisses her for the first time he feels that he lived with her in Alexandria and played on its sands. He asks himself many times if anybody had the right to uproot someone who had grown up in one place and send them to another continent about which they knew nothing, forgetting what he had learned about colonialism and the capitulations that sucked the blood of the Egyptians before the July revolution. He will pursue this paradox, naively assuming certain rights and say, "Aren't the poor of the world the poor of the world, be they Greek or Brazilian?" Had Maggie not been in the picture however, he would have taken the exact opposite point of view, in defense of the land and the nation.

He felt he couldn't stay away from this woman or her rich world. He extended his stay for three days after the conference so that they would leave at the same time—he to Cairo and she to Luxor and Aswan before she joins him. The tour group gathered at six in the morning in front of the hotel, waiting for the bus that would take them to the airport as the sun cast orange rays that lit the edges of the October clouds crossing the sky above the city. Restless movements, hesitant steps, a last minute rush to capture the most sights and hoard them in the heart and memory. The suitcases are stowed away and the organizers make sure everyone is accounted for. The clouds tighten their grip on the inattentive sun. The sky darkens and bids the group farewell with teardrops that come just in time. It was not sadness they felt in their hearts, but waves of love at the height of enjoyment mixed with the pleasure of pain and that certain knowledge that it won't be the last visit.

Omar carried Maggie in his heart to Cairo with the hope of meeting her again soon. He was quite certain that she had moved into his world and that no power on earth could take her away from him. He didn't know the moment he got on the train, leaving her lips as the last things he touched in the city, that he would meet her after just one week, and that she would move into his small apartment and that a few months would pass before they announced their marriage after he made sure that she really loved him, that her feelings were not just a result of her nostalgia for the land she had grown up in.

With their daily meetings he discovers that she is sometimes a mixture of innocence, childhood, and spontaneity. At other times she is a well-organized, bright intellect, raised in a communist party, capable of theorizing and debating. It didn't take them long to discover what they had in common, despite the fact that he had no affiliation with any leftist party, and had a more comprehensive and profound outlook. The idea of commitment to the party was the most controversial at that time, especially the questions of commitment in literature. Maggie had resolved the issue, on the theoretical and the practical levels, a long time before he had, whereas he had figured it out more by intuition than by any methodical treatment.

He didn't pit Maggie against Fayqa or make any comparisons between them, especially after work circumstances separated them, when Fayqa was transferred to another department and he seldom saw her except to make love. With Maggie, there was lively discussion about art and politics and attitudes toward governments. She carried him through her memories to many countries he had hoped to see.

Boredom had begun to set in in his relationship with Fayqa in recent months. He was able to predict how things would go between them, even their exact timing and the words they would exchange. He would hang up the telephone after telling her what time he would come in the evening. She would kiss him behind the closed door, then accompany him with her arm around his waist and his arm around her shoulder to a table set for a hot supper, then a cup of tea. She would be wearing one of three nightgowns which he knew quite well and which she would get out of as she made the tea. Then they would get into bed to do the same things they had done since the first month of the relationship. She would lie down like an upturned turtle and accept whatever he did. She would ask him to do certain things and might ask him to make love one more time if she was not content with the usual two or three times. And they would proceed; coming together in the same position they had started in.

One time only and by sheer coincidence, Fayqa broke the routine. When he arrived that evening he was quite exhausted. He had finally managed to get his own place after a long, tiring experience of moving from one furnished apartment to another. He went through the ordeal of dealing with workers and renovation, getting electricity hooked up and moving the furniture. He went to her in a state of total exhaustion. They had a quickie then he fell into a sleep that was more like a coma; from which he was awakened by a mysterious rocking, her hands pushing his body and shifting it. He heard her voice as if it were coming from the bottom of a faraway well: "Get up, darling and finish the job." He said, "Sure." Then he was overcome by fatigue and he fell asleep again. She awakened him again and he asked her to be quiet and postpone it until the morning. He went back to sleep only to wake up to the sound of her sobbing and repeating, "Are you trying to humiliate me?" He was shocked at the idea and later learned to ask her if she'd had enough.

Deep inside he was looking for a woman, and not just a female. Fayqa no longer satisfied him physically, even though his experience with the other sex hadn't gone beyond his relationship with her. He knew, however, from his readings and getting around, that there was another world out there that he had to explore. And he knew Fayqa in her passivity was achieving the highest form of pleasure for her man as she understood it, not as it satisfied him, but he didn't know what other forms he could communicate to her.

After his return from Alexandria, he went to Fayqa out of habit, boredom, and confusion of mind. He had postponed visiting her several times out of anxiety and vacillation between moods of sheer joy and hope and inexplicable dejection. She welcomed him with joy and enthusiasm, which caused him a few minutes of regret. They did their thing until they had had enough. He lit his cigar as she lay down next to him succumbing to the pleasure of rest after exertion. He knew, as his feelings found some focus, that a crack had developed in their relationship. He hadn't pinpointed Maggie's place in his life and he wasn't certain their incipient relationship would succeed, but he was certain that he wanted to see her and stay with her all the time. He looked at Fayqa, thinking: "Comfortable and happy. I love her curvaceous and effervescent body and all that desire. Maggie gives me other feelings; until now the body hasn't played a significant role. Can I keep the two women? Or, if I make love to Maggie, will I look for a way to disappear from Fayqa's life? How can I tell her and how will she take it? I haven't deceived her. I never promised her marriage, but she's an Egyptian woman who has given me what she believes is the most valuable thing in her life. How do I leave her without wounding her?"

The first time Maggie touched me, I was surprised by her experience. She dealt with my body with a real desire and not just to please me. This feeling was reflected in my growing awareness of my body and her body. She taught me in a few days that reaching climax was not the goal of the burning coupling of the two bodies, but that the journey to that goal was the source of the enjoyment. I learned with her new alphabets: her ability to express her desires, not by asking me to do something but by dealing directly with my body and pushing it to do what she wanted. She wasn't ashamed or afraid of the act of love and she didn't create barriers of any kind. She's a different woman from a different culture. This was in total harmony with the opinions she fought for as she spoke with me about her favorite poets: Neruda, Nazim Hekmat, *The Alexandria Quartet*'s Durrell, 'the great Ungaretti,' as she called him, or when she described the *Guernica*, or played some music by Mozart 'the genius,' or sang to the tunes of Theodorakis, or danced the Greek form of *debka*. These were not acts of the imagination but actual lived reality, no less than her

Egyptianness despite her Italian nationality, her Greek mother and her brothers who spoke Alexandrian Arabic with thick accents.

Yet there was a thread I couldn't break; my feet carried me to Fayqa with whom I was now playing the role of a husband, acting mechanically without asking himself whether she was really enjoying it or just playing that role. The desirable woman that my body pushed me to unite with no longer elicited anything in me but pity. The moment I realized what truly brought us together, I was aroused by a wild desire to penetrate her with strong fast thrusts, egged on by thousands of horses that I felt I was leading, and I felt her galloping hard with me. The room was filled with our panting. I put on my clothes quickly and went out in the street panting and feeling as if my head was under water.

She captivated me the moment I saw her fingers move on the piano keyboard, touching it as if they feared they might wound it, then suddenly attacking it with ferocious strokes as if there were a feverish struggle between her ten fingers and the black and white keys. She let her body sway and her spirit soar as she filled her lungs with air, swelling them until she exhaled causing her body to recede from the black piano, still alive with the melodies. It was as if a whole ballet company was moving on the piano keys, and Maggie seemed to swim away as if she had gathered the whole sea, calm and tumultuous in those fingers that I didn't know were sad because she'd never found the voice she had been looking for. (O Maggie, Maggie, you sneaked into my life behind Time's back and I fell in love with you.)

I forgot Fayqa until I found her in my office one painful day. I borrowed a page from Maggie's book and told her that the end had come. She asked me with tears in her eyes if I had made the decision to leave her before we slept together the last time. I said yes, and I didn't know why she asked that question.

After her arrival in Cairo, Maggie used to come to me after my work so we could go together downtown. She was not afraid of what my friends might think of the nature of our relationship, but would introduce herself simply, without any information about our relationship. We would go to plays or visit art galleries or sit in a café where intellectuals gathered and talked. She was particularly fond of the Café Isaevitch because it had a commanding view of Tahrir Square, and she would sit there for hours behind the glass façade watching the sea of humanity passing by. I was not bothered by her former men, as she called them. She talked to me about childhood romances with boys next door in Alexandria. She told me, as she relived the joy of the memory, about the first love letter she received at the age of nine from a twelve-year-old named Hashim. In the letter, he told her, "I want you to be my love and we get married."

She said, "I waited for him eagerly in the school courtyard but I adamantly refused that he be my only friend as he wanted. We had quarrels then we made up and quarreled again. On my fifteenth birthday, he introduced to me a very beautiful girl as his beloved. He vexed me, but I refused to be his as he had imagined me. He corresponded with me after we left and when he graduated he asked me to marry him even though he hadn't seen me for a long time. I loved his tender feelings, but I shook them off easily as I grew up. When we were young we thought our lives would end if we ever separated."

She didn't feel any shame or regret when she talked about Romario, the Puerto Rican with whom she lived during her university years. She would suddenly remember someone else: "Hercules came close to being my boyfriend, had my feelings not changed at the last moment, when I became certain that he had a fiery temper, that he believed he was the rightful heir to the myth, and that he was violent in all his dealings. He harassed me but I didn't sleep with him." Her directness and simplicity compelled me to deal with her in a manner different from the way I dealt with women who were good at fakery and at hiding their previous experiences with men, thinking that that feigned innocence was a treasure worth pointing out at every opportunity. I didn't feel any jealousy and I asked myself why. She never felt shame or regret or a transgression of any principles. She felt that her experiences were part of her right to life. I confess that her previous experience with men gave me joy and I wondered why men in the east insisted on inexperienced virgins.

This woman, who one day pledged to come back to this land, has returned to me and I deserve her.

"I played music on its stage when I was nine," she said through her tears in front of the square left empty when the Cairo Opera House burned down. "I came from Alexandria to take part in a contest that the Ministry of Education used to conduct every year. The competition between our schools and those of Cairo was intense. I played solo, which was quite something at that time, and I acted with my school's theatre troupe and I got the first prize for music. I was so smitten with the design and architecture of the opera house, the color of its velvet curtains, and the golden engravings on its walls that I fought for a musical career despite my father pushing me to study for a career in foreign service. 'This is the only way to go back to Egypt,' he would say.

"My mother had difficulty getting used to life in Italy; she was homesick for Egypt. We couldn't believe the pains of her homesickness despite her lifelong dream of leaving Egypt. Everything and everyone was impelling me to realize my desire to come back. Tito, son of Mikhailinodis, owner of the printing press in Attarin, came back to Egypt under another identity on a freight ship. Two months later he was arrested and deported. He got a scholarship at the American University in Cairo and when its term expired he went back to Italy and then returned to Egypt as a tourist and stayed beyond his residence permit and was deported.

He applied for citizenship dozens of times and was turned down every time. The immigration people told him, 'We have enough people. Find somewhere else,' but he would tell them, 'But I love Egypt,' and return. His passport looked like a scandal of stamps and cancelled visas, quite a mess. I saw him once after one of those deportations, hardly capable of standing from illness and exhaustion. He almost perished as a result of all of these adventures, but he stayed very determined to fight to return. I don't know the secret of its charm and I am not surprised at his behavior but, praise God, I am finally back."

I invited her to lunch at my house. We went out of her company headquarters together and went to the Tawfiqiya market. We bought some food, which she examined with great expertise and haggled with the vendors. When I saw her moving so naturally there, I couldn't wait. I ordered her, like any eastern man finally ordering his wife, to go with me to bring her suitcase from the hotel because she would live with me.

Crisis

He had loved her in silence ever since he first saw her. She was his sister's classmate. He was attracted to her considerable self-confidence and her gaiety. He waited until she was close to graduating and surprised her by asking for her hand from her father without telling her one word about it. This incensed her and when her father left the two of them alone she asked him, "Why didn't you broach the subject with me?"

"I am broaching it in my direct manner. There's no need to stop you on the street and propose to you or wait for you to visit my sister to impose myself on you."

She turned him down without any discussion. She said he just wanted to complete the furnishing of the house with a bride. Any other bride would have seen in him a model youth, refined and serious; she would have liked his neatness, calm, and achieving his goals without a lot of noise, and also his family's love of him. There was a general sort of admiration, but it remained a good distance away from the heart. She wanted a more passionate, more daring man, someone who would break the rules and take matters into his own hands rather than throwing a bucket of water under them and wait for them to float to the surface before picking them up. She had closed her heart against anything but the illusion of the first love that came only once in life. She said to herself, "One falls in love truly only once. I did and I failed." She limited her dreams to continuing her studies abroad.

He invited her to dinner through her father. She didn't know why she said yes; was it curiosity? Family encouragement? Or boredom? He told her that he loved her and that she was right when she turned him down but that he deserved to be given another real chance, that he was willing to wait until she knew him up close. He sneaked into her life with tireless perseverance until she found herself wondering one morning, "Should I marry the man who loves me or the man I love?"

Agreeing to the marriage stood in the way of many of her dreams and changed the course of her life. She had to join him in Safaga where he worked, as she had learned since early childhood that the wife followed the husband wherever he went. It was a pattern she was quite familiar with since her father, a police officer, had to be transferred every few years to a different town and the family moved with him. She didn't know how she would combine studying with travel, but she didn't give up. She adjusted her life to what was possible.

They decided to postpone finding an apartment in Cairo until his mandatory service in Safaga was finished. Cairo's housing crunch surprised them a short while after they were married, but during the holidays they didn't feel the full extent of the problem since they stayed sometimes with her family and sometimes with his. When returning to Cairo for good was a necessity, they decided to pool all their money and buy a condominium. But Mustafa's mother suggested that they renovate the family home.

"Let's build one apartment to begin with, then finish the rest of the house when we can."

They pooled all their savings and paid off their mother's and siblings' shares of the inheritance and finished the construction. The habits of the family, which gathered around the mother, didn't change. Mustafa felt grateful to his siblings for taking care of their mother. But their return from Safaga came as a shock to the family, which had arranged its life around their being away in Safaga most of the time. In the meantime, Nahid and Mustafa were delighted to be with the family, longing for closeness after years of being away in a small town. When the summer was over and Maha started school, and Nahid got her job at the antiquities department, the problem revealed itself; they discovered they didn't really have a home, it was more like a marketplace or a bus depot. They didn't know who would come or when, and who'd stay for how long. They had no privacy, no rest, no place to study or to write papers or just be by themselves, to catch their breath or take a nap at siesta time. The discipline and order which gave Mustafa success in his work and Nahid progress in her studies in Safaga disappeared.

At the beginning they tried to contain matters in the hope that each family of the siblings would be busy with its own world when school started. But things got worse: some children were enrolled in nearby schools and their mothers came to pick them up in the evening; the husband of a sister who lived in Mansura had to stay in Cairo three days a week for some training sessions. The family gathered in front of television in the living room until two in the morning and asked Nahid to keep the kitchen ready to serve meals twenty-four hours a day.

They discovered the loss of their freedom under the pressure of the unjustified communal living condition, having to wear appropriate clothes before crossing the threshold of the bedroom, the inability to speak except in whispers behind walls that kept nobody and nothing private. They started getting physically tired. The mere sight of their siblings' cars in front of the house caused them agitation before they even got in the house. Then two simple incidents caused a change in the course of their lives. One night, Nahid got up in alarm after hearing sounds in the room. She asked, "Who is it?"

Mustafa's mother's voice came from in front of the wardrobe, "I needed some money and all the money is in your wardrobe!"

Mustafa woke up in surprise, realizing what was happening as he looked at his watch which indicated 5:00 a.m. Covering her naked body, Nahid said, "Money? Now?"

"Yes," the mother said, finishing what she was doing and left the room as Nahid wept silently.

As for the other incident, it was Mustafa's sister traveling to Cyprus with her husband without telling them and leaving her three children at home. They were surprised by the presence of the children and their involuntary responsibility for them. When Mustafa asked his mother why they hadn't asked their permission before leaving, just out of courtesy, she said, "My daughter is entitled to take a break away from her kids. And she left them for her mother and not for you."

"Our living with you requires a different system. I want a house where I can enjoy my freedom just as they enjoy their freedom in their houses. Everyone can come and visit you one day a week."

She said calmly, "Why don't you go back where you were and make some more money to build another story or find a job in any Arab country? I can't live without my children."

"Why did you let me pay all I had and buy out your share and my brothers' and sister's shares?"

"I didn't imagine you couldn't stand your brothers and sisters."

Mustafa and Nahid noticed, after that discussion, that what was happening around them was deliberate, and that the details which they thought were just a difference in habits, were intentional so that they would leave the house or accept the situation as it was.

He went out on the street carrying his effects, and accompanied by his wife and daughter. He was without a specific destination. On his key chain was a key of an apartment that belonged to a friend, one they used to meet in for studying in their student days. He knew his friend had moved out after getting married and didn't know whether he'd kept it or not. He called his friend, who told him he could use it until he got his affairs in order.

Nahid tried to talk to Mustafa about the decision to leave the house, the only thing they owned, to his family, but he said, "She is my mother and they are my brothers and sisters."

"Why don't you arrange that your mother or older brother buy the house? They have enough money to buy it. Then we can get another home."

"I am responsible for the mistake and I will fix it."

He had discussed the matter again with his mother and had suggested this very idea, but she had told him to borrow from his in-laws to build a second story. He refused and had no choice but to leave the house which had turned into hell, without telling Nahid what he and his mother had discussed.

They couldn't change Maha's school for a full year, during which they took turns accompanying her from Kubri al-Qubba to Abdin every day. A single rainy day on which traffic became a mess was all it took for Nahid to get upset and renew her persistent question, "Until when will we live in a warehouse while others enjoy our house?"

She didn't forgive him for continuing in business with his older brother and for tying himself to the family that had cruelly cast him out. The situation erected a barrier between the two of them that they couldn't get over, a barrier fed by the troubles of everyday life in a small house that stifled their emotions. The kindness she showered him with did not help break the barrier, it was a bitter kindness that reminded him that he had to regain possession of his house and that he was unable to take back what was rightfully his. He was provoked by her silence, her crying, and her dreams. In her case, the psychological sense of protection was shattered; she didn't know who protected whom. She stood by him, protecting him against caving in, pushing him to work until he lost himself completely in it, leaving his problem for time to solve. Then, suddenly one day, his mother died and he sold the house without telling Nahid, and bought a plot in the Pyramids area close to where Nahid worked, got it built quickly and moved his family there.

Contact

She followed him with eyes that smiled at the surprise of suddenly see-ing him in front of her, crossing the corridor that separated the two sides of the store. She had gone into the store to buy some special batteries and there he was. She watched him as he made his purchases, then went up to him, "Hani, how are you?"

He took his time absorbing the surprise and as he extended his hand to greet her, she thought of the many years that had passed since they last met. "What a strange world we live in!" she thought, without feeling that inner jolt that she had imagined she would feel every time she pictured her reaction when she met him. She was not worried that there was no jolt; his self-confident ease was reassuring and his usual steadfastness in the face of surprises did not make her angry as it had in earlier times.

During the next few minutes she learned from him that he lived in a nearby building, to which he pointed, saying he had moved there two years after their graduation. He told her that he was living with his wife and his son, Nadir. So, he kept the name of the child that he had want-ed to have with her one day. "Great," she said several times. They exchanged telephone numbers and promised to arrange a reunion with classmates soon. She got in the car and chose a longer route to give her an additional five minutes to call to mind, not the days of their love, but the days she drove her car past his old home in the hope of seeing him by chance, even though she knew where he worked and could go to him at any time.

She wasn't serious about meeting him; she was just recalling a story that had made a real impact on her life even though it was built on an illusion. No, it wasn't an illusion at the time, but that which determined the course of her life. It was a childhood thing, nothing more. Why all this happiness that came over her when she realized that she wasn't shak-en by meeting him, and because she felt he was faraway and a stranger? Did she need all these years to prove that to herself? Yes, because now she was able to stare facts directly in the face. And, because she had been used to having a calm internal dialogue with herself since she was young, she was able to see clearly; even if the decisions she made were contrary to her wishes, she made them fully aware, at least at the moment, of the factors that shaped her decision-making.

She loved him and thought that losing that love meant her losing all love: "For a person cannot truly be in love twice," that's what she always said. It was a naïve attitude that circumstances helped cement as if it were fact. When the family pressured her to agree to marry Mustafa, who loved her and had waited for her for three years, she was crying over her separation from Hani, and refusing to be another's. Then she gave her grief free reign inside her without naming it or allowing it to be embroidered in the image of the one who, when he kissed her finger as he held her hand one morning, caused her eyes to well up with tears under the many taboos that she believed in and did not want.

Finally, after she had tamed her feelings towards Hani, covered them carefully and placed them in a safe hiding place, she settled the matter in favor of the man who loved her, without being able to offer him her heart. She left her feelings in their well, contenting herself with a single thread of sadness out of which life, later on, wove a delicate, translucent web that was difficult to see, even for her, and made of it a trap for other threads that subsequent losses added.

Nahid did not summon the hidden secret from the depths of the well but found it floating in front of her when she met a mutual friend after years of absence, if that friend said something that reminded her of Hani's world. Unexpectedly, one would see her undoing the satin ribbons wrapped around her secret and would let herself go, cursing love and what it did to lovers. She would bring out her hidden secret to the light and cry her heart out, and would take long walks down unfamiliar paths of memory and feelings. Then she'd end up making peace with herself, admitting her right to suffer and to scream. And scream she would, soundlessly, even though she was used to hiding from her own voice.

Then she would calm down and tie the ribbons around her secret to return it to the well where many moons had fallen without lighting it.

Reassurance was not the reaction she was looking for in the scenario of her anticipated meeting, which she had worked over dozens of times in her head throughout the previous years. But the reassurance brought about a feeling of restfulness that enveloped her and enabled her to smile calmly in contrast with her usual boisterous response when she met her classmates. She had followed news of him from her friends; she learned that he got married at the time that he did, and she kept up with news of his career success, and his joining the bureau of an international organization in Cairo. And despite the bitterness of love's defeat, as she called it, she never held it against him. "He's a noble human being, but he's dull. Why haven't I seen this before?" It was a logical question, from her experience, now much richer than when she was eighteen. She knew that what drew them apart was not an external circumstance but rather a combination of circumstances that had led to mutual aversion. "I didn't find something in front of me to cling to." Even the question that kept posing itself without any answer, *why*, which she had expected to ask him one way or another, to hear his story as he had lived it, to know his true, contradictory feelings—even that question did not occur to her at that moment. "I am no longer the same girl." She looked into the mirror and saw eyes that had experienced the world.

Their next meeting was not by chance. They arranged it by telephone without resorting to subterfuge. She thought it was only natural for the two of them to sit down together to find out what the journey had been like. A question persisted in her head as they were shaking hands goodbye, "Why were you so determined to prove your success? Why did you present him with a dry, strong woman who made fun of the feelings of adolescence?" She remembered that she had told him she'd met a mutual friend by chance, and that he kept using his name in every sentence to push her to ask about him. She commented on that incident by saying that some people lived in the delusions of adolescence forever! He didn't reply. "Why did you do that? Was it some feverish effort to prove yourself, to make him regret, for instance? Or was it an attempt to exculpate that which you know so well?"

She turned the page without allowing him again into her dreams. She never saw him in her dreams afterwards. Before that meeting, her dreams of him had been a strange internal means to remind her of him when she forgot him in her busy life. She saw him as he was: vacillating, satisfying neither her feelings nor her mind, putting her on an unbalanced scale whose continually moving pans carried her sky-high only to send her tumbling down the following moment. If she ran towards him, he would meet her with an earnest smile and tied hands. If she waited he would pick her up and soar away. In her daydreams, when she got fed up with his indifference, which wounded her feelings, he would appear to her, without calculation, as a loving, caring man as he told her once in a moment of truth whose memory she cherished.

They stayed in touch afterwards with difficulty. She pushed aside the persistent question. They sought out each other out of a desire to know. She tried to get over the urge to ask him about the past by various means and guises. But in the end she found herself confronting a single question: what happened? Even though she, at one time or another, had realized he didn't love her or, more simply put, that her estimation of that love was much higher at the time than she would later realize. It was a realization revealed to her by a truism that she hadn't known or believed at the time, namely that the other person did not necessarily love you to the same degree that you loved them, or love you at all.

The emotions that she freely shared with others opened their hearts to her, but she didn't realize that opening them did not mean that one should just enter. Therefore, she had imagined that his feelings had matured just as hers had after they both had declared their love for one another, and was quite shocked when he acted as if there was nothing going on between them. She had woven a shared future but he hadn't. He contented himself with the available present when he had the time and he gave his public life and his political activities all his time. They would agree to meet at ten in the morning at the college then he would come at three in the afternoon, only to leave her fifteen minutes later for an important engagement. If she refused to give him another date, he would pursue her day and night until she said yes. He would snatch her away from their friends and from her studies only to go back to the same circle a few days later. Always on a fiery peak for a while, then an ice lake. She couldn't keep up with these changes, or pause long enough to savor either condition, positively or negatively. This even began to affect her body—when he passed closely by her, she felt excessive heat, which turned into cold in a few seconds only to be suddenly hot again. One day a girlfriend of hers on whom she was leaning, on a bench at the college, felt that sudden change and screamed. And when she gave her a calm knowing look, her friend burst out laughing and they both cursed love and what it did to lovers. It was the kind of love that caused you to burst out crying or experience joy and tremendous attraction that in one second turned into blinding fury, then returned to a frenzied search for it. It was a love around which revolved time, events, relations with others, hopes and frustrations; it was life itself.

Her happiness in meeting him, without sharp conflicting feelings, pointed to the long road she had traveled, without her realizing that some of its fruit was now falling in her lap. She also didn't realize that her plan to achieve other goals had woven in her bleeding wound real tissues that closed deep gaps, that opening the wound was not as easy now as it once was, in the distant past. When a hand was extended to shake hers, coldly or reluctantly, or with a bit of curiosity as she imagined, she began to realize that she had been a different person before, and that she was now another, but that these parts of her were related to him in a way she was not related to anyone else. She can at least trust him or so she told herself; perhaps there was nostalgia for a happiness she once loved or for a feeling that she never experienced again.

Even when she met the love of her life, Omar, years later, they were not the same feelings. The sharp shock of live electrical wire was gone, replaced by real tremors of internal earthquakes that shook her to her very foundation despite her attempts to resist. There was a big difference between the two experiences even in the joy each brought on. The joy in the first case was innocent and childlike, even when it tyrannically took hold of her very being. But the joy with Omar had a different weight, augmented by an awareness that made it more profound than the extended calm feeling she had with Hani, even in her imagination. She didn't dare, even once, go further in fantasizing about Hani than to place her head on his shoulder—something that never happened in reality. With Omar, though, she was capable of being overcome with a real desire to merge, body and soul, with him.

"The body, what a tyrant that subjugates those with the strongest of wills and the sturdiest moral character!" she sighed.

She went back to her diary and discovered that, on paper, she was two people, that she had simply pitted her rational half against her emotional one, that she had lived her life wishing to unify them instead of letting them be at odds with each other. She had forgotten about the diary that she had called 'The Black Book' in the midst of her preoccupations. There was another surprise in store for her when she read it with the eye of her fourth decade: the pain of the words vanished in the transparent and delicate feelings which reflected, unbeknown to her, a love of life and an intense desire for survival that the girl she had one day been had. Under the title, "To the Rest of Me," she read:

"(My) longing for the rest of me rends me."

"Can you retrieve it?"

"It's blended with him. I can't tell it apart from him."

"How?"

"We've blended. Our parts are mingled, and when we separated, neither of us could capture the features of the self prior to love. And yet we split. I discovered afterwards that parts of him live in me and remnants

of me in him. Longing for these remnants torments me, rends me."

"Give up what you have of him."

"I can't. It's what's left for me. It is me now."

"You're not looking for the rest of you. You've been looking for him."

A flash of light surprised her, bringing back the feelings of hot and cold which Hani used to produce in her. Her mouth felt dry and her eyes welled with tears, as if time or its shadow had not moved. She regained her composure and kept reading, and the more she read the louder the voice and she got lost in the words, not the thoughts

Ecstasy

"Everything has a great ecstasy at the beginning and also at the end."

"Followed by?"

"Great sadness or great joy."

"And you, are these tears in your eyes?"

"No. My eyes will not cry now that the pains have been drowned in my chest."

"My dear little one: they are showing all over you. So why smother them? Letting them inside you will light a fire that will be difficult to put out."

"I draw comfort from the ashes of the fire."

"So are they the tears of smoke then?"

"The remnants of the smoke will dissipate with the wind and will just be a memory that I imagine will visit me from distant quarters."

"Do you now know where this ecstasy has come from?"

She folded the pages with fingers almost numbed by the cold as her voice, which had stopped, continued to reverberate in the space around her. In the silence she found a pang of grief that spelled his name on the threshold of memories.

That reassurance did not last long. A vague feeling of happiness and longing sneaked in on her as they sat alone one evening at a table in a place they used to meet. She was not ready for this change, and he did not give any indication of how he felt, but she was afraid that her glances at him would betray her, that he might understand. She didn't allow her heart to display joy at receiving a signal from him. She firmly rebuffed her heart's attempt to break loose and act coquettishly. Soon she was back firmly in control, the way she had been used to it all her life—limiting herself to a strict framework that allowed for no intrusion. She came out of that meeting staggering, the question coming back gleaming in the dark of her soul: what exactly do I feel towards him?

She answered with a brevity not befitting her age or the situation, "These are feelings of other humans of a long gone era." But her heart, which was not frightened by the candor of the answer, created in her dreams a long embrace which took her back ten years, accompanied by all the ordeals of a love vacillating between yes and no. She removed all the barricades that the mind had placed before the imagination and allowed him to accompany her to countries that she loved in her travels. She invited him to a dinner during which they were serenaded by slow music and danced with him until everyone was gone. Then she let him kiss her. Another time she invited him again, then withdrew to her room when she felt he was getting too close to her. A short while later he was knocking on her door and then he finished the dance with her on the hotel balcony overlooking the northern Mediterranean. Then she changed the scene to his coming to visit her when she was sick and insisting on staying by her side until the morning. She could only fantasize about these dreams, like sequences of romantic love in which the body is left out of the equation, which she thought was what love was all about. She also thought she would never know any other kind of love. She could not at that moment bring him in her imagination to the African continent where she lived. Rather she accompanied him, crossing vast waters with high waves so blue that the mind got lost in them before they landed on terra firma on some island or another where she could dream of him embracing her gently. She contented herself with that until she woke up at their next meeting realizing that she had now been completely weaned, that she now knew him quite well, even though she'd never asked him about what he did to her: not deserting her but pushing her to desert him. Nor did she ask him the question that had kept her awake many a night, if he had really loved her in the past or was she just imagining it.

She let herself enjoy his friendship and the practical relationship that had developed between them on the margins of their lives without asking the questions. She never found out why he desired to renew their relationship. Was he also in need of the reassurance provided by another human being who had come from the past when kindness, trust, and love characterized relationships during that period of their lives, in an atmosphere in which they discovered that they were two beings who met by chance at a time not their own? She never found out and she subsequently didn't stop imagining a fleeting scene in which a momentary embrace was not completed. She'd smile and her heart would stretch coquettishly, this time without sadness. The wound was not healed and the satin ribbons came off, floating on the surface of the well because the secret treasure had dissolved and the ribbons floated on the water like a colored paper boat, its banner flying like bygone years bearing the imprints of forgiving and forgetting, since life had given her true love which for a long time she thought only a few were entitled to. She would say that to herself fearfully.

Escapade

It was foggy and he could barely see the broad outlines of shapes moving in front of him. He was used to driving slowly under such weather conditions. He felt refreshed and calm in the cool quiet around him. When he saw her running in the street in front of him, carrying her little daughter, he turned the headlights on and off several times to alert her to get out of the way, and when he honked briefly, she stepped aside, almost stumbling. He stopped the car next to her and immediately recognized her. As he introduced himself, he asked her if she needed help.

"I need a doctor. My daughter has a fever and my telephone isn't working."

He opened the car door, telling her about a doctor in one of the back streets, and, unusually for him, he drove fast as he tried to calm her down. "My daughter tried to climb down from her bed but couldn't stand. I put my hand on her forehead and could feel it burning. My shyness prevented me from knocking on my neighbor's door, so I carried her, not knowing where to go."

The doctor said she had scarlet fever and told her to get a penicillin shot right away and directed her to a nearby twenty-four-hour pharmacy. She bought the medicine but the pharmacist refused to give the shot saying she needed an allergy test first. They went to a private hospital but the doctor there refused to give her the injection and refused to do the test. They left the hospital quickly in anger and drove a considerable distance through Cairo until they arrived at Abu al-Reesh Hospital in the Sayyida Zaynab neighborhood. When denied service there also, Mustafa asked the doctor angrily, "Should I get a mechanic to give her a penicillin shot?"

"Sorry, penicillin often produces very serious adverse reactions and the tests are often misleading."

Her copious tears as she told Mustafa that her daughter had had penicillin shots many, many times made it difficult for him to maintain his composure. He left the hospital with her, threatening everyone there that he'd sue them. He asked her about the name of her doctor and where he lived because his office was most probably closed at that time. She asked him to wait until she found out his address from her aunt by telephone since he was a neighbor of her aunt who could also send someone over to ask him to stay if he was at home. A few minutes later she came back, hopeful: "Now I can breathe easy. He lives in Doqqi." She hugged her daughter and refused his suggestion that the girl sleep on the back seat.

She bitterly related to him how she couldn't ask help from her neighbors who closed their doors quickly when she leaves her apartment to take the milk from the milkman.

She said, "Just seeing me in the corridor frightens the women, as if I were a devil even though I don't mix with anyone and I only exchange the morning greeting with them. Every one of them fears for her husband from me, even though I am a married woman, as you know."

He looked at her sideways, anxious that she not notice his glance. He had known her since she moved into the neighborhood. She was the subject of many rumors because of her beauty and youth and the fact that her husband was forty years older than her. Her beauty was not the kind that would ordinarily catch his attention. She was white with pronounced features and a stout figure almost as tall as he but twice as broad. Her long, black hair had come undone due to the movements of her child held to her chest and she looked more tender than she had a little earlier.

"My husband comes only for a few hours at a time whenever he can get away from his responsibilities. He spends some time with me, which is my whole life since he made me stay home from work and close my atelier after we got married. Waiting for him and giving my daughter an education are now the only things in my life."

The city was stretching as it woke up lazily on the day leading up to Eid al-Adha, most of its inhabitants having left for their villages or to Alexandria despite the cold. The stores were closed and most people were fasting, waiting to break their fast with Muslims on the hajj, standing on Mount Arafat.

The light traffic made it possible for them to make it quickly to Doqqi Square, which was still asleep. She was right to feel reassured; the doctor who welcomed them was experienced and precise with a healing smile. He said it was too early to be sure that the girl had scarlet fever and that he thought it more likely a case of rheumatic inflammation resulting from repeated exposure to tonsillitis, and that the fainting resulted from not eating enough. He gave her a penicillin shot and some medication to reduce the fever and asked them to go to a lab that he telephoned to open especially for them on that holiday.

It wasn't the same woman leaving the doctor's building, but a cheerful, optimistic one, moving with an agility incongruous with her weight, holding her daughter's hand. She went to the only open store and bought some cookies which she tried to convince her daughter to eat. Then she turned to him, thanking him for his help, and asking him to go to his work now that there was movement in the streets and taxis were available. He didn't understand why he insisted on staying with her until everything was taken care of. She acquiesced and they went to the lab and had the prescribed tests. They were told that the results would be available before midnight. He gave her a ride home as the city began to put on the joyful colors of the wait for the Eid. He learned from her that the girl was from an ex-husband, that she married the husband of one of her mother's relatives who took pity on her because of her former husband's refusal to support his daughter. Then he proposed to her on condition that their marriage be kept secret so that her aunt wouldn't suffer and his children wouldn't get mad, especially because he was a very wealthy man.

Thus he justified his position. He bought the condominium in the Pyramids neighborhood for her, so she would be away from the family home. They spent the rest of the ride back in silence; he thinking about the coincidence that left such a deep impression that he couldn't explain and she thinking about the illnesses that came to her mind when she saw her daughter falling prey to a disease she didn't know: meningitis, paralysis. She let out a soft moan as she squeezed her handkerchief hard, saying, "O God."

Her voice cut into his quiet. He turned to her, "Have faith in God. Your daughter is fine and I'll contact you to let you know the lab results." She thanked him, "My conversation with my aunt will make my husband get in touch with me right away. Please say hello to Nahid."

He entered his house in the late afternoon and found the whole family waiting for him, anxious to travel to the village before the call to the sunset prayers so they could break their fast with the extended family. He couldn't suggest postponing the trip till the morning. They were used to spending the night before the day of the Eid in the village to take part in the Eid prayers after dawn. Besides, the test results wouldn't be available until 11:00 p.m.

He assured himself that he could make a telephone call from the village and once again thought about his desire to tell her himself. Nahid attributed his withdrawal inside himself to fatigue or a preoccupation about something that he would reveal only after he got over it and chose the right time to speak, if he wanted to. She'd gotten used to the way he thought and lived, and she no longer bothered him with questions she knew he had no answers for.

He spent the Eid anxiously waiting for it to end. He met his childhood friends and stayed up with them until dawn but he was absent-minded and irritable in a way that he didn't understand. His impatience to return was not tempered by the return of his brother from a study leave abroad that had lasted for years, nor by his wish to learn about the details of his trip and what he had accomplished, or by wanting to inquire after the conditions of his family which in recent years he visited only sporadically. Had it not been for some self control remaining to him, he would have returned to Cairo with his children the following day. He also suddenly remembered that he hadn't asked Reem whether she would spend the rest of the holidays in Cairo or not. Would her husband take her somewhere? Would she go to her family?

Feverish sleep. Anxiety. Boredom. He lost his concentration under the pressure seething inside him. He got angry at his son who asked him to take a phone call, saying that he didn't want to talk to anybody. Then he took the call. He reversed all his decisions that he made throughout the three days he spent in the village. He agreed with the children to visit his uncle, then cancelled it and an hour later accompanied them there. He agreed to have a cookout in the mango orchard, then changed his mind, but in the evening he yelled at them to bring the grilling equipment so they wouldn't be late. He decided to accompany them on a Nile boat at sunset, changed his mind at noon, and in the afternoon made the arrangements for the boat ride. Nahid watched from a distance, keeping herself and the children out of his sight, soundlessly.

Several times she was on the verge of asking him if he had lost one of his friends or heard some disturbing news, but she held off. Then she noticed in the following days the famous symptoms of the fever of love but she put them quickly out of her mind, for her husband who hadn't changed his habits ever since they got married still showed that he cared very much for her. She watched him as he prayed devoutly, and concluded, "He hasn't done anything to make God angry at him." And when he calmed down and seemed to be serene, she dismissed the whole idea.

He had made a decision to stop his crazy waiting for Reem to appear in her balcony or to seize upon the chance of her being out on the street at the time of his return. He discovered that he enjoyed his relish for it. It seemed to him as he sat by himself in his balcony at night that she passed by the glass window and stood for a few minutes. And even though the dark hid the direction of her gaze, he had a hidden feeling that it was directed at him. He tried to find out if she appeared at specific times but he could never return home at a fixed time to be certain of that. He thought of knocking on her door with the pretext of inquiring after her daughter's health but he dismissed the idea, thinking it was possible that he might forget about the whole thing and preoccupy himself with an upcoming trip that would last two months at least.

He didn't tell Nahid the story of the girl's illness, and Reem somehow figured this out with her female intuition, so she didn't talk to Nahid about anything. One day he saw the girl playing with other children in the garden in front of the house. He had learned from the lab that the doctor's diagnosis was correct, that the illness was a simple, temporary condition. He did not need to withdraw into solitude to introspect as he had been used to throughout his life. Reem triggered within him a question about the meaning of true love. What, exactly, were his feelings for Nahid? Was he experiencing a midlife crisis? Questions about self-fulfillment and fear of the passage of time without achieving major goals. "But I do love Nahid even though some boredom has managed to sneak in. Nahid is moving away, I feel it. She is moving away in a sad way that I don't understand. Could it be that I haven't lived up to her expectations? I don't think so. I also see her contented."

Just as he had almost given up on a chance meeting with Reem, she sought him out asking for a special favor. Before he had awakened to the fact that he was experiencing this chance meeting at the neighborhood florist's shop, and had dealt with the myriad feelings that came over him and made him behave in a childlike, joyous manner for which he reproached himself, she told him that his neighbor, who lived next door, was badgering her. She asked him to intervene and put an end to this behavior, since she just wanted to be left alone to look after her child. Before he could ask her about anything she reached out to shake his hand and thanked him, turning around to leave. But he stopped her, saying, "Have more trust in the world. You don't need to be afraid of it."

He didn't really want to say that but a wet blanket had drenched his feelings and left him shivering, so he put on the garb of gravitas.

The surprise that was awaiting him upon his return from his trip was not just the death of her husband, but also Nahid's taking part in giving testimony to the police to confirm that Reem's husband had frequented her apartment, thus establishing her rights which she didn't have a single document to support.

The story had begun a short while after news of the husband's death was announced. Nahid was surprised one morning when a distraught Reem knocked on her door. She was not used to visits from her, they usually just met by chance in the neighborhood since it was a quiet area with few residents. Nahid invited her in, but Reem asked her to go with her to her apartment right away, saying, "A police officer has come to verify my right to the place and my marriage. My husband used to assure me that he had secured my future and kept the papers in a safe place. I never asked him to give me a copy of the documents. I was content with his being there with me. I never expected from him anything other than shelter and help with the bare necessities. I was careful not to hurt my aunt's feelings, and I kept away from the family. My father announced to everybody that I had married a conservative man who didn't approve of visits and that I was happy with him. Therefore, no one invited me. Whenever I needed them, I went to our house to visit my father and stepbrothers."

Despite her surprise, Nahid sympathized with her and told the investigating officer that the residents of the neighborhood were introduced to Reem and the man who visited her as a married couple, that the doorman, the neighbors, and the merchants dealt with them as such. A grocery store clerk testified similarly as did two security guards who worked for a government official in a house nearby. Nahid told Mustafa, "I didn't see any of the women neighbors there, just like the time I went to offer my condolences and Reem told me that they all came together, spent half an hour with her, then left, never to be seen again. Not a single man from the apartment building visited her to offer his condolences even though her father and brother were there with her."

Mustafa did not comment and Nahid continued, "A few days later she called me and gave me her telephone number and asked me to stay in touch with her because she was lonely. News spread quickly among the neighbors and everybody realized how innocent and naïve Reem was— she had no marriage certificate, no deed to the condo, not even a lease to the apartment. All she had were a few scraps of paper that she showed to the women neighbors as she wept and told her story in utter, amazing simplicity. On some of these scraps were written a few words: 'Dear Wife, I'll drop by in two days,' or 'I didn't want to wake you up.' He left her these notes if he came to visit and she was not there or if he left after she had fallen asleep, late at night."

She found him before her when she opened the door. She invited him to come in, hiding a desire to throw herself in his arms. He closed the door and before sitting where she invited him to sit, he took her in his arms. He didn't know how, given her considerable girth, he was able to hold her to his chest. He wiped her tears saying, "Everything will be okay." And he didn't move away. As they stood there, he gave her a long kiss on the forehead that was interrupted only when the phone rang.

"I couldn't come before. I repressed my desire with an iron will."

"I knew I'd meet a man who'd awaken in me my feminine desires, but I was obstinately resisting it. My husband was like a brother to me. He came here to talk to me about his problems, his worries, without expecting any solutions from me. I liked his company and fondly waited for his visits, for I had nobody else in the world. Even with my father and his family, I felt I was a burden and a stranger. I knew you were that man when you went with me to the doctor. That's why I stayed away from you so as not to ruin your life. I am not the monster that the wives here make me out to be, as if I would snatch one of their men. I love Nahid, she's the only one who speaks to me and shows me kindness."

"Don't we deserve this moment? Don't I deserve that you be mine and then come what may? From now on, don't worry about anything else outside this little space which unites us, please."

Thirst alone was not the reason their enjoyment was so fleeting. It was his way, which was like that of a rooster: a fleeting moment of eruption that ends the moment the deed is done. She was ignorant; she thought shyness and her longing for a man and his confusion were the reason for this brief eruption. She wanted to sleep in his arms, but he reminded her that he had ostensibly come to offer his condolences, and promised to arrange for another meeting. He asked her to watch the street so he could leave without being seen by any of the neighbors, for no one had seen him coming, and that way he could come another day on the pretext of offering his condolences. She stood behind the balcony door until she ascertained that there was no one around and gave him a signal. He sneaked out and she watched him as he entered his house, reminding herself that it was impossible to move between the two houses without being found out, that even the arrival of a car would cause doors and windows to open.

When Nahid finally realized what was going on, she resisted her desire to confront him. Then she postponed the confrontation, hoping to discover that it was a figment of her imagination, or until she made sure that it was real or that he had stopped doing it. She didn't know when she smelled his underwear one time, commenting that it was reeking of ghee, and wondering what he was eating these days, that she had almost recognized the other woman in his life. She had once referred to that other woman in mirth, using a line from the comedian Abdel Fattah al-Qusari as 'tubs of running ghee.' She couldn't restrain herself from sleuthing, which she did unintentionally most of the time and intentionally some times. Bits of information began to come to her without the least effort on her part—his awkwardness when, lifting the telephone receiver, she would find him on the line with a woman whose voice she recognized but wasn't able to pinpoint. He would tell her that she was a friend's wife asking him to do her a favor, thus changing one of his lifelong habits which was never to justify or explain anything no matter what. There were the long telephone conversations at night even though previously he had only used the telephone for one or two minutes at a time. There was the feigned intense physical interest which failed if she was responsive. There was her constant feeling that his eyes were watching her from afar and when they settled on her back and she felt the heat of his gaze and turned suddenly, she found his eyes averted in shame. She would get up near dawn and find him sitting on the bed, smoking even though he had quit years earlier. There were the inexplicable absences and travel which was now frequent, without real details. There were the sudden disappearances, the boisterous happiness at times, and unjustified misery at other times, as if he were tossing and turning, experiencing heat and extreme cold at the same time.

Twice, by chance, she found out that Reem was traveling at the same time as Mustafa, but she did not make the connection. The precision with which he managed the situation was foolproof, nevertheless she found a hotel bill for a room for two and roundtrip tickets which alerted her dormant antennae and she started compiling a file: the strange scent on his clothes, his visits to his mother which did not materialize, and so on. Then one evening, as she was closing the window, she saw him going into the opposite building after turning off the car's headlights. "So she is the source of the strange smell on his clothes and body!" She withdrew quietly and waited for him in bed, thinking about what to do.

He greeted her, taking the following day's paper to the bathroom after telling her that he didn't need supper. After that she started monitoring his movements with tremendous self-control.

When she saw him sneaking into the opposite building, she quickly put on street clothes. She chose a simple outfit, a light pair of shoes, and strong perfume and covered her hair with a long colorful scarf. She looked at herself in the mirror and made sure she looked beautiful and happy. Then she took a box of chocolate and knocked on the door. Reem opened it, wearing a silk robe suggesting that she was naked underneath. She apologized that she had been about to take a bath. Nahid ignored the remark and sat down and coyly asked for a cup of tea. She had not yet drawn up any specific plan: should she play with their nerves or catch them together? She had thought that Reem wouldn't open the door and let anybody see him there. He must be hiding in the bedroom now and will be forced to face her presence from his hiding place. The thought occurred to her when Reem took her leave to put some clothes on and left her in the living room, feeling his presence with every atom of her being. She knew where he sat, where he drank his tea, where he kissed her. Tears almost came to her eyes, but she pulled herself together and put on a fake smile.

Reem told her that a lawyer for her husband's family had asked her to sign a quit claim for all her rights in return for ownership of the condo, which would be recorded in her name right away, and to pledge not to make the marriage public according to the wishes of the deceased himself. She added that she had agreed to these conditions but was surprised that her husband's eldest son, who was five years her senior, had accompanied the lawyer at the signing of the papers and the recording of them in City Hall, which indicated that there was a large fortune hidden from her, and that by that agreement she had signed her rights away.

Bowing her head, Nahid said, "Maybe they are trying to avoid a scandal."

"At least I am not in the street. I have a home now," Reem replied.

Nahid couldn't stand it anymore. She took her leave and left sadly, knowing that she had ruined the night for them. She thought of waiting for him on the balcony, making it impossible for him to cross the street to increase tension for both of them but she thought that what she had done that night was enough. She liked 'the black game' as she called it later on and she skillfully managed to thwart their attempts to meet. If he told her that he was on his way to visit the family, he would find her at the door beating him to the car; if he said he had to run an errand before going there, she would tell him that waiting for him wouldn't bother her. If he decided to travel, she would get a leave of absence, send the boy and girl to her mother, saying she needed to be alone with him. Tormented by doubt, he lost track of his appointments and became a nervous wreck. She would welcome him with open arms calmly and cheerfully. She filled his schedule with evenings with friends which she arranged first, and then informed him of. She enjoyed the hurdle race until she got bored with the game. She waited for him at the door the moment he crossed the street coming from Reem's house and said to him, "Why should I make you miserable because you cannot see her? She's yours any time."

She left to prepare a supper she knew he wouldn't touch. His shock destroyed his ability to respond to her and he started murmuring some sharp words, rushing towards her until she felt the heat of his shoulder almost encircling her. She ignored his threatening closeness to her body and went on preparing the food, turning once to stop him with one firm glance after which he left for the bedroom without saying anything. He noticed the black souvenir box and knew that a confrontation was inevitable. The following day she calmly said, "I want the whole story."

"What happened, happened. Accept it or reject it."

"I want the reasons so I can choose to accept or reject."

"NO."

He took the refuge in silence as usual. She needed any answer but silence. As she felt the presence of beings choking her, beings of long patience and adaptation to what was possible that she had skillfully woven, she lost her composure. She remembered his denying her the right to physical fulfillment, his giving up their house to his family without any significant resistance, his ignoring every problem, leaving it for her to solve or hit head on, it didn't matter to him. She said, "You will not run away from this life-long confrontation forever. This time, time will not solve the problem for you. I want the truth."

He refused. She tried every possible way to persuade him. She used all possible patience to convince him that she wanted to know, not out of curiosity but to get closer to his world, she really wanted to know him so she could overcome this obstacle whose motives were rooted in some kind of necessity, otherwise why did it happen? The only words that escaped his lips were, "There was something exciting about her, I don't know how, something savage, perhaps, something I cannot figure out, something provocative."

Those were the last words he said about that, even though Nahid shunned him and refused to talk about the possibility of a return to a marital relationship as long as he refused to tell her what she wanted. He spent the worst days of his life thinking of nothing but feelings of hatred towards that rigid woman who couldn't accept the fact that the story had ended. He didn't for a moment think of her torment. He was deceived by her self-control. He held her responsible for depriving him of the passionate feeling that had brought such ecstasy into his life. But he realized how much he loved Nahid when he heard her responding to a comment on Reem's behavior by one of the women neighbors. She said, "She's a poor, lonely woman that fate dealt a bad hand. I wish people would leave her alone to deal with her wounds. It's natural for a lonely woman to look for a man."

Mustafa remembered that Nahid's sorrows took their time coming, that she nursed them drop by drop, calmly taming and deferring them which made her sadness bitter, deep, and silent. The Nahid that he knew as a young woman had not been so capable of controlling her feelings. To the contrary, she was quite spontaneous and demonstrative in expressing joy and cried the moment she felt pain. But time pushed her feelings inside and she seemed to have lost her former gaiety. At the same time, she didn't stop expressing her feelings to all those around her. Mustafa, suddenly feeling the pangs of conscience, and without taking a single step, started to figure out a way of going back to her and getting out of his dilemma. He concluded that time would make the problem go away and Nahid forget it. When three months passed without being able to get near her, he said to her like a child who had been grounded too long, "What did I do to shun me like this? It was a mistake and it's over."

Her inner weakness came from a question that kept forcing itself on her mind about the existence of any established true fact in life. Was there anything that one could be sure actually existed? Why was she living with him? She knew that love was not what bound them together, at least in the sense that she had hoped for with her husband. His love for her was the reason she had accepted the principle of adjustment that she had adopted in her life. So, why was *he* paying the price for her wrong decision to be bound to him so long, as she had agreed from the beginning?

She recalled her intimate relations with him and smiled bitterly: if he cannot make me happy, how can he make someone else happy? She almost went to Reem to ask her if she was able to actually connect emotionally with him. Did he treat her differently because she was not his wife? Did he have another personality that she didn't know, a personality that needed a different kind of woman to come into being? Maybe, why not? She wished she could look at them together through the keyhole to know him as he really was and to believe he was capable of that.

In the morning she discovered that her face was covered with little pimples and that many parts of her body were similarly covered. The doctor said they were caused by nervous tension and recommended long rest.

The mirror tormented her, so she cocooned herself in solitude and tears came to her eyes but did not flow. Instead of pitying her, Mustafa resented her in a childlike anger. He thought to himself, "All I need is a sense of guilt for disfiguring her as well." It was a banner of torment that her body had flown without her uttering a single word.

One night, on his way back to his house in which no word was spoken in anger and in which neither the two children nor anybody else in the family sensed that anything was amiss, Mustafa remembered that he hadn't apologized for what he'd done. He went to Nahid and, pushing the book away from her hand said, "Nahid, I am sorry."

When he embraced her, she did not push his hands away.

Desire

As if crushed between the millstones of impotence and desire, I screamed, "I want to be me! I want to escape, body and soul." I asked myself dozens of times: "What are you waiting for?" I've seen my daughter growing up before my eyes at a slow pace that consumed my years and I fell silent for a long time, realizing in the meantime that what I suppressed and repressed would one day explode within me.

The night did not augur any change. The usual is abundantly available: my daughter is in her room, asleep, surrounded by her dolls and teddy bears, dreaming. Tonight I am immersed in silence and tranquility. I watch a film on television while he is fast asleep. He wakes up in alarm and plants himself in front of me without preliminaries and accompanies me to our bedroom. I go without saying a word, knowing the outcome ahead of time. My body is crackling with desire, expanding like a tree whose coarse bark grows until it cracks from sheer vigor and passion. Here I am. I am ready for you. You enter me absently, slowly, restraining yourself from discharging all your desire at once and getting it over with too quickly. You rein in your passion, which would rather dash off to the finish line, leaving me behind. Your attempts at taming your movements exhaust me, filling me with a frustration that drains my desire during our encounters. I beg you to go back to your usual rhythm, to get to your quick release and not to bother about me, to finish what you began. You say, "No, I'll wait for you."

Tears well up in my eyes despite my feigned forbearance. I go hunting for the swallows of desire. I cast my nets for them; I trail my desire behind me as I await the birth of the fiery star as it makes its way out of the nebula. Your body moves slowly.

I feel that you cannot move with that rhythm that brings either of us satisfaction. I hear disparate ringing sounds that do not resolve themselves into a harmony. The star is born weak and dies before it can shine. A sorrow looms, yawning. I get away from it. I scream at it and it falls away. Once again you hold on to my body hard, afraid that your lips might cling to that which my lips seek, and that the genie of your desire might escape, and that you can no longer control it. I redirect my steps and start anew in the hope of discovering some light on the way out of the tunnel. All feelings regroup in one cloud sobbing its songs, needing just one touch to come pouring down. I cannot tell you, as I feel you waiting. I read distant signals and I hear the melody of release playing in my body. I believe and I run. I climb, panting. I light all the candles. I am singed by the fires of shattered desires. I continue laying the fire of longing, hoping for ignition, gathering my moans and crushing them.

The river within begins to erupt into a flood but the feeble motion of your body oozes boredom. My body loses its way to capturing the signal. I hear crashing sounds in my bones and I smell the smoldering smoke. Out of the dark appears a wall like a hill of sand. I fall down a precipice. I hear the rumbling of wheels on an unpaved road as your body gathers up steam in a few seconds, to give quick, panting stabs, followed by a calm like that which prevails after a train has departed. I swallow my saliva and try to open my eyes, covered with salty sweat that reminds me of drowning. My absorption in the moment recedes, and debris closes passages that had been open only a moment ago, burying still-throbbing body parts. Hope looms with a final attempt on your part and you cling to me in anticipation. A different rhythm comes by chance despite the increasing limpness. My chest opens up releasing the air that had been trapped in the throat in the form of a broken moan, spelling desire. Signals are trying to get through, but are stopped by a growing awakening.

"Try," you say.

I gather up my will, like a wind dreaming to beat the center of a cyclone, going through roads and exiles, dissipating and stumbling through tree branches, stirring up the dust, dragging a disappointment that expands each time a stumbling block is swept away. Clouds of realization gather and illusions of silence are put to rest.

You play a final tune with the notes available to you and my body is crushed under the burden of the attempt—a glow comes from outside and the thirsty body opens up, waiting to be filled, deluding itself, hunting for memories of the certainty of being filled, as if it were a speedy, uncontrollable slide when in fact it is a panting climb. The feeble strokes do not resemble anything; they increase the burning but don't lead to a fire. They constitute an empty glare that makes me lose my balance in the zone near zero, just before going into negative territory, into a murky darkness pierced by feeble points of light making it seem as if it is perforated, but it is nonetheless heavy. I go round then I roll in delusion. I try to recall from memory images of what I fantasize is happening to me, trying to get ignition from my head. My mind is quite awake and each stroke adds to its alertness but does not bring it to the center of lightness, to weightlessness.

I plead with him to help by staying away, saying, "Enough! Give my body a chance to catch the spark."

Marches clamor with forced loudness. The mind perceives that his organ is now completely out of its place. The harmony is disrupted and the instruments scattered. My body parts separate and I feel them as organs moving independently from each other. With each step, my mind takes in the empty space, alertness stings like a light brushing against the tent of darkness sheltering body and mind. Massive tension fills my arteries with fright whose wailing echoes reverberate in my soul and I cling to your body even more closely. Desperate attempts are dampened as if by an increasingly cold rain as the mind absorbs the situation: it is as if I am no longer with a man but a woman. And despite the increasingly nerve-racking attempts, I hold on to emptiness and I realize it's no use.

I turn to the wall in silence. I don't know what was extinguished inside—just the body's desires or the very desire to live? I ask myself, "Why are you crying? What hope do you look forward to?" And like all days, I split into two vicious selves, going in opposite directions.

I look around me fearfully as I hear his calm, comfortable breathing, deep in sleep. The night escapes from my questions and the giant whose features become more pronounced day after day, encircles me like an octopus with thousands of hands, gripping all my feelings, squashing them, turning them to burning fires that cannot be put out.

"Self betrayal is the most reprehensible type of treason."

"Self denial is no treason."

"How can someone who betrays herself be truthful with others?"

"I am out of options."

"What do you call succumbing and submitting to failure?"

I spend the nights trying in vain to tame my insomnia. In the morning, my mirror tells me about the bitterness of the years, reconstructing the map of my face. I spend my days resenting everything that floats but does not swim, resenting all existing life like that, neither crossing the river nor returning where they came from, until they are mounted by other beings, whose roots reach the bottom. I don't want to be mounted.

I observe him from a distance, talking, acting, and making decisions calmly, confidently, and proudly. I try to know who he is. How can he be the same man who turns to the wall so that my fingers might not by chance touch certain parts of his body that are considered taboo? Throughout my life, I was never aware that my body was forbidden or taboo. I see it as part of the package given me by God, in a natural way. I don't understand all the mystery surrounding it or all the efforts to hide it. And despite this openness to my body, I didn't learn anything and I didn't get to know my body in any real sense. Knowledge doesn't come without someone causing it to burst forth.

I feel the vast distance growing wider between the two of us every day. At the beginning of our marriage, I couldn't explain to myself the reason for my anxiety or how to pose the question. I feel that my body needs a different kind of treatment but I don't know which. I wait for it, but it doesn't come. I am ashamed to ask about something that I am totally ignorant of. I hesitated a long time and one night I said to him, "I get ready for something that does not come. I come out from under you empty, thirsty, waiting, looking for a fulfillment that I don't know how to describe. I have an idea, but it's a vague idea. I know that inside me there's an energy that wants to be released somehow, but I don't know how, as if there's a barrier hindering it."

He understood what I wanted to say, but he didn't tell me what I learned for myself not too long afterwards in slow phases of awareness. Evading my sudden description of my condition, he said, "In a few days you will get what you want, on your own."

He didn't realize, or perhaps he did, that at that time, I was still innocently ignorant and unformed. I believed him without quite fully understanding. Years later, I knew that that night laid down the law governing this relationship forever: You'll get what you want on your own, on your own. He broke the link that I thought bound us together without being bothered by embarrassment.

Does a man's attitude towards his woman differ from his general attitude towards life? This will be taken as a sexual reading of history! In other words, does his attitude towards his private relationship with me differ from his public attitude in life, toward work, for instance, or fighting to win in a cause? He is the same man who, in a hotly debated issue that requires a definitive decision, waits for someone else to insist on his point of view. And, if compelled to make a decision, he runs away, leaving it to time to resolve matters. When was he capable of any confrontation when he constantly ran away from facing fateful questions?

Oh my God, what have I done to myself?

Invitation

I hadn't known another woman since I married her. Marrying her gave me the worst parts of both marriage and bachelorhood; I neither had a traditional marriage that gave me a comfortable house and children, nor remained a bachelor, choosing what I wanted out of life and moving freely.

My outburst this time came because of her refusal to take care of Sharif while I was away. His birth had been an accident; she wanted to postpone pregnancy for several years until she was completely settled in Egypt and after she had brought her family back from Naples. I didn't object, but she suddenly became pregnant and I was against abortion in principle, and reassured her as much as I could that we'd overcome difficulties. I did my share in raising him; I learned to bottle feed him after I failed to convince her to change her schedule and temporarily stop accompanying the company tours. She said that work is work and does not change according to circumstances, rather, circumstances change because of work. Thus, I found myself totally responsible for a baby.

I received an urgent invitation from Morocco; that was the first time I was invited there despite having many old friends among its writers. For a long time, I dreamt of visiting Casablanca, Rabat, the Atlas Mountains, and Fez, and meeting my friends Muhammad Shukri, al-Ashari, al-Miludi Shaghmum, Bin Slaim Hamish and Abd al-Hamid Aqar and others whom I had met in the Gulf, in Jordan and even in Egypt. But it would be the first time to meet them in their country. I thought of arranging a visit to Marrakech (known as the Red City) and seeing Fanaa Square and meeting the famous Spanish writer and activist Juan Goytisolo who lived there. I went to tell her the good news, happy that I was invited to an international symposium and worried because it was such short notice. She didn't wait for me to finish telling her the theme of the symposium. She said, "I have a group at the same time. You have to stay with Sharif."

"I have stayed with Sharif every time you've gone on tour. Trade your schedule with one of your colleagues!"

"You knew my schedule ahead of time. Besides, respectable invitations are sent at appropriate times, giving participants sufficient notice to make their arrangements."

"This is a special invitation."

"Impossible."

She went to Luxor, after a quarrel. I got Sharif a leave of absence from school then took him to my mother in the village, knowing that she'd manage despite her age. Her calm response made me resent Maggie's behavior even more. Why didn't I get similar accommodating comfort from my wife? I gave myself totally to the trip and tried in vain to avoid things that reminded me of Maggie. I began to reflect on her from a distance and ask myself, "How did I fall in love with her and why? Was I so deceived? Or was she another woman who changed with the passage of time?"

She accused me of being responsible for her neglecting her piano training even though I never prevented her. She says, "My responsibilities towards you prevented me." I think about these 'responsibilities' and I find that I don't have a home, but an inn that provides us both with shelter, serves meals three days a week in return for my doing the housework and the meals the following three days followed by a free day on which the guests choose where to eat out.

She preferred tourism to playing the piano after the Cairo Opera House burned down. There was only one government-supported orchestra, which she didn't think much of. She kept indulging in the hope that things would change when a new opera house was built, and she knew that would take years. That was her choice, so why? I threw the questions to the clouds before we landed in the Marrakech airport—a small, beautiful one-story building that drew me to 'a place where civilizations met. The architecture was exquisite Arabic-Andalusian style and the walls were mosaics of ornamental tiles they call *zellyj* here. The warm welcome of friends and an old habit of mine which I developed to enjoy travel, leaving other times and places behind, made it possible for me to quickly enter the magical world of Marrakech and the symposium's hot debates.

On the evening of the second day, I was approached by a thin young woman with delicate features and brown complexion like many young Egyptian women in Cairo. She asked me if she could interview me for research she was doing on the modern Arabic novel. I told her I was leaving for Fez early in the morning. Her face became visibly pale and she asked me, "What are you going to do now?"

Feeling sorry that I couldn't accommodate her research plans, I said, "I am going with some friends to Fanaa Square. I saw it yesterday morning and they told me it was more charming in the evening. Come with us."

We entered the world of *One Thousand and One Nights*. We met dozens of Johas, each of them standing there wearing their conical shaped caps as if time had stopped. It was a square displaying obscene wealth and abject poverty. Her hand encircled my waist tightly and I held her other hand so we would not get lost in the crowd. The night was dotted with multicolored lights from the carts that filled the edges of the wide square. There were Berber dancers moving to the primitive rhythms of multipart castanets, a mixture of Egyptian and Spanish styles. They twirled, moving their heads, which were covered with hoods, striped in vivid colors, and sang in a language I didn't know, but which spoke to my African sensibility. There were monkey trainers, jugglers, snake handlers holding harmless cobras, one of which they laughingly placed around my neck. There were soothsayers and shell game players, gypsy women and herbal healers. Badi'a told me that female Hollywood stars came here especially to obtain these herbal remedies to keep their youthful complexion and vigorous health, since Berbers were famous for knowing the secrets of staying young. It was a world that resembled big saints' *moulids* in Egypt, except that here were droves of tourists going around every show in separate circles despite the very dense crowds. It was as if the whole square was one living cell of a mythical animal whose parts were moving endlessly, dizzyingly.

I asked myself, "How did Marrakech turn such a city square, which connotes 'extinction' and has witnessed the crushing of armies, into a square for joy? And how did it bring together the people who have fallen in love with it?" I felt her clinging to my back each time she saw me dazzled with one of the performers in the square. Then she playfully rested her head on my chest as if we had been lovers since Shahrzad had been telling her tales. I danced with her at the dancing circles and we kept going from one circle to another until we found ourselves beyond the circles. Rain dispersed the crowd and every player put his mask in his or her sack and put on another one in seconds.

The square was suddenly empty as if no human being had ever been in it. The carts that sold sweet nuts were covered and the red color that resembles blood began flowing in the streets after the rainwater mixed with the iron-rich soil.

We moved to the bazaar roofed with tattered covers. It was a maze of streets leading to alleys that would keep getting narrower but which would open on a small square that led to even more meandering streets filled with goods piled in heaps. Behind the merchandise stood the vendors using humor to lure you to buy. The smell of the African and Asian spices intoxicated me and left a special taste in my mouth that reminded me of the lustful fragrance of a woman in love. She accompanied me to my room and poured a drink for each of us as I washed in warm water. I loved the steam rising to my nostrils as I stood, eyes closed. I felt her hand wrapping a large towel around me as her body pushed me to a sofa in the middle of the room. She gave me the telephone and said, "Order dinner."

I obeyed as if I were used to her orders and succumbed to a relaxed, liberating sensation as I saw her sitting at my feet massaging them and moving with trained hands to my legs, and there she totally encircled me. I was transported even as I kept track of the time and listened for the footsteps of the room service waiter on the carpet outside the room. She was engrossed, sucking her pleasure slowly. I tried to moisten my lips with words, to no avail. I was totally aroused, torn between options. I wanted to swim to her throne set on a floating island swayed by the wind. I found no obstruction to diving in. Was it the drink? But I didn't drink enough to get drunk. After I found her, I came out, burned on a path I had not taken before and I almost dozed off in a glow emanating from her chest like nothing else I knew.

The telephone rang and I heard the receptionist saying, "Please, guests are not permitted in the rooms."

She didn't wait. She jumped up into her clothes and said, "Don't worry about anything. Don't have any regrets. Tomorrow I'll go with you to Fez."

I saw her off, and my whole being, which had been suddenly awakened, still desired her. All this longing, why? I looked around me and holding on to her fragrance, I fell asleep.

We traveled to several cities. She spoke a little about places and a lot about the characters in my novels, and about her long admiration for me. She told me that she had chosen a research topic that would make it possible for her to meet me and that she would be coming to Cairo soon. She said, "You'll be waiting for me, right?"

She didn't know that she'd broken a strict rule that I'd committed to with Maggie. I hadn't known another woman since I married her. We had agreed that if either of us succumbed to a whim, we'd tell the other. I decided not to tell her. When I crossed the threshold of my house, I knew that what happened with Badi'a would happen with other women, that the barrier that had come down could not be restored. I didn't feel guilty and had no pangs of conscience. Rather, I felt, as one of my friends once told me, that I was 'too married.' I said, "Good evening," and she returned the greeting tersely. I didn't care. I went to Sharif's room and put his gift there in such a way that he would see it as soon as he entered the room. I counted the hours remaining until morning when I would go to my village to bring him back. At that time I felt I had returned to Egypt, to someone who was truly waiting for me.

Morning

I was watching him with shocked, tearful eyes from behind the glass of the intensive care room as contraptions pumped oxygen into his lungs and read the movement of the heart, while he lay there resting comfortably, his eyes closed. The bird of death erupted on the scene, wanting to drain him of life, spreading its wings, filling the room. My father signaled me to come in, despite the doctor's warnings. He put aside the oxygen mask to talk to me while I begged him not to.

"Why are you crying, Nahid?"

I couldn't say anything; every cell in my body was shaking.

"I am happy with my life's journey. I've lived ten times as much as anyone has. I've enjoyed every second and achieved what I wanted to achieve. If only you'd learned how to hold on to life and pluck its fruits."

He pressed my arm so hard it hurt and the tears disappeared from my face.

"Every moment is a gift from the Creator. Live it. Don't ever let me see you crying."

I left, knowing that he would defeat the sudden stroke with his spiritual strength and he did. The second time it defeated him. I didn't know, as I was silently saying goodbye to him, that his departure would play the most important role in my life. I was beset by the question that attacks people in midlife: What have I accomplished and what do I want? I hadn't yet reached forty but I had prematurely aged despite the fact that whoever saw me laugh believed the deception.

Serenely and without a single moment of regret, I took an inventory of what I'd done to myself and I asked myself, "Why would anyone decide to walk in a direction opposite to their destination, despite the awareness that they are killing the spark of life in themselves and clinging to all that is imposed on them? Why would one even invent reasons to defend that which is imposed on them and call it 'adapting'?"

The answer was the details of my life that I made with full consciousness and will and also with a cold heart, even though I never felt divided or rebellious or had self-pity. Perhaps all I felt was that I patted my crushed heart when it broke in pain and told it simply, "I understand."

My father's departure released the genie that I had long thought I'd locked up in the bottle and thrown the key into the ocean. It now appeared to me in broad daylight and said, "Adapting is no longer possible as of today. Your true will and nothing else; and no reckoning for the past."

My decisions surprised all those around me. They thought they were illogical, unreasonable, unnatural, and the opposite of what they had known about me all my life. The change was not as sudden as my husband imagined. I had been playing its tunes for a long time, but now was the crescendo.

I wasn't seeing him in this light for the first time that night and he didn't change the way he behaved with me; on the contrary. But I was a different woman without his realizing it. When he came on to me I allowed my desire to climb and I dropped it the moment he was spent and done, leaving me at the height of my arousal. I moved away, telling him that I had been just a refuse can the whole time. Then I began to cry in a choking voice, "A hole. A mere hole."

The gap between us grew so wide it swallowed me as the words tried to come out of my throat before they were choked to death. I pushed him away from me but he didn't understand and asked in an innocence that I still envy him for, "What happened?"

If he had understood it would have been easier, perhaps a few more moments of surrender might have resulted, but his failure to understand cut the matter short and accelerated my outburst. I screamed, "I will not be yours after today! Each time, you promise to be with me and then forget me the moment you enter me. There are doctors and psychiatrists, even friends. I am saying this for your sake, not for things between us to be righted. You've enjoyed my waiting for your mercy and my acceptance of my lot and that will not happen again."

I cried over my long years, my failure, my emotional hunger and loneliness. I cried the burnt inside and the terror of the knowing backwards glance.

"Oh my God! Have all these years really gone?" I cried.

He began to dry my tears and talk. The words gathered as a meaningless cloud, neither dispersing nor coming down as rain. I got a grip on myself and hid behind a transparent veil that shut him out. I realized that I was talking to myself, that there was no chance he'd understand.

The morning brought me a plane that flew me to Europe, to Athens. I gathered my books, and closed the doors to a raging fire. I put on a smile and a self that I said was at peace, as if I had a date with an awakening. The light outside me was white with clouds and the plane started its descent along the sea. Are you the same sea where I played with its last waves on the edge of another continent? Are you the one who knew me as a young girl and young woman? Do you still know me? If I could jump from the sky into you, I would. I don't know where I got the mask of irony that hid me and I wanted to look at the world from its most interesting angle, but the mask soon cracked under the hammer strokes of questions. How do we prevaricate and run away from ourselves? There's no room for you now. I've left you behind in gray Cairo as I held on with a hand and trembling heart to words between the covers of a book, divulging to me what they hide from others, as if their author, when he wrote them, many years before I saw him, was entrusting me with a secret that I would discover in time.

Understanding

She will not be able to persist in this separation from her husband. She is weak toward him, and he has rights, and she knows that quite well. If he acquiesced to her wish, it is because he is letting pass what he knows to be a short-lived tiff that happens often between husbands and wives. He will consider it a temporary quarrel and will keep trying until he succeeds. Their long history together proves his ability to win her over. As for her fantasies about resolving the matter for good because of her hospitalization, it is just one of those romantic fantasies.

I don't have any doubts about what she says; I have no choice but to believe her, despite the difficulty of the situation, but ultimately I disagree with her assessment. I admire her courage and his grasp of the crisis and his letting it pass. It seems I haven't underestimated his love for her. What makes a man accept a situation like that? There's something mysterious about the matter, the source of which I don't know. Is Nahid hiding something from me or is that the actual extent of the story? There is a sadness in her that has something to do with her relationship with him, something that she is not divulging. She is evasive and I can't pin it down. Is it shyness or long training to hold back private matters? I appreciate her situation, but I am not that romantic. I know that our relationship will not go beyond a year, maybe two years, and as usual will end up in boredom, leading to damned indifference which is the real end of life, not death. I love her as I haven't loved anyone else, ever, but my natural caution prevents me from taking part in big visions for the future that I see her drawn into, even though I am about to divorce Maggie, a decision that I have postponed several times because Nahid entered my life. She listens patiently to the problems that Maggie causes and calmly guides me to ways to overcome them, absorbing my anger. After a while, I noticed that the quarrels at home were one-sided. I no longer needed to respond; I have an oasis that gives me shelter. I pass the time there absorbed in work, somewhat reassured about the future in a way that I was not used to.

Curiously, Nahid panicked whenever divorce was mentioned. Her panic caused me to doubt whether she seriously wanted to commit to me. I reflect on how she talks about our house, the world that we will travel together, the life that she will provide for me so I can write my most beautiful novels and how she reacts like someone possessed if I decide to leave home or even think about it. She keeps after me until my anger subsides then she makes me promise to postpone any action. She analyzes what I have told her and shows me where I went wrong vis-à-vis Maggie's reactions. Then she makes me swear that I will make some concessions and causes me to go back, most of the tension gone. After awhile she says, "I won't ask you to divorce her. The relationship will consume itself without me, so why should I be a part of ending it? My presence in your life is pressure enough." I assure her that fights have been going on since the early days of our marriage, that my relationship with her was a natural result of what I have suffered over the years.

I read in Nahid's eyes a question which I avoid answering. Sometimes I comment on my intimate relationship with Maggie by saying that it stopped a long time ago, hoping that that would happen. Nahid talks about an unconditional commitment in the future. When will that future come? She is not specific. If I am separated from Maggie, she will ask for a divorce at once. The real paradox though, is in Maggie's flip-flopping desire: ardently wanting me then totally forgetting me, rejecting my desires, even running away from them. The mad lust she had at the beginning of our marriage is gone and her need to be with me has turned into short and far between encounters. She doesn't even ask herself about my wants and when I remind her, she remembers, then forgets after a while. Staying away from her awhile restores her old lust for a few days, then boredom creeps in again. I don't understand the reason for this paradox, which as time passes has become a fact of life.

I ask Nahid once, "Can two people live together when all that ties them is the ability of each of them to poison the other's life?"

"Yes," she says, "because what unites them is some kind of love."

"Love?"

"The provocation here is not hatred, rather it's a desire to excite, desire that's full of life."

She looks at me with understanding eyes and adds, "Yes, darling. You cannot leave her and she cannot leave you. And I love you with your whole world, with her and Sharif. I don't know if you can grasp that."

I look at her unable to respond. Am I supposed to accept *her* world and love it? Impossible.

Enticement

She is still turning the pages of Omar's novel *The Maze*, sitting alone in the quiet garden, reading it as if she were sipping a rare vintage wine.

He continued to watch her from afar, trying not to give himself away. He sensed her tensing up when she discovered that he was watching her and he was upset at the feeling that brought him back to reality. I haven't seen Nahid so beautiful before. She's become curvaceous, put on some weight, as if turning from a virgin to a fully-developed woman and her face is glowing. Is it possible that a woman reaches the zenith of her beauty in her forties? Or is my deprivation making me see things in her that aren't there? No, the gleam in her clear eyes, the curves of her lusty body aroused me greatly as she was trying on diamond earrings before going out to my sister's wedding party. She had stopped changing her clothes in front of me some time ago and if she had to, she'd cover her body shyly which made me feel like a stranger to her.

I asked, "Shall I zip you up?"

"Please do."

He reached out his hand and pushed her hair aside then planted a kiss on her bare shoulder. He felt her body quiver and he was aroused. He embraced her back. She acquiesced in silence, but he didn't know whether she was responding or not. She slipped out of his arms smiling wordlessly and began to replace the earrings on her ears, then, taking his arm, she announced, "I am ready."

She engaged with everyone at the party and danced with him a long time. He thought, "I know that she loves my sister and that she's happy she's getting married, but tonight she is particularly radiant and vibrant. She has something that makes me long for her so much, something that is setting my passions, which I had thought had turned to ashes, on fire. My waiting for her is killing me. I am trying to forget it, but it erupts in front of me when I see her moving gleefully among people and when I see them envying us for our happiness and when I believe the kindness she shows me. How can she be so nice and yet keep the distance that she has decisively drawn between us?

"She's become like a flower garnering all its energy before its short life comes to an end, vigorous and giving off raw femininity. I am suffering from her extravagant breasts that seem to have thrived by being away from me, as if they had drunk from another well and turned round in flagrant defiance of me.

"She is no longer as conservative in the way she dresses as she used to be. She loosens up a little to show off her charms. Is she making up for her deprivation of men by pretending to be satisfied and full of love? How come her body is oozing with lust like that? Why do I smell her desire now when I used to suffer her constant escape before? How did she manage to fortify herself against the cries of a body like that?"

"I want you. Nothing compensates me for losing you," he kept repeating to himself when they went back home after the party. She hurriedly changed her clothes before he went into the bedroom and put on a simple nightgown that made her look even more beautiful. To him she seemed like a lustful filly with her unruly hair and her shimmery makeup that she was removing with a cleansing cream. Her face gleamed with a dark redness that gave her tan color a youthful look that took her back years. He remembered that her face turned rosy when she had an orgasm. He tried to embrace her. She asked him if he needed to eat something. He said no and clung to her even closer. She said that the party had exhausted her and began telling him stories about the family and the wedding, ignoring what he was trying to entice her into. Then she suddenly said, "Good night!"

Before he could answer, he saw her turning to the wall assuming her sleeping position, her eyes closed. He thought, "This ability of hers to shut me out, my desire for her and her insistent rejection kills me. I wanted to wake her up to tell her that I wanted her now, this instant. I reached out to drag her by the hair out of the bed and make her stop ignoring me and beat her if need be. But I heard her breathing irregularly. She cannot deceive me—she's only pretending to sleep. She's suffering just like me. I still love her and I know that she loves me, so why the obstinacy? Well, actually I hate her. I hate her just as much as I was able to love her once." There was nothing left to do but to leave the room, now that the bed has turned into a battlefield seething with muffled anger.

Celebration

I grew tired chasing after the officials of the cooperative society from which I bought the apartment, which I intended as the home for my newspaper office. They lied to me and promised me things that never came to pass. I discovered the extent of the theft in the co-op. I found out from a woman who lived with her children in the building next door, that an influential notable had an interest in the development and used his influence to prevent all attempts to resolve the situation. He sent thugs around to terrorize her when she objected to anything, because she was monitoring everything about the development since she was there all the time. One day she disappeared and when I asked, the newlywed told me that a group of men stormed her house and that she took her children and ran away until things calmed down with the co-op officials. I tried to find out specific information: they said that differences in costs among different contractors caused the development to stop, even though the members had paid the price in full and the co-op could not cancel the contracts with them, nor could it fund the completion of the construction of the buildings.

The newlyweds surprised me with news on account of which they had a celebration, to which they invited the two of us, although we didn't want to get involved with them in anything that might expose our real relationship. "We got electricity!" they both shouted when they heard the key turn in the door of our apartment. They hugged us and pushed us to the living room of their apartment then to the bathroom and we saw an automatic washer in the corner with a white lace cover embroidered with bright colored flowers.

"Finally, electricity and a baby!"

The bride, laughing, said that they were expecting the first baby after they made sure that things needed for normal life were secured and that they were going to buy a motor to pump the water up, thus getting good water pressure.

Escape

He turns off his car lights and sits smoking his cigar slowly, waiting for me. I do my best to get out of talking with a colleague who met me at the door of the guesthouse. He wants to discuss something that requires time. I promise to talk to him tomorrow, because I am late for an appointment. I escape before he realizes that I will not get in my car. I walk past Omar so that he'll understand that the coast is not clear. I turn with the road then enter a store to buy whatever they are selling. I ask myself, "How many of those standing in front of me, in this narrow space, have known true love? Is it possible to measure how true it is? How many experiences did each of them have?"

I look at the misery creeping over the faces as I study them. I know that love changes the features, gives the face joy and strength, defiance and recognition of how splendid life is. My quizzical glances seem to worry a woman who thinks I am staring at her. When the sales clerk asks for the money, I come to and I notice both him and her. I give him the money, and I begin to muse about the woman: Who are you? Have you accomplished what others couldn't? Did you know what they offered you or did you break the barrier and choose what you wanted? In the beauty parlor and on the metro women chat. How many of those women confided to a friend about their passion or infatuation with a man, and said that they looked forward to transgressing? I quickly return to Omar and before I close the door of the car he speeds away. We burst out laughing, like children playing hide and seek, instead of bursting out crying, for I don't want to spoil my only available moment.

The world opens up before me and I cling to it despite the misgivings of the heart, which declares its revolt against the tangled circumstances. More doors open up before me when I see in his eyes that great longing to embrace me. We chat about news of the outside world, as we call it, because when we are alone in our oasis we don't allow it even to knock on the door.

I am surprised by my constant insistence that he pick me up after my evening shifts. I could take the government car or my own car and avoid going out at the same time as my colleagues who know him well. Despite all precautions, chance often spoils the joy of the moment, when I see in front of me one of my colleagues standing there to shake his hand. I mumble some lame attempt at explanation and Omar looks at me so I won't explain or justify. He accuses me of attracting attention by being afraid. We turn our back to the city and take the Nile Corniche route to Maadi. I ask him several times to stop at one of the spots along the way where we can rent a boat, but he doesn't agree. One night, after watching a ballet by a famous Russian troupe, we took a walk and discovered a quiet path in the island, wrapped in greenery and silence. I begged him to continue exploring the path on foot. I held his arm and clung to his body without saying anything and whenever he tried, laughing, to get me to say something, I shook my head, gesturing with my hand that I was soaring in a different world. He didn't know how much I suffered because I was not able to walk next to him, taking deep breaths and getting all the questions off my chest without waiting for answers from the world!

Body

"I love your body as I haven't loved any other body. My relationship with it goes beyond lovemaking, and that hasn't happened with any other woman."

"Because you love me."

"I loved Maggie, but I didn't linger so much over her body. I've known bodies that are beautiful in themselves. Neither love nor beauty is the reason. It's something else that I can't define that ties me to your body and makes me follow it passionately at all times."

"You are now more mature, more knowledgeable about life. You're aware of feelings that you were not aware of when you were younger and with other women."

"Deep reflection is a possible explanation, and so is lingering, but the main reason might be my feeling that as much as I desire to possess you,

you offer yourself up so completely and so unconditionally to me that I feel that I own your body and can deal with it exactly as I want to."

"Perhaps touching it gives you a different sensation, therefore you love it."

"Touching it cannot be compared to touching other bodies because with others, touching ended the instant lovemaking was over. She and I turned into two independent entities, separated by an invisible distance. And that hasn't happened between you and me; the moment of our cleaving together continues even after you move away, out of my reach. The nakedness which we insist upon has given us another dimension, a visual tactility, if you like. The eye is no longer only an instrument for seeing; it has turned into a tactile organ, just like my hand or any other organ. The relationship here is not with one organ but it is a total relationship in which organs and the senses are intermingled."

"Isn't the response to touching different from one body to another? I mean your feeling when you touch another body, even if you were performing the same act?"

"Speaking in general, with other women, the feelings were almost the same and I knew the outcome as soon as the relationship became steady and making love became a regular practice. It would begin with a certain rhythm, then it would ascend in a steady manner whose goal is an orgasm. After that would come instant separation, and awareness of the body would stop. Within that duration there are no transformations or unexpected sensations, just an intellectual movement until the end, devoid of peaks and valleys, of varied speeds. Therefore, all the inner strokes produce expected and constant reactions. With you, this mechanicalness has not been there, or rather it has changed its pattern of movement; the main goal is no longer the orgasm, but the journey itself with its winding roads, its ups and downs; a journey that takes its time, during which the two of us immerse ourselves, exploring our evolving desires. One of us would do something that sets the other on fire or drowns the other in a sizzling lagoon, or as you put it so often, makes the other go crazy; creating an earthquake that smashes all feelings of complacency. That shapeless feeling that is created has the distinction of being in our innermost depths. I doubt if it can ever be seen or observed from the outside; and even though it is buried deep down, it opens paths of passionate, quivering delights."

"I know that and I also know that it doesn't take place between just any two bodies. Each body has its own specificity, a need for a very specific other body, to have this feeling with every touch and stroke. Therefore, despite Maggie's understanding of the details of the journey of lovemaking, the result was different, perhaps because· of the difference in sensibility; she probably needed a different kind of touching. Why not?"

"Between you and me there is a specificity in every thrust and the response to it. With another woman, even when love is present, all the strokes have the same general feeling, rising in one direction. With you every stroke has its own meaning, has qualities which I feel even before it reaches you and it differs in strength, in mode and angle, in the way you receive it, in the way you prepare to absorb it, in the way it dissolves and vanishes. I feel your opening up for it and your absorbing it before you release it for another stroke. Here each thrust has its own entity, separate, almost independent and has its own personality."

"I think its duration also plays a role in determining its form and the signal it gives."

"The law of variety and sudden leaps in time helps keep longing alive."

"Yes, from slow to sliding to body-shaking force."

"I now have a constant desire to see your body in its various cycles, not just the internal but also the external ones."

"I used to be afraid of our many reflections and discussions. I thought they threatened that desirable mystery that gave making love its magic, but our dialogue has, on the contrary, made us open up regions that transported us to a different phase."

"I am aroused by the dazzling change that happens to your eyes: from total alertness as you sit next to me to not being there in less than one second. The moment I am inside you, the black of your eyes gets lost in the white and it drowns into a deep sea that sucks it inside, despite the calm surface whose screen is clear and relaxed and accepting, waiting for a far-off destiny."

"You can see clearly, but I don't have the strength to see what happens to your eyes. I don't have external focus. I sense what happens to you, and by intuition I know that what happens to my eyes sums up what happens to my whole body."

"If that is what happens to the eyes, what happens to the rest of the body?"

"Withdrawal generates an internal vision of the movement of the two bodies together; the apartness is rejoined and I feel that all the organs belong to my body. Your hand gets the signal from my brain. I see the thrusts and where they are moving and where they end. They explode inside me a feeling of a live wire that has lost control over its inner strength, and as it winds its way, it lights sparks in a meandering course with stings in unpredictable places. I see the thrusts on the screen of my eyes which have blurred and closed half their curtains, turning on a warm black light outside and opening the inside windows to all the colors. They heave with a motion governed by the law of recklessness, the connection of contradictory feelings sending the electrical stings in a direction opposite the expected one. I follow them with delectable fear, trying to predict their locations, savoring their flow on the edge of moments, before they disappear. I ready myself for them the moment they are born and my body finds their melodies in a different place."

"Fulfillment is not just spiritual, it's also physical."

"One can find fulfillment with one person only. And despite the terror contained in fear of the thought of loss, it is the truth as I saw it when I was a young girl, not fully understanding its dimensions and as I see it now at my age. Did I tell you that your thrusts cautiously touch my soul?

Yes, it is possible for that physical feeling to reach my soul, here in the place where all the sparks of feeling crackle under my ribs or here near the heart or here where my neck meets my chest in the middle of this triangle. Where's my soul? Where your thrust is, as it should be!"

Crossing

Torn between two worlds, I try to balance, to be truthful in each of them. I train myself to forget my first world when I cross its threshold, so that I might totally enjoy my entry into my new world, which grows day after day to become Life.

I realized that I needed to train my mind so that it might annul the details of home, motherhood, and the responsibilities towards the children and the family, since merely remembering ruins my feeling of my own being and the truth and nature of my existence, making me like a very small sparrow in a large snare. Omar doesn't understand why I become invigorated in other cities or what happens to me when I take off my clothes, which I can't stand any longer, and totally give myself over to him, as if I've never stood on a land other than his, nor known a world other than his, as if I were a blank page, unschooled in the reckoning of hours. I love my children because they are my children without facing any questions about choice: Love or them? Their needs or me? I believe that I will remain in that situation and that city forever. Therefore, he was surprised by my outburst one day at the airport in Asyut.

We had passed by the village of Durunka, where devastation had taken place due to a massive flood. I don't know what came over me when we finished the procedures before boarding the plane. The moment we stood in line, I held on to him and, crying loudly, I begged him that we go back and postpone the return trip. He embraced me tenderly as he pushed me very gently to keep walking so as not to slow down the moving line and sadly indicated that we would attract attention.

"For the first time in my life, I don't care what people think. I don't want to go back. Let's stay a few days, please."

"No matter how long we stay, we must go back. We'll solve the problem soon. Have no fear," he said resignedly.

I clung to him even closer as he fell silent. His body, which appeared strong on the outside, began shaking. I could feel the tremors of anguish.

"I thought you were much stronger than that."

"I love my weaknesses with you because it makes me feel human and because it makes me feel like a woman."

He held me tighter and sat me down in my seat as if I were a young child, and he did everything for me: he fastened my seatbelt, adjusted my legs and put my bag in the bin. I rested my head on his chest. I don't know what took hold of my mind, sleep or absence. Moments of fitful wakefulness threw me a crucial question as I thought how very similar my situation was to the village devastated by the deluge of change brought about by the flood: Do growth and renewal require mandatory uprooting? Can't life renew itself by slow, studied change? How can slow, studied change be possible in my case? Given the choice again, I wouldn't choose any path other than the one I have taken, I wouldn't do anything but tighten the shackles of my enslavement by the world that I created one day with my eyes wide open. It wasn't just one choice, made once and over with; it was a choice that was renewed at different phases in my life. Maha was four years old when I decided to separate from Mustafa, after I had totally given up on the possibility of things working out between us. Instead of informing him of my wish and discussing the details with him, I decided to give in to my daughter's persistent request that I get her a brother. She would plead and beg, saying that she was lonely. Yusif came into life to force me, very consciously, to provide him and his sister with a stable house that could withstand storms. How cruel I was to myself and my needs!

I was in need of someone who would pull me, against my will, away from and defend me against the other Nahid, no matter how she railed against my suffering and despised it. I needed someone capable of understanding my real me, without masks, one capable of crushing my ability to bury my desires alive, one who insisted on the essence and brought it to light without breaking the shell. All I needed was a lover who understood my motives, who understood that I was a mother, that I cared for Mustafa, one who could reach me, fix the mirror so I could see the truth as it was and not as I feared it to be.

The airport in Asyut was not the only line that I refused to cross in an outburst, after my days had turned into a series of dislocations as I crossed the isthmus between the two worlds. I tried to prepare myself for the questions I'd face and the people I'd encounter. The landmarks on the route between Omar's Maadi and Mustafa's pyramids reminded me of the drums of war strongly heralding the moment. I hear the clamor of birth. Does death also have a clamor? I try to remove from my body its desire to give in to the warmth that enveloped it a short while earlier. I close my ears to my body's pleas to doze off holding on to the moment of the soul's release and its mastery of the world. It's as if I am urging the cold to come quickly and announce the reality of my existence, and to return me to the required legal present. The radiant fire recedes from my cheek and gradually the heat in my limbs escapes as the landmarks indicate the remaining time and distance. I make up an issue to which I surrender my mind, waking up its veins, pushing it to remember a work program for which I prepare, to get lost in it. Sometimes I succeed and sometimes I don't, and I pray to God, as my heart fights to get out of the cage, to help me cross the threshold, and I turn into a butterfly paying the price of shedding and molting. I remember, all at once, all the creatures that mature in several phases and how they pay the price once in their lifetime, whereas I pay it every day. I see the house rushing towards me; perhaps it cannot avoid colliding with me. I take refuge in a world that doesn't exist. I believe it exists or I annul all existence, real and imagined, and I sing in an attempt to flap my wings and fly to some kind of sky, a heaven or a hell. My soul quivers and my mind wanders off and I imagine that I have fooled it into arranging itself to the tunes of songs of love and loss. When I place the key in the lock, I discover that I have been fooling myself the whole time. So I meet the place and the people in it in silence and I totally forget the world I came from, and the world that I swam through emptiness to cross. I find myself surprised as if I am seeing them and perceiving their existence for the first time.

My mind could not get used to it and my soul did not accept the constraints of the cage. Life surprised me once, when by chance I bought a cassette of Byzantine music from a museum that was able to sneak into my heart and close it, and drown me with the mystery of the universe, and to worship at the altar of the unknown. The music came to be like an intoxicant enabling me to get over the pain of crossing, so I crossed the threshold of the house semi-absently. It made me forget that I was coming from a world that I love and want and going to a world that I love, but do not want.

Ethics

I avoided Mustafa for a long time, until circumstances would force me to meet him. I needed information about a new discovery in the area of the village where the workers who built the pyramids had lived. I heard the news, so I decided to cover the story, and I sought Nahid's help and her contacts to facilitate my task. I rang her up and Mustafa answered the phone. He gave her the receiver. We agreed to meet in a cafeteria in the city. Until she arrived, I found myself preoccupied with Mustafa's sense of security, and how could I betray this taken-for-granted, blind trust? How could I break it or continue to break it and meet him face to face as if nothing was happening? Nahid surprised me by telling me he had given her a ride to the cafeteria in his car. I repressed the thought that in half an hour she would be in my arms, naked, and he would go somewhere to wait for her then come back to take her home after our meeting. He brought her to me and will come to accompany her without knowing anything. I wonder who would put up with such egregious deception? He doesn't know, but I know, and she knows, and we insist on it. What are the lines between right and wrong? Which of us is wrong and which is right? And where does he get this absolute trust in the world and people? And how do I allow myself to betray it in this manner?

I said to myself that his ignorance is a merciful thing, for who could bear knowledge in this case? And who could pay its price?

He didn't know that she had cried at the airport in Asyut, that she didn't want to come back, that she was clinging to my chest the whole trip and she did not dry her tears and that I was terrified at the thought of his seeing her at Cairo airport with tears still in her eyes. By the time we found him waiting for us, I had almost fainted from the unanswered questions in my head and the unresolved issues. I was perturbed by the question: how could she be taken away from me, just like that, to the other side, despite my knowledge of their separation under the same roof? The situation seemed to make little sense, looked at from his, her, or my point of view, or rather it was akin to an absurd play that we couldn't get out of or break away from. He will never imagine and I will never forget that he would meet her while she was still wet with me, that there was something wrong, not inconsiderable, in the continuation of this situation, impossible for us, but for him, the utmost of deception. Is it possible for the face and mask to be one? Or for all the masks to be taken off so that we can see each other for what we really are without illusions? Who could handle that?

But the alternative, the constant alternative that I thought was just an exception, is very painful, as painful as a slow poison. I have no doubt that he is consoling himself with the thought that their relationship is still alive, though moribund. He doesn't know that it has died several years ago. He doesn't want to believe it or see it. It would've helped me if he could see it and it would have put an end to the tough questions I am grappling with.

How happy he looks with her! That sometimes makes me doubt the veracity of the way she described their relationship. I'd say to myself, "This is not a man who has had no relationship with his wife for years; this spontaneous intimacy, this kindly regard for her every move and this unblemished warmth—how can it square with all that she tells me?" Thus, every time I see them together, I come up against a thicket of thorny questions about him, about her, and about our relationship and what entitled me to ruin *their* relationship. Who gave me that right? How did I usurp it for myself? Next time, I am going to tell her I can't go on like that. I can't stand it anymore, even if the price is going back to the old emptiness and the old misery and my barren desert.

I don't know . . .

Curse

"Don't move before you purify yourself. Every step you take, the angels will curse you a thousand times. It is as forbidden for you to deny him access to your body as attributing a partner to God."

I didn't understand this paradox. How can our physical union, so blessed by God that denying it is tantamount to attributing a partner to God, end when he ejaculates? And why do the angels curse my steps after I have fulfilled God's will? I want to sleep in my bed, enjoying the warmth inside. I don't want to shower and take that away in a few seconds.

One afternoon an angry woman followed me and accusingly asked me, "You've gone out in the street immediately after the afternoon prayer without bathing?" I was too dumbfounded to ask her, "What business is it of yours?" She yelled, "You'll bring ruin to the house and everyone in it!" With difficulty, I was able to muster enough presence of mind to ask her, "How do you know whether anything happened that would necessitate it?"

She sucked her lips and went on, as if she hadn't heard my question, "I tell you, no single step before purifying yourself."

I was not used to complaining and I didn't say a thing but I began to notice that Mustafa agreed with the idea—he would slide from the bed to the bathtub just a few meters in the corridor to carry out our forefathers' instructions. Deep inside I didn't have any desire to honor this ritual. Even when I took a cold shower at dawn, it was out of fondness for water and the way it rejuvenated me body and soul, the way I have always felt ever since I was a child. I never imagined that it would cleanse away any impurity from me, even though I mechanically recited the declaration of faith every time I took a shower after I married.

Impurity. I was able to grasp the meaning they wanted to convey to me after I became a woman. When Mustafa's father died one morning, the men ordered some hot water to be brought to the room of the deceased. I got up to prepare it because they were all busy grieving. A woman ran after me and said, "Only a virgin can prepare it."

"Why," I asked.

She came close to me and whispered as she tried to place her palm on my mouth signaling me to lower my voice, "Because her purity is guaranteed."

She led me by the hand like an impetuous child and got me out of there, pitying me for my ignorance which went beyond her wildest imagination.

All the women's attempts to convince me that something in me had changed, that I had entered a new world with new conditions when I became a woman, failed. The way I looked at my body remained unchanged; there was no undue awe or affected avoidance. The organs meant nothing but their functions. My body did not concern others, just as others' bodies did not concern me. I couldn't exhibit fake bashfulness because I didn't understand how my body could be desirable for anyone or how its allures could be public. I'd thought a long time ago that any desire came from within, came from one human being desiring a specific other. I totally forgot that my ancient grandfather desired all women and that my ancient grandmother gave herself to every man she desired.

I needed to spend all those years of my life discovering new meanings with you; the joy of savoring our feelings together, slowly; the joy of warmth after the blazing flames and that serenity that envelops us when our honey blends and flows and plays with our bodies like the brush of a skillful painter, dyeing our souls with color and fragrance. The ritual continues until it satisfies my inside which voraciously wants you, and stays inside you and wants me without quenching the thirst.

Anger

We don't know how much pain we feel when we miss each other as we do when we meet after a date we had to cancel. We rush into each other's arms without giving consciousness a chance to take in the feelings slowly. We embrace, letting go of ourselves to each other, unable to pause even to look at each other's face or give ourselves a chance to find out what has happened since we last met.

I missed our date because I had to take Maggie to a gynecologist. After we settled down, I noticed that Nahid was worried about Maggie. I reassured her that it was just a matter of age, the doctor's wish to change the birth control method, and Maggie's apprehension at trying a new, unfamiliar method. Nahid looked at me for a long time without saying anything but her color darkened as if she had acquired an instant tan. She waited for a reaction from me which I didn't understand. When the silence continued for a long time I asked her, smiling, "Where's your question?"

"I've heard you many times making fun of colleagues who lead a double life—a wife and a mistress; one woman providing a proper social status, a home and children with secure traditional behavior and a mistress with whom they realize what the wife doesn't give them: love, under-standing, and conversation. You'd add sarcastically, 'Strangely enough, they cannot leave the wife and choose another woman. Even more strangely, some of them even brag about loving the wife and being unable to do without the other woman.' I've heard that from you dozens of times and I didn't ask you to describe your intimate relations with Maggie. But you volunteered by telling me that it is an intermittent rela-tionship: long months of separation then going back for some weeks which you can't endure in a natural good mood and that you were no longer capable of coping with that roller coaster-like life. As you put it, 'Maybe we could get together once or twice a year.' My question is: Why? Why this gratuitous lying? Is it necessary? I know that you are a husband and that our circumstances have made this unnatural situation inevitable. When you told me that your relationship with her had broken down, I told you I won't ask you to divorce her. I told you to do what your relationship requires you to do. I want to live with you in truth and in truth alone. We are paying the price of a situation that we conscious-ly choose together. I don't want any falsehood in my life, otherwise, was what we've done necessary?"

"We didn't know each other sufficiently to broach the subject."

"How many years do you need to know me?"

"I mean, the reactions. I don't like to see these tears in your eyes. I've lived a tumultuous life, with more anger than calm. I don't want a colli-sion for any reason. I avoided critical areas for fear of problems erupting between us."

"But I didn't ask you."

"It's much more complicated than that. I told you once that you'll have to pick the thorns off me, so I can be purely yours. My life wasn't easy."

"You're defending yourself against something I didn't do. You shoot the sharp quills of a scared porcupine that pretends to be brave."

"I lay down my arms at your doorstep, so don't be unfair to me."

"You've wounded me. You'll never realize what changed in me today.

You would have preferred anything to my paying this price without a single justification."

I buried my head in her bosom, trying to compress my body. I wanted to hide as her tears washed my forehead. I wanted to take away her pain, but I couldn't. I never trusted that she would understand this double life. And at that moment I did not believe we were capable of leading a life in total truth. I spoke to her without a sound, hoping that somehow my words would reach her, "I can't totally be yours. Longing pushed me to immerse myself in this love but I am haunted with doubts. What if I am wrong and you are capable of stabbing me, walking out on me, or your love is not what you think it is now? Life has taught me to leave some room, some percentage for the fickleness of treacherous time. And you, in your naiveté made me your eternal man. How? If you had met another man, he'd have exploited your naiveté to amuse himself at your expense or get together with you for a few days or a few months, then leave you. I know how difficult and thorny that can be and I fear for your simplicity. Also, if you put me between a rock and a hard place, I fear believing you, letting my world be in someone else's hands, giving myself totally over to you and enjoying the blessing of not knowing, or keeping part of my mind awake, leaving room for caution."

Bitterness

One day I awoke to a very disturbing idea: how could I stand anything related to Mustafa? How did his body odor turn into something that greatly bothered me and his touching me feel like hell? I was like someone taming an unruly child to deal politely with adults, then others, then his peers, taming him to get used to the idea that I am an other that is no longer his. I quietly slip away from my habits that have accumulated over fifteen years. I attend to his needs mechanically, figuring out what he will wear and when he will eat, his schedule and the children's schedules. All of that I try to organize in a detached manner until the moment I dread every day despite our separation—getting into my bed.

Until now I haven't been able to ask him to get another bed, because I don't want anyone in the family to notice what we are doing. I want quick secret decisions that do not allow anyone else to intervene or cause my children undue worries. Therefore, I accepted sharing his bed as if nothing has happened. He was used to going to bed hours before me as I needed the quiet of the night to do my research, then I faced the moment that I need to keep my nerves steady so as not to awaken him.

I get into bed, hugging its edges, leaving half my body outside it. When I ascertain that all is quiet, the other half of my body creeps onto the mattress. If I succeed in not disturbing him after he has slept for several hours and almost had enough, my journey to control my breathing begins. First my breaths would be very quick, keeping pace with my heartbeats quickening with fear, echoing in the room. I try to muffle them but to no avail. I fall asleep half conscious, leaving my antennae on to watch out for his hands which out of habit reach for me during his sleep and unconsciously hold my body. I cannot wiggle out of his grasp so as not to wake him up; my heartbeats race, wringing my stomach. I acquiesce, forgetting my body's rebellion until I reassure myself that he is fast asleep and I turn, moving his hand away or I succumb to sleep.

Before he comes in, you can almost hear his fiery breath. He greets us with muted anger and I know that I am in for a period of tension that will end only God knows when. I bring him the food and sit in front of him until he is done eating without speaking a word to me or answering a single question about his day. He just nods or shakes his head, chewing his food with difficulty. I withdraw to my study and he to his bed. I know that I'll see him within fifteen minutes. I wait for him with a trembling heart, not understanding a word of what I am reading.

I seek refuge in Salim Hasan. I place my palm on the volumes of *Ancient Egypt* and everything he has taught me flows into me without rereading the actual pages. I let my eyes roam the pages of Claire Lalouette's *Textes sacrés et textes profanes de l'ancienne Egypte*, Pierre Montet's *Everyday Life in Egypt*, Barry J. Kemp's *Ancient Egypt: Anatomy of a Civilization.* When I get to James Henry Breasted's *The Dawn of Conscience*, my mind comes to and I read the words that I've almost committed to memory: "And as for the Gods, they had forsaken this land . . . if men prayed to a god for succor, he came not . . . if men besought a goddess likewise, she came not at all. Their hearts were deaf in their bodies."

He passes in front of me, stops at the newspaper and magazines and leafs through them, then carries some of them without a word. I follow the movement of his feet to the place he chooses. He bursts out angrily at our daughter who asks him if he wants a cup of tea. I jump from my place and gently push her aside telling her, "Your father is tired from work." I pat him on the shoulder waiting for him to say anything even though I know he won't. He utters not a word. I leave the place, unable to go back to my work. I answer the telephone which seems this moment like a godsend while following his aimless movements around the house. I give the wrong answers, I make mistakes in gender—he becomes she, then the letters get jumbled in my mouth. It becomes impossible to continue the conversation with the person on the other end of the line who is surprised at my incoherence. I turn on the television, paying no heed to what is being shown. He comes and sits next to me in silence, surfing the channels, looking for something or another. He makes a cup of tea even though only a little earlier he had refused one from his daughter. After an hour of smoking without saying anything, he leaves the smoke-filled room for his bed. I guarantee that for at least three days he will not try to touch me. I know that he will sleep fitfully. I lie next to him, awake and aware of his tormented wakeful breathing which banishes sleep from my eyes. I hear the dawn call to prayers after some dark hours and I hear his footsteps in the family room and the sound of water and I fall asleep.

His eyes pierce me in the dark even though he takes pains not to turn. I become alert to his awakened body which resists desire in silence. I close my eyelids on my sudden awakening. I try to summon calm to my body which suffers internal spasms of fear. I try to persuade it to sleep as the mattress, the mirror, and the armoire, even the turned-off lamp seem to radiate pain. I wish to pat him, but I can't. I know he knows I am awake even though I haven't stirred. We still have this umbilical cord despite our separation.

I ask myself in confusion, "Who created this situation? I've paid the price a thousand times, so why doesn't he try, just try to realize my sacrifice and inability to cope?"

I feel his hand consciously getting closer to the shoulder that's closest to him, after I'd turned over so I wouldn't be vulnerable to him. My eyes open wide, praying to God that he would stop there, feeling the heat of his body before he clings to me. He embraces me hard without saying a word and his fingers reach to parts of my body seeking an arousal that does not take place. I lie still as if I am not part of the scene. After failed attempts here and there, he withdraws to the other side of the bed. I can almost hear his burning body crying.

I wish I had another body other than the one worn out under the pressure of this constant torture. His pain hurts me but I am unable to open up to him. I ask God to give him another woman, to wean him from me. I seize every opportunity to hint at this idea but he rejects it saying he knows his own needs.

One night, I wake up to his body trying to penetrate my clothes. Before I completely come to, he has ejaculated the desire that had been repressed for months, before reaching the place where, for long years, he discharged his solo pleasure.

Division

Nahid had to spend her nights all week long at the guest house. I tried to lure her to spend one whole day with me but she skillfully evaded my attempts. When I pressured her, out of my longing to spend more time with her, she said as if dealing with an unruly child, "I love you, but you know my responsibilities. News about the jewels we found scattered during the dig has spread like wildfire in the neighboring villages. The peasants think the workers have found a treasure and that it is finders keepers. Security is spotty and the guards don't comprehend that the discovered treasures are far more precious than the value of the gold or the gems inlaid in it. I alone am responsible and I have to supervise their protection in person."

We spent the day together until six in the evening. I went to an appointment at the Zahrat al-Bustan café. No sooner had we sat down than Maggie came. I saw her in front of me before my body's wetness had dried or Nahid's scent disappeared. I felt the heat of both our bodies on my face and I seethed inside but remained calm on the outside. I was like someone caught *in flagrante delicto*, even though she didn't know anything.

I was haunted by questions the rest of the night. How can a woman not be sure, when her husband is physically and mentally separated from her, that there is another woman in his life, despite her suspicions and the death of love between them, and his body's giving off his beloved's scent? How does she not get that when she washes his clothes, shares his bed, and opens her eyes in the morning to his grim presence? How does she not notice his clamming up, his not permitting anyone to get near him before drinking his coffee, smoking his cigar, finishing his bathroom rituals, shaking off the shrouds of his sleep little by little? How?

An Arrow

We celebrated the publication of Omar's new novel. We had a boisterous party. I don't know of any joy similar to the joy I feel with a book of his. I know how hard he works preparing and writing. I feel him pouring himself in the work, to come out crisp and compact, and when he is done, he is very close to collapsing. I hover around him, dying to know what he is writing. Sometimes he gives me a few chapters and sometimes he holds back, saying, "I am not used to this. I prefer to have it finished first." But when I persist, he lets me follow his progress.

Omar decided to buy a refrigerator and a table with the advance for the novel. I wanted a bed. We were sleeping on a foam-rubber mattress on the floor, which we called 'the bridal furniture' and laughing, would say it is more healthy.

Omar refused because he wanted to buy a whole bedroom set when circumstances permitted. I said, "The bed will come in handy in the future. We will put it in the other room for the children. I will redesign the house to accommodate the three children with us."

"What children?"

"Sharif, Maha, and Yusif. Sharif and Yusif in one room and a couch for Maha in the dining room."

"The children won't live with us. Maggie will not accept parting with Sharif; he is her only family in Egypt, as you know, and she'll never give him up. Maha and Yusif no longer need you. They can live with their father."

"But I am a mother also and I can't part with my children."

"Who said you'd part with them. Stay with them two days a week in grandma's house and visit them one more day. We'll figure this out together and they'll get used to life this way quickly. They're not children."

"Maha's at a critical time in school. I don't want her to face the divorce of her parents, her mother's re-marriage, and perhaps also her father's, and the secondary school certificate exams all at the same time. I have to supervise the schedule of the private tutors and help her realize her dream of going to pharmacology school, and Mustafa doesn't go home at regular times."

"I cannot live in the midst of a school schedule and an arrangement that keeps you busy and keeps the home where I write busy. Besides, the place is far away from their schools. Nahid, I've escaped to you. I've had it with Maggie's clutter all this time. I have arranged my life to be alone with you to start my deferred projects. I am planning for an epic novel that will require all my time and attention for years and I cannot start working on it before I separate from Maggie and live with you in isolation here. I am even thinking of getting a leave from the newspaper and moving to a coastal town in which we will both devote full time to writing. I'll finish my project and you will finish your research. I dream of your taking care of me and in my dream there's no room for the kind of life you are suggesting."

"But you didn't refuse before that the children live with us. I talked to you about my dream of furnishing the children's room; I told you that Yusif and Sharif were close in age and that Maha would soon leave us to get married. I never once heard you object. So what has changed your thinking suddenly?"

"I haven't changed anything. It was *your* dream and a picture in *your* mind."

"You want to postpone the divorce then?"

"Who said that?"

"Because I am not going to leave my children at this age without taking care of them."

"Their grandmother can take care of them."

"Please reconsider. You are killing me, between you and them. I am not going to choose parting with my children and I am not going to leave you now."

"Don't postpone the divorce, but don't make a rule of the exception, because it is an exception. And things might change any moment because of a silly coincidence."

"I know the gravity of our situation and I suffer from it. I hide my pain from you so as not to add to your worries, but I am torn trying to balance the two worlds. Our life this way never occurred to me before, but it came as a temporary solution until the children no longer need us so much."

"Don't make me wait long. Things that come too late are no good. Sartre turned down the Nobel Prize saying, "It didn't come when I needed it. I don't need it now.""

"There's nothing to be done. Perhaps you'll change your mind later."

"No. I know that in your eyes, your children will remain children for life. You have to know your real needs now and I won't object to your decision and the way you choose our relationship to be. I want *you* in whatever arrangement."

"You are not giving me much of a choice."

4

Questions

Nahid's relationship with Mustafa was, for me, a big question mark. Things on the surface suggested a woman settled down in her marriage, content, anxious to drop the names of her husband and children in conversations with others, as if she were carrying them with her wherever she went. But on the other hand, she doesn't talk about the nature of the relationship, just a few suggestive references and it is up to the others to figure out the significance of these references. She was getting very close to me, and very fast, without saying a word until she found herself in my arms, saying to me, "I love you," without explaining her relationship with that other man.

Early on, as I contemplated her equanimity, I had a dilemma: should I approach her as a friend or is she going to open the door to more than that? There were no signals, no hints, but she kept getting closer and closer. She'd spend ten hours talking to me, looking happy and content, then she'd go home and spend several more hours on the telephone with me. We'd discover that we'd almost spent the whole day together. Where was the husband in all of this? He's the one absent, in the far background, except for a few words—more like statements of facts that at the same time indicated respect and appreciation for him. But I resolved to forget this situation entirely and the unresolved questions when we kissed for the first time without premeditation. Anyway, it doesn't matter anymore, for I discovered their relationship in that first kiss. As for the details, they will come later, intermittently, in different places and different times.

Talking about that relationship brought nothing but chagrin for her and I became torn between the desire to know and the desire not to dig up the painful past.

The first time that I saw them together, he seemed inappropriate for her, at least as far as looks were concerned—his dusty, swarthy features were not handsome. When I got closer to them to shake their hands, I wished I hadn't been introduced to him. And even though I met him only a few times by chance, I noticed one time that she spoke to him affectionately and I also noticed that their hands were moving together freely, and I was made to feel like a stranger between them. What was my place? These two have affection for each other, so what am I doing there? Is my intruding on their life ethical? I never wanted to see him again or see them together or have a close relationship with him so there wouldn't be any moral responsibility toward him. Had I had a closer relationship with him, my relationship with Nahid would have been undermined.

For a whole year I thought they had a natural, normal relationship. I accepted that and banished it from my thoughts. For a whole year, she spoke to me about a romantic past before marriage, but she never got close to talking about her intimate relationships that I took for granted.

Rejection

She opened her eyes to his fingers stoking her body, then she coquettishly closed them as she smiled. She was overcome by an enormous desire to cling to his chest, to slowly savor a calm pleasure that seeped through her soul after they had exhausted their bodies in lovemaking. She coiled up like a snail and began to wiggle slowly under his fondling finger, clinging ever closer to him without undoing her fetus-like position. She gently pushed him away, trying to keep his palm from awakening her sleepy veins, but he tried again and kissed her tenderly at first, then more and more ardently. She slipped from his hands and turned to the other side, giving him her naked back. He returned her to her earlier position. She begged him to leave her alone for a little while as she smilingly drifted into sleep, barely following his moving to the edge of the mattress and picking up and lighting his pipe.

She had become increasingly aware that he had bowed his head, raising it from time to time bitterly to exhale the smoke, making a sad hissing sound, and that distracted her from pleasurably succumbing to the mystery of the moment. A momentary awakening claimed her attention and revealed to her the seething within the stillness. She didn't understand the reasons as she struggled against falling asleep. Once she managed to wake up sufficiently, she threw her body onto his back and hugged him strongly despite the laziness of her sleepy fingers and rested her cheek on his naked shoulder.

"Don't do that again."

She was taken aback by his firm, almost angry tone.

"Don't reject me again."

"How can I reject you when you are all life to me? I just succumbed a little to a desire to enjoy myself slowly. I am tired but happy, savoring my feeling of love for you."

"You denied me my desire."

"Who taught me to reflect on feelings rather than skipping them?"

"Nahid, listen to me. I ask myself a lot: is your desire for me real or is it just a desire to satisfy me? I recall what happened in your life before we met and your aversion to your relationship with him and the paradox surprises me. Are you repeating what you have endured your whole life?"

"The situation is different. I chose you with my free will and I am staying with you because of my desire for you. The secrecy of our relationship has eliminated societal pressures. So why should I endure that which I cannot? We are not together because of children or social form or joint interests. What we are doing is something that we want and love. Time is not on our side, Omar. I don't have time for another failure. I have time only for truth and the truth alone and what we really want. I will not accept half measures, as I've told you. You were not the reason for the change in my life. The reason was a pledge between me and my father that I made the night he passed away. I will be nothing but myself and I will not accept pale colors and wishy-washy positions or repression even if it were the repression of my love for my children. I had expected time to pass without meeting a man who would fulfill me as I wanted, one with whom I could be myself. I would have accepted such a deal with life and fulfilled myself some other way. But life wanted to tell me: you deserve my passion because of your perseverance. That's why I met you. Chance alone could not have made this love, but both our desires, which we had matured. People who are oblivious or indifferent to love do not fall in love, only those totally ready for it. Do you remember the song by Fairuz that says, 'I have longing, I don't know for whom?' That's a woman about to fall in love, to whom the world sent a wave of longing so that everything about her would be waiting and she would recognize him at once and would love him, not from the moment she saw him, but from the moment she felt that unknown longing and she would be telling the truth when she tells him that she has known him for a long time."

"I need to believe this. Assure me of your feelings; repeat it many times. I don't have time for new wounds. I don't want another rejection. I don't want to have to go through that again."

"You never told me what is tormenting you and I was afraid to seek to know your intimate relations with her because I won't be able to put up with the consequences. I don't want your picture together forcing itself on my imagination. Put your head on my chest and say what you want."

"Maggie has used my burning desire for her to pressure me. She used it as skillfully as the most lowborn women in Cairo's poor neighborhoods. But there's a drastic difference between the two: the poor woman haggles coquettishly to obtain small favors and she knows that if she doesn't get them, she will not reject her man. She will give him the same pleasure and tell him that she expects to get what she is requesting the following day. He knows that the rules of the game require that each of them believe the other's role: he believes her anger if he delays delivering what she requests, and he believes her joy when she obtains it, and she believes that he accepts haggling in principle, so sometimes she plays hard to get and other times lets him have his way. This is part of the ritual of flirting, like the dance of the birds. Do you know a creature that doesn't perform flirting maneuvers? My love for her prevented me from understanding. I imagined that what was happening between us was just a game and I took into account the difference in environment, culture, and character formation which sometimes made her act in a dry, rigid manner. But a long time of living together proved to me that we didn't blend together, we didn't turn into one entity, but remained always two. And the things I had thought were unconnected, were in fact connected. I didn't connect her rigid ideas about women's liberation and equality, and removing feelings altogether from the issue and her precise separation of our finances and her ability to use sex to pressure and extort me, even though the picture is quite clear to me now. She considered our natural relationship one of her weapons in her battles with me. And instead of our desire turning into a means of restoring our intimate closeness, it turned into one of the reasons for my outburst. She played the game very skillfully: she'd lure me and when I got ready, she'd broach a thorny topic and demand immediate answers. Before I understood this game plan, I'd ask her to postpone the discussion a little and continue to swallow the bait and lower my defenses. I would try to seduce her, but I would find her more alert, a sharp and ready mind moving towards me, taking me out of the amorous mood. With time, I noticed the mechanics of the way she dealt with me and I took cover. I stayed at least partially alert and yet I often fell into the trap because I truly desired and loved her, and my body demanded its pleasure with her and I didn't see any reason to deny myself. Many a time, a tempest would blow up for a trivial reason or around a purely cultural issue that could have been post-poned for some other time: Shakespeare, is he a real English poet or a myth? Is he one poet or a group of poets who wrote using his name?"

"But that's an interesting question that hasn't been fully answered. Some scholars have posed it and its validity has not been proven."

"If I said that, the night would be ruined. She would leave the room and bring to bed scholars' opinions. And maybe two months later, I'd find a new book in the mail or photocopies of papers from different books or periodicals to support her position to prove to me that *she* was right, then she'd reopen the subject; when she felt that I desired to hold her, she would leave me and go off in a different direction to prove that I needed her. She did that so smoothly and carefully that I didn't figure out what was happening for some time, then she'd turn vicious; for days on end I couldn't even just talk to her. It would be a house where you couldn't hear 'good morning' for days, then when we finally made up, I'd find in my arms a woman with a voracious appetite for sex which she would have lustfully several times, and so I'd forget what happened, and once again I'd believe that she loved me. I'd convince myself that I am delusional and her game is totally different from what I made it out to be. It's a case of very strange compensation: her body opens up all its secrets to me and gives me splendid, unadulterated pleasure.

"She'd enthusiastically play the piano again, beautifully, and with great ability and agility. You'd feel a joyous mood in the house and a defiance of obstacles; you would sense success and gaiety; she'd welcome people and make peace with them, forget their drawbacks, happily go out with me, read what I wrote without suspicion, and love the characters in my novels. Then in one moment—an explosion. I don't know how it starts or why, and she accuses me of being the grievous mistake of her life.

"It was a chain of eruptions and moods that I got used to receiving in silence after I'd tried everything to stop them at a level that would allow us to recapture our happiness. Then I realized that she went through nervous cycles with definite speculations: if the anger begins, then it must reach a zenith, a fraying of the nerves that she cannot stop, months of solitude more merciful than daily skirmishes. She had no family to whom she could run to for support, and no real friends. The inevitability of our staying together established rules that we both knew at times of clash. We'd each go to a neutral corner and keep quiet, engage in a sort of silent divorce, in which she imagined that by denying me her body she would force me to make concessions or make me her equal because she believes that equality means separation and power, not integration and mutual affection.

"Perhaps what you give me is one of the reasons I love you, this mercy and intimacy. You don't have that blind fanaticism about equality."

"When part of me gives another part of me something, it does not need reciprocation. And I am part of you, so how can I expect a return? I don't need a declaration of equality because that would be a desire on the part of two people, each of whom is measuring how much they have, and that sets up barriers because it assumes separateness the whole time, whereas we are one being. I want you always, Omar. Your desire for me is love for me, you give me something very precious of yourself, not the pleasure alone, but the blending. I've made love without emotion because of the body's needs and because of the circumstances I found myself in. But what is happening between us has other specifications. I wish I could find another name for it that would separate it from what happens to others. I will never be Maggie, but just give me the space to be tired, angry, quiet, wanting to be alone with myself. This is quite natural and you are not necessarily the direct cause for it, for I move, I get excited, I get sick. This is not directed against you."

"Say that you want me before crossing the doorstep after an absence of even a few hours."

"I will wear a bright red pendant around my neck that says I desire you forever."

"I want you now."

"No."

Unplanned Communities

I was able to uncover some facts having to do with the Maadi Construction Cooperative Society. The society was finally forced to hold an emergency meeting during which its board of directors decided to go ahead with the project, financing its completion at revised costs, the balance of which would be borne by the member-owners. It seems there was hope for solving the problem. All we needed in our apartment building were the utilities, since the Administration of the Governorate of Cairo considered the development an 'unplanned community' even though it was that same Administration that had sold the units, and waited for the society to pay a specific sum of money to get the utilities up and running. But in its present circumstances, the society couldn't pay. My efforts and those of our bridegroom neighbor resulted in an agreement that each member pay a sum greater than the price of the electric meter to cover the cost, and thus we were able to solve the problem of electricity. But the Water Department refused this solution, saying that we had to collect the money from all the members or at least from every building. It was then that I discovered that each building had fifty units whose owners I did not know. The society manager refused to give me a list of the names even though I told him it wouldn't cost the society in money or effort. I didn't understand the reasons for this obduracy. But when I began my campaign in the newspaper, they gave me the names grudgingly and resentfully. My bridegroom neighbor and I began a journey that uncovered for me much of what I didn't know about the suffering of Egyptians, no matter how much I claimed to know hundreds of cases of misery and sacrifices behind the doors that were forcibly closed to people. The apartment building also witnessed many mysterious sales, and we'd get in touch with a buyer only to discover that he had sold the apartment to another person.

The whole thing seemed absurd. One day someone knocked on the door of my office and asked me to move my ownership to another unit in the development. Despite my urgent need for the office to obtain the license, and even though the other unit to which he suggested I move was more finished and had better facilities, I insisted on staying and following up on what was happening. I was writing my new novel, so I took a break from my journalistic work. Besides, I really liked the apartment, the love oasis that had given me my most beautiful times.

I had, over time, moved most of the things I needed to the apartment so I could work there whenever the opportunity presented itself. I could not, however, get used to being there alone. I would wait for Nahid to finish her job and then we'd go together. Today she caught up with me after a long inspection tour. She arrived exhausted.

"Take a hot shower and a nap until I finish my work," I told her.

She carried out the first part of my suggestion but not the other one. "I didn't want to waste time sleeping," even though I tried to convince her that sleep is wonderful when we are both there.

She came out refreshed after the hot shower.

"Are you translating an article?"

"Yes, one by Robert Fisk, under the title, 'The Evidence is There: We Caused Cancer in the Gulf.' Fisk is a British journalist who writes in *The Independent*, which is one of the major newspapers in Britain. He has visited Iraq several times and wrote angry articles, about what he saw in the hospitals in Basra."

"Did you finish the translation?"

"Yes, and it's an important article and really frightening."

Nahid began to read the article, which reiterated and elaborated on the link between the use of depleted uranium shells by American and British forces during the 1991 Gulf War and a noticeable increase in cases of tumors among Iraqi children. She was particularly struck by his description of the condition of a nine-year old girl from Basra.

"This month," Fisk wrote, "I've seen enough Iraqi children with tumors on their abdomen to feel horror as well as anger. When Hebba Mortaba's mother lifted her little girl's patterned blue dress in the

Mansour hospital in Baghdad, her terribly swollen abdomen displayed numerous abscesses. Doctors had already surgically removed an earlier abdominal mass only to find, monster-like, that another grew in its place."

Nahid could barely continue reading but she stoically went on following Fisk's rebuttal of a letter sent to *The Independent* by Lord Gilbert, Minister of State for Defence, in which he characterized Fisk's earlier accounts as a "willful perversion of reality." Fisk cited statements by some British and American officials intimating or confirming the existence of a link between the use of DU and unexplained and "potentially terminal illnesses" and cancers suffered by "tens of thousands of 1991 Gulf war veterans . . . and thousands of Iraqi civilians, including children unborn when the war ended."

Nahid was still quite taken aback when she came to the end of the article: "Translated by Omar Mamun." When she was finally able to look up from the page, Omar was holding a book which he handed to her: " Take this book also. It will explain to you how dangerous depleted uranium is. Its title is *Depleted Uranium: Metal of Shame.* It was published by the International Action Center in New York in 1997 and it contains articles by a group of scientists and testimonies of soldiers who took part in the war against Iraq. The book was published in English as part of a project to publicize the knowledge of the danger of depleted uranium and of the fact that the Pentagon had exposed soldiers and civilians to radiation by using weapons shooting this metal during the Gulf War in 1991. I intend to review this book in the paper and hope it will be published."

"It's unbelievable what's happening to Iraq. We should all speak out against it," Nahid said.

Telephone

I impatiently wait until a moment presents itself to me when I need to hide in your arms. I shoo away the crowds, the requests, and the wishes of others. I know that you are now sitting in front of the computer typing, staying in touch with your characters and Sharif and the silence. I want to disappear inside you. I postponed picking up the telephone several times until I couldn't wait any more. I took it to a safe and quiet corner. When your voice reached me, I gushed forth, expressing my unbearable longings. Your dry words were lost in the heat of my ardor, so I didn't notice that you were in a different world. Then I realized that my words were hitting solid walls and bouncing back. I mollified my words, for my desire for you was greater than my understanding of what was happening. When the sarcastic tone you used to make light of the situation I did not understand finally reached me, I had fallen into feelings of loss. The seconds rolled dryly by and the conversation ended with formal words and good wishes.

I got lost in a maze of incomprehension. I wondered if you were the same person who is mine when you are truly mine or whether I was laboring under some kind of delusion. I review in my mind the meaning of crowding that you try to convey to me in code and I realize the time is not appropriate for conversation. I get over it and patch up the gaps that open up as a result of our strange situation, but today I didn't understand. Circumstances were not so totally difficult that you couldn't reply with an appropriate word if even obliquely. I didn't understand the reason for the aversion.

I succumbed to a troubled sleep that made me even more hungry for sleep. I awoke to a state of being with no taste and no color until your still sleepy voice came to me, "Good morning. I miss you. I couldn't talk to you because I needed you more than you needed me, so I was afraid of getting into a mood in which I would lose my self-control. Only a few minutes before you called I was holding back my desire to call you and tell you to come right away. And when I was able to control my feelings, I heard your voice and almost threw all caution to the wind and told you without any restraint how much I wanted you. Sharif was standing there with one of his friends joking with me and teasing

Maggie from afar. I almost told them, 'This will not jeopardize your security.' But all I could do was restrain my desire for you and prevent a single word from coming out, so that the river might not rush in an unstoppable flood.

"Had I been with you at the time, I would have held your head to my chest and hugged you like a baby, feeling the warmth of the breast and, falling asleep, continued to dream of suckling. I prevented myself from speaking to you for fear that you would sense my streaming tears vying with the words. I know you can control yourself and I know how much you suffer, and I can see the tips of your lips quivering so gently that only I can see them, because the quiver begins in my heart. Anyway, I just miss you so much. Go now and make yourself a cup of tea and wash your face then call me, for I love your intimate, rippling voice that no one but me hears, or so I imagine my rights."

I was lost. I didn't know whether I was crying for myself or for you. How come I didn't trust your feelings? Why was I assailed by doubts? Why am I always waiting for you to desert me, and dreaming, not that you are kidnapping me, but leaving me? Is it an internal wish that I cannot express but can only see in my daydreams? And why do I give in to these dreams? Do I wish for a solution that comes from you, that you leave me? And, can I live without you?

It's as if I want a *force majeure* to resolve my crisis. Do I really want my two lives at the same time? Do I want my home and my children and Mustafa and Omar, as he says? That's impossible. My fear for Mustafa and my caring for him, despite the separation, can be justified on the human level: there is the shared life and the friendship but there is also the inability and the fear of the unknown. Yes, I fear illness. I fear old age after I leave those I gave my youth to. Why don't I trust Omar's ability to look after me when old age comes? Perhaps because I know very well that he is easily bored and if he is confronted at any time with my inability, he'll find another woman and skillfully hide it from me, and that will kill me.

I've always imagined that a male pigeon cannot do without his partner until one day I saw a beautiful female pigeon cowering in a corner of the coop, looking very meek and her male partner in another part of the coop amorously pursuing a younger female. I watched them for days until I found her dead one morning. I didn't know whether she had taken sick so he left her for another or she died because he left her for another.

Omar says, "I don't want a solution that comes at the wrong time, I won't need it and I won't feel happy about it. It will be too late." As if he were the voice of reason and I the voice of madness. I know all of that and more. I know that life might complicate circumstances after a month or two. I know, but I am afraid.

Goddess

She watched his quiet after all her efforts to provoke him to fight in the hope they would make up afterwards failed. She wondered in puzzlement how he no longer needed her. Have their needs changed suddenly and is she now the one doing the chasing? She knew that he had no patience with his body, that in the past his desires had made him end the quarrel. She hated the quiet reigning in the study, as she hid her resentment of his ability to totally disregard their relationship. The ringing of the telephone broke the silence. He picked it up and started talking to someone whose identity Maggie could not determine. Suspicion bored its way into her heart as she followed his talking about details of daily living that she knew he never cared for. It's a woman. It has to be a woman. She tried to sort things out in her mind, puzzled by the incongruity between the long time he spends at home and the isolation he imposes on himself, ignoring her being there, glossing over any clashes and poring over paper, writing his novel day and night, and the days he totally disappears and she cannot track him down at the newspaper or anywhere else and his accusing her of silly unjustified jealousy. His life has turned into a closed box in which he lives alone.

She picked up a book from the table nearby and felt in it a letter addressed to him that she had received the day before. She was strongly tempted to open it and find out what was in it after her suspicions were aroused by its dainty envelope and the feminine fragrance wafting from it. She hid it until she made up her mind about it. She kept looking between it and Omar, who got up to buy the newspapers. She turned the letter over and saw the Moroccan stamp. How many times did he go to Morocco this year? She knew that if she opened it, she would provoke her husband terribly, but she gambled anyway for the sake of knowledge and confirming her intuition in the face of his denial. She tore the envelope open quickly and nervously to prevent herself from changing her mind. She read the love words written so fondly they made her mad and she couldn't finish the letter. She looked for the name of the sender and found it to be Badi'a Hilal. Omar hadn't mentioned that name to her before. She went back to read where she had stopped as blood rushed to her face, which was now burning more and more as she continued reading. The woman was expressing sexual desire with an ardor that Maggie had never heard of.

She had barely finished the last two lines when she heard the sound of the key turning in the door lock. She raised her head to him as the tears pouring from her eyes choked her screams, which he heard but didn't understand the cause of. He became apprehensive before realizing it had to do with a woman as she handed him the letter.

He asked, "What happened?" His question came late as she collapsed on the chair crying the loss of love, the collapse of the relationship forever, and his betrayal. She became more tense while he became cool and calm after finding out the woman's name. He put the papers on the desk and reached in his pocket for a cigar and a lighter. Then he placed them on the desk and sat facing her, taking off his shoes after slipping out of his jacket. She followed him with alarmed eyes as he kept reading the letter to the end with a light smile on his face that turned into a full grin as he looked at her. "Where's the problem?"

She swallowed the tears pouring down her cheeks as she felt her pride hurt and she fell into the uncertain region between returning the insult and growing doubts, between belittling her and her opening a letter addressed to someone else. But she had made sure the name and address were correct. So where did he get such audacity? She wondered as she took the letter from him, as she almost got up to throw anything within reach at him.

"Read it again. It is from a woman who knows me but who I don't know. But she certainly is talking about herself and not about us." She snatched the letter from him and began to re-read it and discover the trap she had fallen into.

The words did not fully confirm anything with any degree of certainty but sort of pointed in a certain direction without being explicit. She read the letter for the third time and recognized in it the intimate talk of a woman in love. She didn't refer to shared memories or promises to him. She was just expressing her fervent feelings for him and expected him to write to her because she didn't know of his visits to Morocco in recent years. She swallowed the anger screaming inside her and kept its roots seething there. I know there is a woman in his life. My feelings never lie. She followed his retreat into his closed world, arranging his papers on the desk, going into the kitchen to make tea and his question which she couldn't help thinking was provocative, "Shall I pour you some tea?" and her unthinking reply in the negative.

She couldn't carry her body, now beset by fatigue and worried thoughts, to bed. She resisted appearing defeated in front of him until he was totally lost in the screen and his fingers kept tapping the letters on the keyboard. She sneaked into bed without saying goodnight. She picked up a magazine but quickly found it boring. Nothing gave her joy anymore. Insomnia spread its cold white on the ceiling of the room. She curled, seeking warmth in Ovid's *Art of Love*, which was always within her reach beside the bed and began to peruse the pictures accompanying the poems and skim them, heedless of the meaning of the words which she had committed to memory when she was much younger. She contented herself with the inner rhythm of the poetry which she almost sang without sound. The music provided her with a soft cover of tranquility which the gods sent her.

They have all the evils of humans. They are not gods but real humans acting naturally, governed only by their desires, be they strong or weak, cruel or kind, she thought to herself as she succumbed to the playfully haunting specters, and longing carried her asleep on a magic carpet towards the unknown. When she closed her eyes, she saw black circles with gray edges emanating from deep inside the eyes, vanishing only to be replaced by others. A magical opening reveals an expanse. She looks behind her and sees flocks of birds running away from the intense heat and hiding in the tops of tall trees. Omar comes, appearing to be exhausted, seeking rest after weariness. He rests his body on the shaded grass after he secures his quarry. She knows his clothes and does not know them. And the place, where is it? It's a forest she has visited with her mother. Water is flowing at the spring and Omar is thirsty but cannot get up to drink. She recognizes her grandmother's house at the foot of the hill. There are hunting clothes and arrows lying next to him. His lips move, whispering, "Come to me quickly and relieve the heat of my throat, Aura." The opening closes and the dark returns. "Does he love a Greek woman?" Her face became pale and she felt her body bleeding. "Blood invalidates the vision,"—isn't that what they say? This is not your heritage, right? She hastened to the grove to catch him in the act. She remembered the net that Vulcan made with skill and precision to capture his wife Venus with her lover, Mars. And when the two were caught, naked, in the net, Vulcan called all the gods to witness the two but he regretted that later on as they both dashed off, after they were freed, to another place to meet and openly enjoy love. There was nothing to fear anymore.

She hesitated for a few seconds, but she gathered up her courage and sped to where he was. She saw the imprint of his body in the grass and she hid behind a tree, afraid to draw near, unable to stay away as she heard his footsteps. He arrived alone, panting from the heat and sprinkling water on his face, saying, "If only Aura would cool my body!" When Maggie clearly heard the Latin name 'Aura,' the wind goddess, life came back to her veins which had been dried by her desire for revenge. She hurried to apologize to him but some leaves under her feet made a sound that Omar thought was a beast, so he jumped up and shot her in the heart with an arrow. Her body succumbed to the ferryman's boat carrying her to the river of death. Omar's sad face, covered with tears, moved away and the light disappeared as the boat went farther into the darkness. She no longer saw Omar on the riverbank. The echoes of her desire rang out in the horizon of the unknown: can Omar cross to the underworld and restore me to life? Dark-colored birds flocked around the boat mockingly. She discovered that they were his women friends: writers and artists, Arab, Greek, and foreign translators, all naked. She saw them pushing her into the darkness. She gathered her strength and began to shout at the ferryman to return her to land. It wasn't unfounded jealousy; he met Aura, wind goddess, at dawn. Aurora, the goddess of dawn, had seduced him. Silence prevailed as the ferryman wearing a pale-colored cloak calmly went downstream.

Suspicion

He no longer knew how to define his feelings toward her precisely. Is it jealousy or anxiety? Or what is he expecting of her? He knows that he is dealing with a woman who is hard to force anything on. He is not going to rape her, of course, and he is not going to consider the present situation permanent. She, at least, hasn't asked for divorce until now. He has a suspicion that she might have met a man: then why isn't she advancing the separation and making it public, and marrying the other man? I am surprised by her defense of the family and its stability. I think that, for her, the family is more important than her personal happiness or her desires. And she does not dare break taboos. She cannot, as a wife, even if the marriage is only on paper, have a relationship with another man. But sometimes I feel she's planning something and when I become more certain of it and get close to the truth, she does something, maybe a very small thing, that dispels the conclusion I had reached.

I fear her when she falls silent, when she shuts me out of her world so I can't know anything about her schedule or what issues concern her or the atmosphere she moves in. She depends on the changing nature of her job, between offices in the Department of Antiquities and the dig sites, and her accompanying archaeological missions that last for years. She didn't accept such jobs when Maha and Yusif were very young because the contract between the Antiquities Department and foreign missions stipulated that the Egyptian inspectors stayed with the mission full time which meant day and night work. Now she is working as if there was nothing in her life but work. In the years of our separation she made great progress and got fast promotions and was given tasks that very few archaeologists got.

I noticed, last week, that she was frequently away from home and tense for no reason that I knew. I tried to get her to talk about it but she didn't respond. Then I discovered that she was crying silently alone at night and avoiding talking to me. She no longer even bothers to come to the second floor where our room has stayed the same; one bed, shared things, and a husband and wife who have been separated for years.

She is now used to going into her study on the first floor, then into the garden where she spends many hours, reading or meditating until she sleeps. Does she have another place to sleep, the mission guest house? Maybe.

Her work begins at 6:30 a.m. and she gets up at five to personally supervise the day's meals and the needs of the family members. She rarely comes back before midnight, five days a week. When does she get any sleep? She sits in the garden looking at the sky, wide awake. When I decided to ask her, I was surprised to see her at home before I returned from work, ten days in a row, coming from the site before noon, as if she knew that I was going to ask her. She pores over her papers, finishing a number of articles that she publishes in leading American and French periodicals. I know, by chance, that she is studying German on a regular basis. When, Nahid? When? Has your day turned into forty-eight hours? Or are you feverishly using up your life by escaping from the reality you dragged us into?

Pity

I take pains to stay in the same condition I am in after I come out of you: your scent, our mixed sweat, the taste of your body, your groans and last screams. I want to cling to all of that until the end; I mean, until we meet again.

So I go to the farthest spot in the apartment after I return, in the balcony that overlooks nothing, to be alone with myself and with you, away from any intrusions. There's no problem with Sharif intruding, but she is the problem. She comes near me and I try to get away from her until she goes to sleep in despair or something like that, as if I am afraid that she will discover you in me or to take me out of you. At such times I have no desire for sleep; rather, I wish the night would never end so I can preserve that feeling profoundly and uninterruptedly, for a long time, until the moment of sleep, alone with you on the couch in my study without any other company or the threat of company. The following night it might be different; I may have been able to strike a balance between my secret world and the public one, able to combine them and deal with them rationally.

Last night, like so many similar nights, when I came out of the bathroom, I thought she was fast asleep. The lights were out and only a narrow strip of light escaped from the bedroom to the corridor. Everything was quiet, giving a sense of security. I went into the room cautiously, avoiding making any noise that might wake her up and I lay on the bed getting ready to sleep: bringing you to my bosom, feeling your body and its contours cleaving to my body. As I get closer to sleep, I feel her fingers sneaking across the distance between our bodies. "Take me into your arms," she whispers. It is difficult to commit any crudity no matter the reason. She embraces me then clings to me as if she doesn't want any part of me to escape from her. I freeze in my place, making sure that I do nothing that indicates any encouragement, but I feel the arousal in her body spiraling spontaneously. Her hand reaches out to feel my body then sneaks under my clothes and tarries in the places which she knows I am most excitable. The hand keeps going down slowly until she can't stand it any more and totally loses control.

I watch her from inside and study the situation from the outside, as if the body is not mine. I realize at the same time that she has reached the point of no return. I am haunted by the images of last night and your naked body against my chest and my insatiable lust for you, and I don't know what to do, but she takes the initiative—she takes off my clothes and moves away for a second to hastily take off her own clothes and slide into the bed again before she loses the moment. Once again, she feels my naked body and once she senses it is responding, she explodes as if her desire had been repressed for a thousand years.

A feeling of pity comes over me. How is it possible to accommodate the bodies of two women: one body that you keep wanting till the end and another that you don't need? How can you satisfy a woman out of pity and compassion rather than out of desire? I notice the onset of limpness, so I decide to finish the job peaceably with her and harness my energy to complete it. I search my mind quickly for the positions that are most arousing to me in general, I increase the pace of successive strokes and I reach out my hand to those parts of her body that she cannot resist so I can get her to orgasm; I push her relentlessly to the climax until her last scream in the dark. I gently withdraw from her and quietly catch my breath, then I sneak to the bathroom to remove the traces of what took place and go back to the bed to sleep as if nothing had happened. But the questions keep coming: is it possible for this situation to continue and for how long? What did *she* do wrong? What's to be done? How can a man live with a woman whose kisses he runs away from?

I wonder sometimes how I loved this woman at one time, how I longed for her, waited with bated breath for the moment she took off her clothes, happy with the touch of her hand on my body. Is it the same-old woman or another, a stranger I do not know and I do not want? I look at her with the eyes of a spectator as she moves about the apartment. What brought us together? Where did the common ground on which we both stood at one time go? And the glowing nights of love and lust that kept us up till morning? She says to me, "You've changed." I evasively say, "Everything changes. You're looking for the old love and I am too old for it. It no longer fits me." Other times I say, "I no longer want it, it doesn't appeal to me anymore," or "I am just comfortable like that, without it," trying to establish a basis for her to give up on me. But on those calm days without skirmishes, she tends to ignore all of that completely and expect closeness. How is it possible for a man to discover, after years and years, that he cannot stand the scent of a woman with whom he lives affectionately or with whom he used to live affectionately.

Training

She comes in filled with excitement, talking non-stop about the discoveries by the French mission with which she works of a small pyramid at Saqqara, built for one of the royal wives of King Pepy, one of the last kings of Egypt's Old Kingdom. Before that, they had discovered a tomb of one of the king's officials, whose name was Weni, in which he recorded the honor of being charged by the king to uncover what he called, 'The conspiracy in the royal harem.' The discovered text says that he was proud of King Pepy's trust and his charging him with the investigation. But the result of the investigation was nowhere to be found.

Nahid was hoping that the new pyramid would uncover details of that conspiracy for her. She is so taken by the information that she talks about it the whole time, even in our bed. I feel that she prefers staying with the mission to staying with me on such days.

Today I waited for her for a long time, trying to write. I was thinking of our relationship and how far it has gone. I wanted to write about Nahid before I met her, and discovered that my knowledge of her relationship with her husband was quite scant. When she settled into my arms I asked her. She was evasive as usual.

I couldn't control my anger as I repeated my question and said, "You want one soul without paying the price of this wish of yours. You ask me to bare all then you draw the curtain on yourself; you escape from confronting the past and refuse to disclose it. You introduce me to a maze of analyses and long explanations of one theme—that you hate your earlier feelings. I cannot touch a specific event, but rather swirls of wind that sting as they go round. I see you grinding emptiness between the millstones of your desire and your fear, and all that comes out are effects rather than causes. What's that terrible thing that you fear, as if it has never happened to any human being before? Your silence will undermine your aspiration to this relationship, which is open as any can be. Let me enter your secret world with you. Tell me how his touch felt on your hand, on your breast. How can I be a path to your knowledge of your body? Why are you annulling the years as if they had never been?"

"Believe me, it is not annulling of events that pain me and that my memory runs away from, nor is it negating what actually happened. It's much more complex than an escape. I taught my body not to feel. Don't look at me like that. You're opening a door to hell inside me that I'd closed. Don't rush me."

"Rush you? After six years I am rushing you?"

"I was not myself. Do you know how much I have suffered?"

"How, when I know how your body opens itself to me before I even get close to it?"

"I taught it absence, not just not being an active party, but non-existent at all. What good is it to be present in an act that crushes me? I didn't reach this decision easily and I didn't recognize it as soon as I perceived it; rather I recognized its features slowly. I paid its price in years of bitterness and pain until I decided to begin my journey in training my body to nip its feelings in the bud, teaching it not to respond even when it is dying to come undone."

She fell silent and I waited for her. I saw her looking abstractedly at a glimmer that appeared to her. She spoke as if she were speaking of another woman, in words that she had committed to memory, "She is burning like a flame anticipating the purest of blue. He looks at her and she burns even brighter. He comes closer, pours oil, and the flame gets red hot with black edges that contain its light. She asks for more so her heart will find release which can only be achieved by a total pouring out of ecstasy, followed by burning tranquility then translucent blue. It is a fire that feeds on itself to achieve purity. The body demands more burning and plays higher notes looking for a harmony that will make her open up. Before she realizes that the turning has begun and that she is now uncontrollably hurtling down a precipice, he finishes his leap with one fell swoop and reaches his climax. The din dies down and so do the loud marches, leaving nothing but a defeated moan and a soundless gasp that dares not declare its presence. All traces of heat disappear, as if the fires of love had never passed here."

She catches her breath with difficulty and her eyes emit a strange light—neither shining nor dull, but a piercing light radiating sadness. Her voice becomes so soft it gets lost; he feels, rather than hears it.

"I was cheated so many times. Every time he came near my body, I deluded myself that my yearning would cover the distance in record time even if I didn't like my satiation to take the form of a sudden downpour, without a course of time or space and without leaving any marks on a road that should be taken in a swinging, voluptuous gait, getting out of the body all its enriching, coquettish song and dance. My waiting piles up in flaming cracks that want to come undone before I physically sense his desire for my body. So when he enters me, I am already on fire. I wrap my arms around his body, and I don't know how it starts; so cold and without warming up, he pours out all his lust in one mad rush and nothing remains in that room except the hopeless ashes of his spent desire."

He embraces her without saying anything at first, then coaxes her, "Can we have more facts and fewer metaphors, please?"

She instinctively knows what he wants but she also knows the barriers that she has to overcome. He hears her whispering, still in his embrace, "Reluctance crept its way into my desire night after night. My desire grew greater when night prevailed and was lost when pride prevailed, until one day I discovered that I was hiding from myself how much I feared his coming close to me. Fear replaced my desire for the body's dance. The pain of emptiness erupted the moment I felt his gaze or the smile trembling on his lips as if he were afraid of its birth. I taught myself not to feel his hands as they felt my face, to ignore them as they then moved on to my breasts or slid over my belly button. I taught my nerves to withstand sensual onslaughts and I threw the flowers of lust into the well there to die with all the feelings I had already drowned there. I trained my organs to channel their responses to things other than what excited them. My mind was the master of that game, standing there like a giant playing a very serious role, giving signals of understanding, directing every organ to a function other than its own, changing the roles until it got exhausted. I asked it to depart and create another world whose components were not that room, that man, or that bed. Its components might be a war in Nicaragua or the discovery of a mine in the Balkans. My mind? It would be in another place altogether: in an island with sea shells that a boat is carrying me toward, to take me to a man whose features I do not know, who pushes through a dense growth of leaves to reach me. As I eagerly await him, I don't know whether my husband has finished the task he began until I hear his regular deep breathing which tells me that he has been asleep for an unknown period of time. I am relieved, maybe now I can join my man in the story."

She wraps her body around him, and they intersect and intertwine. She feels that her body is light. He wishes she would divulge more and passes his fingers through her hair cascading over her bare bosom and she goes betwixt and between wakefulness and sleep.

"Your problem is my mind, which I've long trained to unfocus; I trained it to superimpose one picture over another, to make up characters and locations and broad smiles peering from a large screen. I got myself a thermometer to measure my body's ability to be steadfast. If the thermometer indicated high temperature, I opened for my mind, a window away from the place, unrelated to what was happening to me. All I hoped for was that my mind not begin to wake up before he finished his leap. At that time I hear the roaring movement of a train squeezing the cross ties under the weight of its iron, exhaling with neutral crudity and slithering in the midst of tranquility, unaware of the illusions crushed under its wheels. I get out from under it totally devastated. Here it comes, heavy, very heavy.

"My body no longer suffers; it was able to wear a bright but dead body glove. It's my head that suffers. I suffer the pain of the amazing question that I avoid, even though I know it is lurking in my mind, residing in my heart: 'Why do you accept?' At that time I see the train and hear the cracking of my bones and smell the smoke as the questions keep coming like the train on the cross ties. Why does he accept running alone in my body? Doesn't sharing mean anything to him? Don't I give him any pleasure when I interact with him?

"The sound of music rises next to me as a blonde takes over the room and sings: 'Barbie, it's Barbie's plastic world.' I feel that I am just a black shadow—if only it were plastic! Like Sisyphus, I once again dream of being whole, even though I know it is impossible. I dream and believe the words he coaxes me to go along with. I once again take the same road to climb the mountain. I jam my intuition which no longer accepts the mere thought of it. I deceive it, then it shocks me that I cannot touch any of his parts, cannot fondle him because if I do, he'll come undone, and if I don't I will remain as dry as the summer firewood in an unlit fireplace. If the deception of the illusion is complete, I try to steer away from the idea of pushing the kind of ecstasy to fly when I cannot even release it. I shoo away my thoughts, begging them to move away and leave me. I need to be whole; one touch is enough to light the sparks of feeling, the bird dashes out forcibly without my being aware that I had reached the shore of pleasure alone, that my panting, which fills the room like a soft morning, is feeding the tree of misery rather than the tree of life. I clutch the air; there's no one with me; I am nowhere, suspended in a space ending up on the ceiling of the room which I feel is not mine. It gets narrower and narrower. I feel the walls are going to crush me. I look for him and find him gone, not to sleep but to comprehension. When he is upset by my words, he doesn't answer, leaves the room or my presence. His silence deepens and runs away from the question. Isn't there a doctor? A friend? Anyone who might have an answer?

"He says, 'I don't know what happens. Maybe next time it'll be better.'

"I get fed up. I can't get close to him or kiss him. His breath reminds me of my inability. His kiss reminds me that I cannot lose myself in any feeling with him. Little by little, I began to shy away whenever he came near me. Everything of his began to repulse me, to cause me to run away from it. I suddenly discovered that I'd come to be repulsed by the smell of his skin, his sweat pouring into my eyes the moment he reaches his climax. All of that has made me feel that I am not a woman, but a mere captive in a cave and at moments like that, animal odors fill my lungs and they get constricted. I no longer let him ever reach my lips. What's the point?"

Diaries

Suffering

I had a hard time with you but I was lucky in that I met you after knowing some liberated women whose multiple past relationships played an important role in understanding the relationship between women and men. I pushed you to get out from under the yoke of taboos and the forbidden, that old world and the barbed wire you so surrounded yourself with during our meetings that they became second nature to you. I pulled the words out of your mouth to make you express your feelings as all women do. I tried to break the sexual mold you'd imprisoned yourself in, the mold of stasis that turned you, without your knowledge, into a passive entity, like a beautiful statue that refuses to move. I didn't want an act that had the rhythm of my desire or your desire but a shared rhythm of two bodies equal in freedom.

You came to me without a voice and when you got one, for the first time, your resistance to having it showed. It was more like meows muffled behind your pursed lips that you made sure remained closed. Once, I saw the strangest sight when I opened my eyes at a moment of ecstasy. I found your mouth closed on the sounds that were struggling to come out, while your whole body had opened itself to me.

I told you hundreds of times that I'd like to hear you scream. There came a moment when you said as you were drifting in and out of consciousness, "I am afraid others will hear my screams." Fear is still living strongly inside you. I don't know who said "There is no ecstasy without exultation."

Let all your inner strengths wrestle so they can appear as they are, and forget the outside world totally. You are naked in the arms of your lover. What brings others into our bed?

If You Were an Illusion

Nahid thought to herself, "I don't know why when you are away from me, even a few meters, I feel the whole story never happened. I begin to miss you as soon as I turn and move in the opposite direction, alone. If a night passes, then another night, apprehensions relentlessly assail me and when your voice comes to me over the telephone, I miss you even more and my certainty that you, Omar, are the same man who sums up for me the meaning of life, is shaken. My longing for you takes away the certainty that the two of us actually exist."

Omar said aloud, "At 3:00 a.m., when I am alone except for the thought of you, when the distance between me and the world grows clearer, I feel my need for you, my desire to say just one sentence—'I love you,'—or to hold you without saying anything, or telling you all the things that fill my head and my heart, I look around and I find you only in my imagination. I can't call you or get in the car and kidnap you forever. And I ask if you, Nahid, are an illusion. I discover in a short while, that that is the only correct word for this love, whose greatness we both know. I delude myself that you are mine so I can maintain equilibrium in my life. I delude myself that you will be mine in the future and forever, as we both want, so I can bear reality and mull over the days. We dream because we do not accept reality and because we don't change it. We content ourselves with the illusion—what a sweet word, because it means that you actually exist and that I love you and that you actually love me and that one day you will cover the distance to settle in my arms forever."

"Oh my God, you are so near and yet I miss you even though you live in my blood."

"Nahid, please, let's get out of this trap. Life is wide open to us. Have no fear. I'll stand by you. If only you knew what we are missing out on!"

Containing

"You are the container, Nahid."

"How can I be the container and the contained at the same time, when I love my weakness towards you, and adore your containing me so much that I get so small I almost disappear, then dissolve in your orbit closed around me?"

"How can you hide inside me when I am the one who gets inside you? You hold me so tightly, lighting sparks of transformation in me, so I almost don't feel that part of me has gone through your protective shield.

I lose consciousness of our separate existence in an ever changing present, incapable of dealing with wakefulness. When I am inside you, you encircle me and you become the inner and outer container. I exchange with you awareness of our organs so much so that I don't recognize my own. The game so blends the parts that I don't see them. I enter your weakness meekly and I feel it as I've never felt it with a woman before. I see you internally declaring your need for my protection and I rejoice even more when I see how modestly you present your great independence from others. You change orbits and revolve around me rather than around yourself. You come close and delete the 't' in 'there' to become 'here.' I bury my head and I feel the milk pouring into my mouth from my mother's breast. Your fire guides me to union and you become the container and the contained all at once."

Mask

I am afraid to get used to wearing this false mask. This schizophrenia has interfered with my way of thinking; I now invent details to replace the real details; I can no longer tell truth from lies, reality and deception. I will get used to this way of life; it will not only apply to my relationship with Maggie. One day it will apply to my relationship with you and to my whole life. Which mask should I put on now? Don't make the exception the rule, for this is dangerous. I won't tell you what price I pay when I come in with a false face, speak with a false tongue. Falsehood has crept all over me and is choking me. I am torn between the masks. I don't see the use of this illusion and this masquerade.

The Revealing Mirror of Love

I looked closely at the fine lines of your face which radiate a beautiful serenity, which reminded me of the works of great painters whose portraits we love but we are not sure why. I discovered that your face is beautiful, at this moment, because it reflects what lies deep down inside you and conveys your feelings, not those of the moment but the real, clear, deep inner feelings. I've read the cells jumping around under your skin, revealing the splendid feelings you are having now. My gaze is fixed on this soft quiver in your eyes, which without words, gives me the meaning.

Does a moment like this come to other people or is it just ours alone? I wish I could capture it forever. I remember your words to me when you see me after a moment of ecstasy, "I am almost certain that not a single creature has seen you as I am seeing you now, Nahid." I close my eyes in a coquettish smile and open them to a happiness that is a mixture of serenity and explosion, a serenity that envelopes a fire that does not eat it up but preserves it. Yes. It's impossible that a creature had ever seen me like that before, because I was never like that with anyone other than you and I will never be, because at this moment I realize what it means to change and to be renewed, to be completely re-created. We are not the same persons at another moment because each moment has its parameters and because a few moments ago, I had not captured this particular moment. Suddenly I remembered 'love's blind mirror' and discovered that whoever said it never knew love, because the mirror of love reveals the inside that is impossible for others to see.

Trap

"I didn't realize what was happening. I entered a state of anticipation impelled by my uncertainty about predicting your next move. Something unfamiliar alerted my senses, and even my mind, which I usually keep out of our lovemaking, felt it had a role to play in this game from which it used to be barred. I felt you several times getting ready, armed with a burning rush. I imagined that you were about to reach your climax, but you hadn't given the signal yet. Then you slowed down the tempo and took your time and the moment kept extending, then once again you were in such a rush that I was almost certain that it was the climax, but then you softened and I went back to a slower rhythm."

"Today I let you get caught in a snare that I set up for you out of my long experience with you, when you want me again. I realized that your desire often exceeded your energy. I began observing it patiently trying to figure out its structure. After some time, I was able to take hold of the helm; every time you got greedy, I varied the tempo to suit your ability to continue. Today I noticed your high level of energy and hardness. My desire increased and I was overcome by wanting you even more, so, whenever I got close to my climax, I indulged in the hope of getting possibly a longer-lasting pleasure. I began to spin the threads of desire and lose myself in its tempo until a net was formed, and then I undid the spinning to start with you anew."

"Are you the same woman to whom I extended my arm one day to adjust the folds of the sleeve, who couldn't extend her hand and kept smiling shyly as she turned her face to hide her confusion?"

"I still feel that same shyness and savor the beauty of the moment: longing to touch you but unable to. What a beautiful moment that was!"

Fictional Autobiography

In your new novel, where fiction overlaps with autobiography, I began looking for what I was able to change in your sternness. I found that I didn't get very far. I saw that you were still committed to a condition of primitive wildness which has never left you since you were a child, stifled by numerous siblings, or a boy running to the fields, or a young man independent from the family.

I began to look for the causes of that condition: is it a desire to live life on an instinctual level? A reflection of the pain you suffered in your life? Or did the one who gave you life trample on you so the two of you could survive? In the autobiography, your father, whom I have never seen, used to gather his strength whenever he came home from the desert in his monthly journey to spend four days with you, which was all the time he could stay away from the oil drill. And once at home, he could spread terror so you would remember that he existed and behave. Then he would get into bed to give you yet another sibling. He was not like the Moroccan novelist Muhammad Shukri's father who tried to stop his young child's crying, so he cut off his head. That frightened Muhammad forever and he lived in the streets. But your father left a thorn feeding off a wound I see deep down in you, which appears to me when I am unaware of it. I almost wonder, am I really safe with you? It appears like a hot tattoo so fresh I can smell the flesh and hair burning, as if you are a thoroughbred on a rampage. I believe I can prevent the pain from that tattoo from reaching your heart, that pricking which stirs in you the lust to rage relentlessly against whomever, even yourself. I imagine I am capable to treat that and when I believe it, I see the arrow piercing my arm. I cry in silence or scream in the wilderness: *I am not coming back to you*, knowing that I will come back even before my tears are dry.

Gypsy

One day when I returned home at midnight, we had had a fight before I left, and I found her sleeping in Sharif's room. My room was like a war zone, as if the Tatars had been through it. My clothes were strewn all over the floor and my papers covered the bed. I looked at the anger written all over her face and I asked myself, "How can anyone burden their sleep with fighting and rage?" It was then that I realized she was not the gypsy woman that I had looked for and about whom I learned from the writing of Pushkin, who said that when a gypsy woman loves, her love is free of the constraints of place and laws. Love becomes the Law. When she loves a stranger, she takes him to her tent and he becomes her man, but after a while he finds her in the arms of another man, whereupon he reverts to his city roots and kills her. The Old Man teaches him the lesson: he did not learn anything all the time that he spent among them. He clung to the city's idea of possession, not to the idea of freedom itself, which constitutes the law for the gypsy man and woman. Thus, I found the gypsy wagons smashed, their fires out, and beautiful Zemfira's body parts strewn about, and I gathered up everything and wept.

Single Role

I looked at the movement of his hand, which he rested on the back of the chair, with the two eyes that grew in the back of my head and transmitted their feelings to my body which felt a calm comfort, like that of a mother patting the cheek of a baby sleeping at her bosom, even though his fingers hadn't touched me. Our laughter rang out in the place and a cloud passed overhead that removed layers of gray fog in my chest. He didn't come very near, just near enough for me to catch a ray of his warmth, covered with the awareness of one who knew that he had something precious that he feared might be scratched. I didn't move away and I didn't get close; I stayed on the edge between the two desires, happy and content except for a small craving that his palm would reach out and glide lightly over my hair. I carried my desire and went home. I put him in a dream that came on its own in which he played a single role—he hugged me and left.

Features

I get tired of driving the car at rush hour in Cairo. Nahid and I travel through the city from north to south. I get exhausted from constantly pressing the clutch, sweating with my shirt clinging to me. I remember our oasis to which we hasten joyously. Today we noticed some young trees scattered in front of the buildings, as our presence attracted a few scattered residents. And whenever a new resident moved in, we saw the appearance of balcony railings changed. Lights were on in various places in 'the project building,' as we called it. Our building was dubbed 'the journalist's building,' another 'the doctor's' and a third one 'the grocer's.' Thus, the neighborhood acquired features that became more pronounced over time but very slowly. One day we found workers putting up a sign for a café and we wondered, who would come here to sit at the café? Then we discovered that it served the drivers of the huge trucks that went through the highway in the back. We saw huge trucks with trailers whose owners or drivers lived in some of the apartments, some of which were leased as furnished rental units for the first time. I didn't like the developments in the area, which was well on its way to acquiring the incongruous mix of an outcast's features. Poverty was not its only trait, but escape from society also. Weren't Nahid and I one such example?

Fact

Nahid said, "I want you as you are, the whole truth, no matter what the price."

Omar replied, "The truth is painful. You might imagine that knowledge is more important than pain, but you are not ready for that."

"I don't accept that others share something with you without me. I don't want to deal with a picture in my imagination, but with reality, which I love without falsehood."

"Listen then: there is another woman in my life. I don't love her, she is nothing to me."

"Since when?"

"Three months. She invited me to dinner at her house. I was lonely and confused and you were away. I confess I enjoyed being with her and she with me. But I thought about what being with her meant and I knew that our relationship was in danger and that it wouldn't have happened if our relationship had not been going through a crisis."

"You are one half of the relationship, so why didn't you try to save it?"

"I didn't know we had a crisis until I found myself with her and I realized what I had not been aware of."

"Why didn't you tell me at the time?"

"I feared for you. I thought I could get over it, then talk to you. Then I traveled and decided to stay there and start working for a London newspaper. And before the conference was over, I got tired and bored. I couldn't stay. I came back because I want you."

She didn't know how the conversation went, nor where the little fires burning her skin at that moment came from. She shooed them away with a calmness that did not fit the event and painted a smile that soon faded away from her face. His words turned and moved in a different direction that she saw on his face before he said another word. He suddenly looked like someone who had fallen into a trap even though she hadn't said anything.

She heard him describing his fear for their love and she took note of things that seemed strange to her: he feared the consequences of what happened in our story, he feared that our relationship might collapse because of a passing moment which would not have taken place at ordinary times.

"Why do you imagine that our relationship is so fragile? Of course it will endure in the face of all risks it is exposed to. I am your friend. Who would you confide in then?" she asked.

"I cannot separate my friend from my lover. I do not see the line between the two women who would trade places in no time at all. One moment you won't be able to bear it."

"If your lover broke down, your friend will embrace you. Have no fear; we'll get over the crisis."

Three days passed. They meet without mentioning the forbidden subject. They have short, quick dates during which each treats the other gently as if it were the last time they will see each other. He showers her with warmth and she showers him with affection then they part, each looking at the other with pleading eyes, begging for hope in tomorrow's meeting. She mulls over the minutes and takes her time, no sleep and nothing much to do except trying to reconstruct what happened over the past three months. She sees him in her embrace asking if she is tired of his advances. She imagines Salma Abed in his arms and she burns. She staunchly refuses to cry when in fact she wants to scream. She plunges into the sea of the moments they spent together and recalls them drop by drop: "He goes through a crisis about which he complains and moves away sadly. I stay patient until the problem is solved. I protect him from knowing about my problems so that I can meet him smiling and calm, and he runs away to another woman."

He immerses himself in his work to run away from his thoughts. Unsure of her reaction, he wants her to feel secure by any means and he pursues her by phone everywhere she goes, telling her the details of his day without her asking him. He receives telephone calls from Salma and notices the amount of empty chatter that he hadn't noticed before. Time kills him. He stays away from Maggie, determining the distance between them, and is comfortable with the silence which prevents her from starting quarrels. He stays in front of the computer until the morning and gets into bed when Sharif's alarm clock goes off. As he begins to doze off he hears Maggie's instructions to Sharif before he goes to school.

The explosion came on the fourth day after she had stayed up all night telling herself, "He tells me 'I love you' and says that Salma was not a sudden desire for a woman, but the result of the collapse of our relationship. How?"

She asked him, shaking, "Do you feel lukewarm towards me?"

He dodged the question, looking at her like a child who wanted to run away from his mother at that moment, but later come back to find out that she had forgotten what he had done. But at that moment, Nahid was the lover, not the friend or the mother. She was prepared to understand his lust and his weakness for a lonely beautiful woman who desired him. But she was not ready for him to blame what happened on their relationship.

"You have an evil strain in you that I close my eyes to and often forget, but it surprises me despite myself , in its depth and virulence."

"You wanted me as I am."

"How cruel! How did your heart go along? How could you? Didn't you remember me at the time?"

"If I remembered you, it wouldn't have happened. It was a moment between a woman and a man alone. This won't happen again. We will preserve our love and forget what happened."

He ran his fingers through her hair as his hand pulled her head to his chest. She melted the moment her lips touched his shoulder. She began to hallucinate as thoughts swirled around in her head haunting her with the image of him embracing Salma. She felt lost and small in a world that was too big for her to cope with.

"If your love is dwindling, tell me now and I'll be able to take it. But I will not be able to live with you and see it dying. Tell me that your feelings for me are no longer what they used to be and I will leave without remonstrance, but don't let me tend its death."

He hugged her hard, their words overlapped and intertwined without either one of them waiting for the other. Each was talking to himself.

Omar whispered, "Don't ever say that. Our responsibility is to recapture and keep what we have.

"It's not the beginning of the end."

"No, it's the crossroad, we either go together or love will be lost. Hold on to me, please; don't leave me. I need you now more than any other time in the past."

"I love you but I want to understand, just understand: how can you love me and run away from me? How were you able to embrace her?"

"Sex for men is not the same as sex for women. I told you that and we've discussed it together many times."

"It is the same. I still say it is the same; the differences depend on the individual."

"I have known women and dealt with them without loving them, just for pleasure. But you can do that only for one man. Believe me. It's a passing matter and will not affect us. I am over it and I know that you will be over it too."

On going their separate ways as she crossed the isthmus to her other world, she asked herself, "Why don't I hate him? Is my love for him a sickness?"

Moment

She said, "The moment was not ours."

He looked at her with that penetrating gaze that controls his reactions so they won't show against his will. She felt apprehensive about what that gaze, as it looked for meaning, hid. She contemplated him and contemplated her own tranquility and wondered about that splendid thing called Time and how it created a neutral climate and cooled down a raging fire.

"How?" he asked.

She said, "Yesterday, when we were together, despite our passion and burning desire, she stood between you and me, between your lips and mine. A question came to my mind: was he giving her of himself what he is giving me now? You made yourself available to her; what's the difference then? I recoiled and my body writhed in pain and I shook and you thought it was the throes of desire, so you held me and we played two separate tunes that, by chance, came from outside, from the same rhythm. Did you say the same words to her? One question followed another. Did you also bring her to my bed?"

"If she had come we wouldn't have finished what we were doing. The presence of the other woman breaks my union with you. How were you able to finish what we started when, as you said, there were three of us?"

"You haven't answered my question. Don't play with words."

"I don't remember what I said to her. It was a fleeting moment."

"I know you and I know your dictionary and how you excite your woman to express what she feels inside. Yesterday, while we were together I contemplated for the first time what we say in our moment. I discovered that I express different feelings with just one sentence and that my dictionary is very tiny and limited. A touch may arouse me and release in my cells an uncontrollable energy and I tell you, 'I am going crazy.' After that comes a different kind of craziness, of feelings that cause me to lose my balance and put me in a place of indeterminate features and again I say to you, 'I am going crazy,' even though it is not the same kind of craziness. It's another meaning that the language somehow manipulates. So you must have talked to her as you talk to me."

"I have never been with another woman the way I've been with you. You tell me 'I've never known myself except with you.' Maybe it's lack of experience and not knowing anyone else but Mustafa. But I've known various women, some casual, but I've also tasted the love that you haven't before with another. And with all these experiences, I haven't known what I've known with you. Even in a direct, natural meeting, there is a difference between a moment motivated by desire. I may have dealt with professionals, I don't mean prostitutes, but experts in dealing with the body and capable of taking it to peaks of ecstasy, but it's just an act, a mere glow that disappears totally the moment it is over. With you, we love what we do and what we convey to one another because it comes from a depth that cannot be replicated anywhere else. This is what I'd like you to know. Close this page forever, fold it by sheer will so we can live our love like before. Ignore the fleeting and hang on to the true and the permanent."

She felt the bitterness that his calm words gave a sugar coating to but couldn't quite conceal. She wished he would reach out and embrace her and make her forget all that had taken place, but he didn't move. She thought to herself, "All this experience in life and knowledge of the female, and yet I discover at a moment of weakness that he won't use the magician's trick that will enable him to kill my despair. Just embrace me. Oh my God, there is a huge gap between the man and understanding his woman that he doesn't even want to enter!"

She said, "I feel I have been robbed. She did not share you with me only when you entered her. She is sharing my being with you now, she is sharing our most private moments."

He said, "I'll tell you something I may not have told you before when we started out many years ago. Many questions came to mind about your relationship to Mustafa: how could you touch him, talk to him, react to his body's attempts to engage you? But I didn't bring these questions to our bed. I thought of them alone, when you were not with me and I gave my imagination free rein to try to know more about you. When I asked you, you answered very grudgingly and with difficulty and pain. At that time I didn't understand the reasons, and with time, some scant details which had enabled me to form a picture of your life before us fell off. Believe me, I banished them decisively and willfully because left there, they would have grown and torn us apart."

"Ever since I've known you, I have appreciated your human under-standing. It's one of the reasons I love you. Your understanding of my pre-vious feelings didn't give me pause or fear. I was sure we would get over them quietly as I appreciated your way of thinking and assessment of mat-ters. You also know that I made a similar effort to know everything about you before we met and I listened to you for many nights telling me what happened to you, about your women, about Maggie, and your love for her. I pestered you with a persistent question out of fear: how can love end up where the two of you have ended up? I imagined, before I met you, that a relationship based on cohabiting alone would break down. I was not dis-turbed, even for a moment, by what you had given to another woman before me. But the difference between the two experiences is huge. You have taken a step outward, to another woman, and said that *our* relation-ship was the cause. So what did you feel towards her? And what brought you back to me? I want to reassure myself about the psychological mean-ing, the true texture of words that you use to express love now, because love is not one being and feelings are never the same. Where, then, would I run away from the words you told me throughout the three months that you knew Salma and which had the meaning of absolute love? How can they have the same meaning? And how am I supposed to take them now? How do I free their real meaning from the mold into which they are cast?"

"Nahid, why torment yourself? These attempts at understanding might lead to a catastrophe. Many questions have no answers. I don't know the answer."

"You said you were bored, feeling lonely when I was busy with my doctorate, but you were continuing our relationship and you were at your best. You didn't feel like a stranger; you felt whole. So why did you go out, things being the way they were, to have sex? And why did you come back?"

"I didn't leave to come back. The problem is, you don't know what 'casual' means in a man's life. It wasn't three months but a fleeting whim. A time spent entirely in curiosity and conversation. My love for you didn't suffer, didn't change. I contemplated what happened and I rejected it and decided to stay away from her and not repeat what happened."

"My problem is, I need the complete picture to make sense of it. I cannot understand something full of holes. What do you mean you contemplated what happened? And how did you see me when you stayed away? And what did you see that made you resume what was? How do you form your real feelings?"

The doorbell rang loudly. The doorman brought the groceries so she took them to the kitchen and began to prepare the meal. The time was appropriate for the questions to fly away into distant space and leave her. He came and held her by the waist and kissed her on the head, accompanying her to the table. They both forgot what they had been arguing about only a few minutes earlier.

Pain

She came armed to the teeth with costume jewelry and loud colors, with heavy coats of makeup to cover the arrows of time with a skilled hand, chewing gum with obvious lust. She attracted the attention of those gathering at the headquarters of the Historical Society for Antiquities with her Spanish peasant outfit—a wide skirt with ruffles twisting under several layers of fabric, a white sleeveless blouse and a scarf with long tassels that she fixed over her hair, leaving her locks dangling. Perhaps it was the body movement that alerted everyone. She swung her hips between the tables then headed directly for Nahid, who received her with the usual welcome.

Salma said, "I was on an inspection trip, hard but very necessary. You know how antiquities need to be guarded and how neglected they are."

Nahid contemplated her: could she be telling me that she was on a trip with my lover? She followed the lines of pain that time has furrowed in her face. She saw black blotches creeping on her neck. The coats of paint are deceptive; they can cover the bitterness of wounds and defeat, but they can't cover lies. She tried to find out all she wanted to understand but repressed her desire with a tranquility whose source she didn't know.

"Take care of your health, Salma."

She made a half turn while still standing between the tables saying in a loud voice not meant for Nahid alone, "Don't you see the change? Am I not better off?"

Nahid smiled as she nodded and thought to herself, "You promise yourself a love story with Omar when you are certain of our relationship. What a wondrous thing self-deception is!" The conversation turned to men after a man present commented on Salma's outfit, that she wanted to do in all Egyptian men.

"Men are like Kleenex tissues. They are used only once."

Everyone laughed and Nahid managed a smile that tried very hard to conceal her bitterness. She followed with her eyes the banter between Salma and those at the different tables in the garden, saying to herself, "How dare you say that? And why did you approach Omar? Was it the desire to steal a man from a woman he loved and who loved him? Or was it an attempt to boost your ego, by proving that you can get the man whose love for me everyone's talking about?"

The voices got louder but Nahid was not able to make out what was being said exactly. She fixed her gaze on Salma's eyes which gleamed with many meanings, suggesting an anxiety that reminded Nahid of the desolateness of a forest, fear of danger, and the indifference of the slaughtered for the death they're heading toward and the life they're leaving.

Nahid continued observing her and thought, "Are we playing the game of knowing together? You know about me that which I don't even imagine, just as I know about you what you can't imagine I know about you. Did he tell you our story? How did he describe me? And how did he depict the end of our relationship? For it is inconceivable to try to put on a new outfit without first discarding the old one. Did he tell you that the old outfit was worn out and no longer fit him? But you undoubtedly don't imagine that I know the minutiae of your story with him; how you got ready for him, what you said to him, how your fingers touched his body. What have we done to ourselves? Was I crazy when I demanded the whole truth from him, so I could torment myself, or do I deserve punishment for loving him?"

A mutual colleague arrived and Salma started talking to him, then asked him in a loud and clear voice, "Do you know who is responsible for leaking information about the introduction of equipment that is undesirable for security reasons into equipment imported for the protection of archaeological sites? If you know who that is, I'd like to reach him anyway I can."

He answered evasively as he pulled the edge of her scarf to undo it as she fidgeted seductively under the movement of his fingers, "Why?"

She frowned as she tried to gather her hair which had come cascading down over her shoulders and she hit him hard on the shoulder, "I just want it. If you don't give me the name a thousand others will."

"Who do you want it for?"

Salma adamantly refused to name the person who'd made the request. He kept shifting his glances between her and Nahid. He knew of her close relationship with Omar, with whom he always disagreed, and an intelligent question showed on his face: could Omar be behind this request, and therefore Nahid pressed Salma to get the information? Nahid looked at the man's angry eyes, but she was really preoccupied with Salma's request which had come to her as a shock. Omar had mentioned to her the desire to obtain some clues to information he had gathered for a scoop about a company that exploited its orders for imported products to saturate the market with equipment used by terrorists. He had spent the night with her thinking about how to follow some leads that he had. "So, he's still in touch with her even though he has sworn that he had broken up with her for good. So, she knows the details of his life to the minute." She was torn between what was happening in front of her and responding to the concerns of those sitting with her about the changes she was experiencing, as blood rose to her face which turned into a ball of fire, despite all her attempts to control her agitation. Salma accompanied the man outside, agreeing with him about a way to contact him to get the information. Nahid fled the place after two minutes, the longest she could stand it.

She went out to a street crowded with people and cars. She held back her tears with an iron will. In her chest there was a huge being that wanted to scream, but her only desire was to open her mouth to let that being out without a sound to the wind, to God, to the universe, to people.

She remembered two moments of pain, one of which she saw with friends and the other with him. The first one was part of a performance of *The Persians* by a Greek company which she had attended in Spain—ballerinas dancing and writhing in pain in silent screams, lamenting the defeat of the Persians. The picture etched itself on her mind for years of admiration; how was the director able to express that tragic sense in silence using a black stage and black costumes except for a faint light that showed the faces of the actresses filled with grief? The other moment of pain that left quite an impression on her she had seen with him only a few days earlier in the movie *The English Patient* as the hero carried his beloved, whom he had left wounded in a cave, and she had died before help could arrive. He was screaming on the mountain without a sound, and bitter hesitation reached her. Omar was sitting next to her the morning after he had told her of the Salma Abed escapade. "What made us sit together in front of a movie screen showing a splendid love story when we knew that we have enjoyed even greater love? Which of us felt the pain of death, the heroine or I?"

People avoided Nahid as she walked totally oblivious to their presence, be it burdensome or warm and friendly. "Did he realize how much pain I'd suffer? Was his pleasure worth what I am paying now? Love, lust, it doesn't matter. Curiosity for knowledge followed by a single moment of weakness. No, sir, don't delude me with what my mind will not accept from now on. The two of you had a prior agreement to mislead me, a deliberate one. And that I'll never forgive. Only a few days ago you asked me to cling to love when you were still in touch with her. When I ask you how the relationship with her will end, you say, 'We don't discuss the future of the relationship, so it doesn't have a future. It's a mere casual meeting between two persons, nothing more. It will end as it began.' I ask you, 'How do you know that that is how she looks at the matter?' and you say, 'Because she never asks me.' I accuse you of naïveté and now I discover how naïve *I* am."

The summer evening, lit with loud neon signs on the storefronts downtown, made room for an unexpected breeze. It reminded her of standing in front of the mirror for an unusually long time to choose an elegant outfit as she got ready to go to the Historical Society for Antiquities to see different friends and to lose herself in their midst, to escape her pain, hiding behind elegant but simple clothes in hopes of gaining psychological balance.

She was followed on the street by a young man, at least five years younger than she, deceived by her neat appearance. She didn't notice him for quite a long distance, even when she stood in front of the store windows not seeing the wares they displayed, just trying to open her mouth so that the fiery being wreaking havoc in her chest would get out freely. She caught a glimpse of him as she turned to cross a narrow alley, trying to prevent her tears from pouring down out of fear of attracting the attention of passersby. Then she noticed that he waited for her until she was done looking at a store window. When she stood in front of a sparse display he came close to her and whispered, "An admirer."

She raised her head and saw him, the first image she actually registered since she left the Society. Then she averted her eyes and kept walking, aware of his footsteps behind her. He came so close to her that his shoulder almost touched her shoulder as she tirelessly stared at the store windows. She wanted to ask him his name and imagined a dialogue between the two of them.

"What if I told you that I've just been slaughtered, that my pain is beyond anyone's imagination? What if I told you that now I am going through absolutely the most difficult moments in my life? And that, as I live at the summit of love, having my highest feelings, when he tells me, 'I've never loved like this, I've never known a woman like you,' he uses another woman to kill me.

"What if I asked you: can a man in love have a relationship with another woman? And how can a whim come at the peak of love? How does he go back, emotionally, to his woman or meet her and touch her? How do squeals of delight leave his lips? Does he see me now as a fat, old woman? Is he bored with me? Has the story ended in this dreary manner?

"I want to tell you, the stranger trailing me in the street, how tired and miserable I am." He came closer and asked, "Are you a student at Ayn Shams University?"

She turned to him in an imploring tone that she had never used before, "Please, leave me alone."

She said it almost begging him to speak to her about anything so she could tell him of her pain. But he saw her frightened, imploring eyes and backed away saying, "Sorry, I didn't mean to . . . ." He then turned back walking fast, running away until he was lost in the crowds as she repeated to herself, "What did he see in my face?"

She arrived at her house by intuition and the familiar route. She didn't know how she got in. She cast a cursory glance at her desk by force of habit and saw a small scrap of paper on her desk. On it was an unfamiliar telephone number and a message to please call Omar at that number. She contemplated the piece of paper, re-reading it several times to absorb what happened. "Omar doesn't leave messages at home except in real emergencies." She gathered her wits without being able to banish Salma, the Kleenex men, the betrayal, and Omar's making light of her feelings. She dialed the number in bitter sarcasm. His voice came over the telephone, tired and sad; it stung her. She shooed away the sudden wakefulness that found its way to her tired heart and her half absent mind, "Where are you?"

"In Kafr al-Zayyat. My brother was injured in an accident."

"I hope everything will be okay, God willing. I met Salma Abed today at the Historical Society for Antiquities."

"His condition is critical."

She sensed the gravity in his voice, "Is he in the hospital?"

"Intensive care."

"Do you need me to come? Do you have enough money?"

"In the morning his condition will become clearer. But the doctor is not optimistic. He bled a lot."

She forcibly prevented herself from running out to the street to take the first car to him.

He put down the telephone not believing what he heard her say, "I tell her my brother was injured in an accident and she tells me, 'I met Salma Abed'? My God!"

He was choked with grief, not the absurdity that he thought at the beginning, a profound grief like that of those bereaved in southern Egypt where he was from. "If I had said what I said to a friend, any friend, his feelings would have been different. It's unbelievable that anyone could be closer to me than her, but this moment—I can't believe it!" he thought.

The morning revealed the loss. Omar took his brother's body in his car to their village Ahnasia, near Beni Suef. Nahid learned the news from the hospital early in the morning and headed for the village right away. She noticed the villagers gathering on both sides of the road waiting for the arrival of the body and scrutinizing the cars. She drove slowly out of respect for the sad gathering. She shuddered as she saw the women marching in their coarse galabiyas. She got out of the car at the entrance of the house and met his family, not believing that she was there where

Omar was born and grew up. She met his mother at the moment that a message came from Omar asking the mother to have his brother buried without bringing him into the house. The mother ordered the bearer of the message to move the body to the house before crossing to his grave on the other bank.

She said, "He will not leave the house, never to come back. That's impossible."

Nahid tried to understand the meaning of it as she admired the strength of the mother. The messenger came back with Omar as the car stopped in the street. He kissed her hand and begged her to let him stop the car in front of the door of the house so she could say her farewell to her son and to let his brother who was already shrouded go to the peace of his death.

She accepted. He patted her on the shoulder and kissed her hand and she kissed his forehead. He gave a signal to the driver to go up to the door of the house and the mother went to the car leaning on Omar's arm to see her son for the last time. The widow collapsed and the car sped away to where the men were as screams filled the air. Nahid had not seen grief like this. Omar cloaked himself with a silence stronger than death. When he came back from the burial she gave her condolences and returned to Cairo counting the minutes until his arrival. When Sharif told her that he had gone out and wouldn't return until the evening, she almost lost her mind.

Omar locked himself up in his room, refusing to speak to anyone, giving instructions to his family to tell his friends that he was away for three days. Whenever he heard that Nahid called, he had doubts that he could communicate with her. He got bored, thinking about the absurdity of life. He sadly remembered happy days with his brother, recalling his picture as a child, as a lad, and as a boisterous life-loving youth who fell in love and announced to the world he would marry his sweetheart. He felt an overwhelming desire to hug him but held nothingness in his arms and was devastated. Sharif comes in to tell him that Nahid and a group of colleagues would like to visit. He shakes his head and wonders, "Can't I be left alone with my grief without anything else? Can Nahid comprehend that?"

Rebellion

She was perturbed by a logical question, "What are you going to do?"

She asked about him for days after she gave up on waiting for him. Every time Sharif said that he had left early in the morning and wouldn't return before evening. She was assailed by doubts: why didn't he send me a simple signal or call me from anywhere? Where can he be? Did Salma summon him to relieve his pain and he found her company an escape from what happened and from my questions which tormented him? Why are you deceiving yourself? If your pain really tormented him, he wouldn't have done what he did. He is selfish and doesn't realize what others offer him. If an idea took control of him, he would carry it out right away regardless of consequences. That's what first attracted me to him—his impetuous independence, his rashness. For what is the use of a sharp straight line that is alienated from life and breaks sooner or later or is forced to bend? How, then, do you love this impetuosity of his, but lose your mind if he tries it on you? This is not a contradiction because I see him as a rebel against true love. It's a dangerous moment. It means that inside, you don't accept rebellion against constants, which is the opposite of the traits you claim to love about him.

She began to address him in anguish, then picked up pen and paper and wrote him a letter that she never sent:

I confess that I had decided to live with you as I hadn't lived before, to be my real me and not the one I used to present to others bound by lines that imposed a distance separating me from them. Nakedness is what used to frighten me about love; it is what prevented me from getting involved in a story in which I would be wounded, because I realized quite consciously that I could not achieve total union with an other except naked, nerves and the inside exposed, with open memory, willing to concede my old constraints so that each of us would flow into and meld with the other. It wasn't a totally romantic idea, even though it was untried, perhaps because of the long time I spent reflecting on my psyche or per-

haps because of an old wound that I had thought totally gone, but which surfaced the moment I discovered your deception of me.

When I look at others around me, especially creative people whom I know personally, or those I know through their creative works, and sense them burning between what they want and what they can have, I realize that their moment is made up of moments and that the escaping glow that comes from the other does not negate the original. Perhaps I thought that our needs were too big for just one love to fill our being, that we needed tributaries to feed it. But I could never do that, not out of rejection of it, but out of my knowledge of my passionate love for absolute melding. Therefore, the others pass by when I am with you; they bring superficial happiness, perhaps just a smile insufficient to put my feelings on fire. I am happy to lose myself in loving you. I am satisfied and full with you; I see you coursing through my cells, pushing me to savor the fullness of life. When rebuke rears its head in the midst of the flood of happiness and despair of changing our strange situation stings me, I push it aside, saying, "Life hasn't offered me what it has by coincidence or at random; I must pay the price, no matter how exorbitant, because it is the price of my very existence because I saw existence in you." And, on the other hand, I saw the pleasure of being close to another man to be a pale pleasure.

Even before we met, some men passed by me. Some were special, but they didn't scratch the outside of the heart, despite my loneliness. There was the pleasure of discovering the other, a free moment that ended as we turned to go our separate ways. You've often asked me, "Why didn't you let yourself go for a complete experience?" And you never liked my answer. I kept myself back from the dazzling passerby who never possessed me and I remained alone. Even that daze disappeared the moment we met. Do you remember? What pushed us, each on his own, to that certainty that the other would play a major role in our life the very first moment we were introduced to each other? Why were we so certain that it was not a casual encounter, no mere whim? For me, it was the long wait, the loneliness, and the hope that came exactly on *time. You were bored, frustrated, with confused desires, wasting your time in the company of those willing to stay up with you until dawn. Now, you want to flee to another continent. So we've come back full circle.*

A train going to southern Egypt at the height of heat, starting the journey of a group of archaeologists, journalists, and public figures, each of us promising ourselves some time away from the atmosphere of Cairo, which is filled with petty problems and besieged by aborted desires. There was a little hubbub among the intellectuals and their comments on the treasure of Dush that they would see in a few hours, on the expansive desert that every day uncovered something new and dazzling. Chatter was everywhere in the car, taming the rough ride; there were even some lively songs. When we came close to one another by chance, I didn't let go of the thread which extended, looking for your pictures in casual encounters before you started covering archaeological conferences. I remember your love of Alexander the Great and a book signed by you about something not in your area of expertise. And I asked myself is he the same man? I had only read some of your stories in magazines. When I was sure that something had started between us, I introduced myself in such a way that would allow continued dialogue.

I waited for you, knowing that you were torn between the desire to change your life and revolving in the orbit of a wandering star that pushed you to the clamor of night life and staying up aimlessly until dawn. I didn't hesitate long and there rose in me the certainty that you were mine. Now, after all these years, we go back to the start. A woman flashes something that dazzles your eyes and whether this attraction is real or a mere whim, it has dashed my hopes and scattered the tranquility that I thought I had.

He found her in front of him at the newspaper. The moment their eyes caught a glimpse of each other they knew how much they needed one another. They ran away to Maadi, disrobed without a word, and became furiously intertwined. Then they subsided next to each other in a calm that enveloped the intimate room, in the isolated place in their forgotten world. He said, "Yesterday I was thinking of calling you and I asked myself if I could touch you and drown myself in you. I found myself answering quickly—impossible. Because once I began, I wouldn't be able to continue. But from the first moment you touched me, a volcano erupted inside me, wanting you, reminding me only of my desire for you, of being mad about you. So, this fantastic thing happened."

"After I went to your village and after I met her, I knew that I couldn't touch you before asking you if you really loved me. The answer would have determined whether I could or couldn't. When I saw you and the family, I was ready to throw myself at you, for it was impossible that you could have discarded me from your life so easily. The part of me that remained in your life was enough for me to compensate you at your hour of grief for all that was hostile to us, and to meld with you and return you to life no matter how hard the road to you. I did not remember her or see my wound. On the contrary, I saw you tired and alone, I saw you as part of me and I didn't see the distance that the events had created. I saw you as I used to: pure love, real and sincere madness, and a knowledge of the inner energy that united us, and which I know at this very moment that we have used up only a very minute part of, and the rest is too huge to even comprehend. I remember, every time we reached a new peak in love, how we came out surprised like two naïve happy kids, not believing what happened. We'd ask, 'Is there something else new that we don't know about? What is this love?' And we found out that our love had peaks and whenever we ascended one peak, it opened another one to ascend. So I was not surprised by my awareness that we have energy that will overcome all difficulties."

"Energy?"

"Yes."

"It makes sense."

Dejection (Nahid)

I am bored. I don't want you. That's a conclusion I never imagined I'd reach. I feel I have wasted something precious. I let myself bleed as I tried to have you back. I staggered between the stab I received, which pushed me to hide in a shell of grief, and my love for you on the one hand and your betrayal and the loss of your brother on the other hand.

As if life refuses to give me the right to grieve, or to be aware of grief, I sip it slowly and even keep its texture forever. It didn't give me a chance to reflect on the moment of betrayal slowly. It deemed that to be too much to give me. Your brother's accident made me push aside the Salma Abed affair to assuage your shock. I didn't want to forgive then, nor was it possible at a time when questions were still digging a bleeding course, and the contradictions in the story creeping in to remove my ability to regain control of myself. I ran to you, begging you that we forget what happened and to know how much I loved and wanted you. My moment turned from drowning in the knowledge of what happened to us, to the madness of pacifying you and being kind to you and restoring comfort and tranquility to you.

I didn't realize at the time, that on my way to you I would lose myself, that the deeper I went in retrieving the profoundly beautiful moments that we had lived in the past so we could recall them together and relive the feelings anew, the more I missed them. I chased what was left for me of that love story and caught it with the skill of a hunter, and discovered that they were just butterflies whose condition for living was liberty. They died the moment I held them in my hand. If only I had left them for their time!

How could I know that when I tried to recharge the moment with the heat of old times, I was depleting their energy. I talked and talked until love glowed and you forgot your pains, and forgot the moments that happened to us, as I watched you half-conscious and half-slaughtered. The distance of consciousness between me and you was the knife that tore through me. It meant that we were not living the moment, just putting it on like a clever actor who wore the costume of the part he played and was through with it the moment the last word in the dialogue was uttered, and then eagerly went back to his own self. He removed from his shoulders a heavy burden, washing it away with a cold shower, with a few maniacal laughs with the first passerby, and he staggered as he drove his car between himself and the character. He listened to some music and stopped briefly in front of the Nile to contemplate the expansive horizon until he felt that he has shed the character, and then he went back to his sweetheart.

But I couldn't shed it. Our old intimate times made me cry when we recalled them together, made me feel how much I'd lost. I ask myself as I contemplate your comfortable sleeping face after you pull out of me, "Have I really regained him?" And for a few moments, I feel that I have you back and I silently cry my joy and my anguish together. I discover, after a little while, that you belong to me only at those moments, because when you wake up, without knowing it, you mention something casual and contradictory that releases the genie that I try my best to return to its bottle, and it wreaks havoc in my chest. I ask you cautiously, begging God for support and you for understanding, "Just one question with a yes or no answer can restore my balance. But the problem is, can you answer this moment?"

You looked at me with sad apprehensive eyes. You expect me to broach the subject of Salma. I see that and I get confused because I am totally absorbed in you and I don't want a third person and you are fed up with bringing up the forbidden topic.

"Do you love me?"

"Yes."

"Are you capable of realizing the meaning of this answer of yours? You might be telling the truth at this moment but I want an eternal answer."

"Nothing is eternal."

"I know, I mean a conscious and profound answer that nothing can change at least in the foreseeable future."

You look at me silently and sadly. You get self-absorbed as I await the answer, which I know is exceedingly difficult. Your hand reaches for your cigar and you draw in its coarse smoke. The moments get longer as I get lost. You are wearing nothing, stretched out on the carpet moving one leg on top of the other. In a fleeting moment, I see your toes stretching nervously and calmly at the same time, I mean slowly nervous. I don't know. I almost scream at you as I wait.

You keep drawing in the cigar smoke and you say, coldly, "Yes, I am able to pinpoint that now. Listen, we have a long, profound relationship that we built together with patience and other things that you know and for which we paid exorbitant prices. And like all long relationships it passes through crises. This is one such crisis. Do you remember when I decided to go to Brazil and accept a temporary transfer?"

"You were going through a crisis at work and one with Maggie. I agreed to your going there, despite my fear of your being away, so you could rest."

"Well, actually, I was not concerned about my relationship with you. The crisis passed and after that we lived some of the most beautiful years of our life and realized how much we loved each other. This is a similar crisis. Please make it a thing of the past and calmly close the door behind it. And don't mention Salma again."

"I want to know the moment you left her. Are you really mine now? Or what? Where are you?"

"With you."

"If I have the certainty, I will ferociously defend this love even against myself which refuses to accept what happened. I will force it for the sake of the authentic and the permanent, no matter what the price might be."

"It will happen that I will get bored and lose sight of the facts and tell you I don't want you. But bear with me, because after a little while I'll go back to my old self, but you would have believed the words about boredom and left."

Contrary to my expectation, his words hit me like a blow from an iceberg. I discovered the enormity of the iceberg's body hiding under the surface and realized the depths inside him, and my pain. He is asking me explicitly to accept what he does and to wait for him quietly. He doesn't care for the relationship, and I pat him; he goes to another woman and I don't have the right to suffer even behind his back. If I depart from this scenario he gets fed up and turns his face away wondering why I move away. Who are you?

I didn't say a thing. All my cells were asking, "Do you really know him?"

An endless stretch that had no form or color loomed and told me as it was about to fly in the sky of the room: ride me and I will take you away from here and forever. Without moving or answering, I saw him moving away. The distance between us grew longer. I froze not out of fright but out of desire.

Masks

He wrote in his novel *A Maze*:

From the couch in the psychiatrist's office she said to her, "I suffer from a double life: I cannot separate from my husband and I can't do without the man I love and am committed to. I suffer from a foolish jealousy towards my lover who loves women and considers all the women on earth his property, if he can. Whenever I think of a decision that would guide the boat of my life to his safe haven, I fear for my two children and the stability I have in my life now, even though it is a cold stability that gives me nothing, but rather pushes me to find someone else. I know that the future with the other man is not totally guaranteed, that it will end sooner or later under the wheels of another woman. At other times, I say to myself, 'What is guaranteed in life?' And I can't find the answer. I am torn between the two worlds and I can't choose."

She leaves the office after long, bitter weeping, agreeing to come back soon for another session. She feels a mysterious relief. After several sessions she sits in the waiting room, anxious. She thinks to herself, "There's something evil about this doctor that I grow more certain of after every session. Sometimes she meets me in a sympathetic mood and easily understands my words. I feel this mood of hers whenever I am tired and want to talk about the split in my life between the two men. She asks me in a friendly way, 'Why don't you try to regain the husband you are so protective of and take such good care of?'

"I cry and tell her that I fear for his feelings, that I don't hate him but that he does not fulfill me in any way. The man doesn't necessarily have to be bad for the marriage to fail. Isn't the lack of fulfillment enough? I give her many details and she is sympathetic and kind. But when she gets out of this mood, during which we are like the ends of a stretched rope, I see her eyes looking for the lover I told her about and she sets herself up as a moral arbiter. And when I stay away from her for some time, her nerves almost reveal the enormous suffering she experiences from attempting to repress her question about him: do I still love him very much?

"I don't know why a desire to probe *her* private life grew within me. I wanted, one time, to ask her to consider me her friend and to tell me about herself, especially because I found out by chance that she had marital problems, which made me understand why she was interested in me, and why sometimes she was responsive and sympathetic and at other times, she just gave in to the desire to take me to task for what I had succeeded in getting, I mean love, despite the double life with all its bitterness.

I told her, 'I know, Doctor, that my crisis does not stem from looking for the roots of the problem within me, but my knowledge of my true feelings toward those around me and toward what I actually do and the route I have taken playing with masks. These masks were transparent at the beginning, shielding me a little from the world for protection, then they got stronger as time went by on the same pretext. Then they became solid and dark. Sometimes I believe them more than I believe myself, which has turned into layers upon layers of frames, so much so that I no longer recognize my original face or live life without masks.'

"One day I surprised her with some questions and her answers were evasive: 'To what extent can we wear masks and live life as we want to? How can one stay in touch with oneself behind the mask? Is it the truth that I don't feel afraid, or is it that I practically die of fear but only wear the mask of courage? Will my husband kill me one day?'"

Decline (Nahid)

Yesterday's meeting created a great confusion in my mind. My questions gathered but I didn't get a sufficient answer. I was choked inside a firmly closed cocoon. He lay down next to me and entered me as I was drowning in questions. His thrusts were not able to free me from the hell of mental alertness. We began to play the natural game of love, each of us aware that the other was half with him and half against him. But our bodies, used to erupting together, trained to probe the secrets of the senses, began to play a tune that sounded distant and then came closer and gradually lost its crudity until it achieved perfect harmony. We came out wet and imbued with incomplete rest.

"It's as if I haven't touched you for a year or longer," he said.

"I still miss you," I said.

We both knew we were lying. He was choked with my questions and I was burning for knowledge as I saw my trust in him and security with him fleeing. I wanted to ask him as he was kissing me, "Do you see what we have lost?" but I couldn't. The warmth of his restfulness and the preliminaries of his sleep, which began mirthful and laughing until he actually fell fast asleep, were enough to make us forget all the pain in the world. We were coming out of the same moment, loaded down with something heavier than cheerfulness. On the road, I tried to escape from the words that were besieging my mind, but to no avail.

I no longer feel the love that was. My questions no longer had the same meaning as we clung to each other: "Do you love me?"—"I adore you."

The questions were no longer playful but doubting. "Happy?"—"In seventh heaven."

Happiness was no longer happiness but something else. I contemplate your feelings and in my head your words to me mix with your words to her a few hours later. Peace of mind is gone forever. I awoke to another feeling which was neither love nor hate, neither despair nor life, but rather an abyss at the edge of which I stood, the bottom beckoning me to fall down. You can push me to my death and you can save me. You come close and you tell me that you truly love me. I believe you right away, until you take one step away from my body, or fall asleep, or turn to look at the road, and my mind breaks down everything we said and scatters it in my face guffawing like the devil. What have you done to us?

"You talk about your desire to know me as I am. You take joy in an author who related all his whims and escapades in his autobiography, and when I tell what happened truthfully, your anger erupts like a volcano," Omar said.

Nahid said, "You fall silent and I drown in pain. As if you are waiting for me to bless your betrayal. The distance between us widens not because you told me the truth as it was, but because I didn't feel sincerity in your words. I am still waiting for what you are hiding. You, as you told me in a moment of weakness, don't know what you want and that you'd end your life if I left you and ended our relationship. When you say that, I rush to the precipice; I cry and I rave about what was and what will be; I protect you with a fence of my love and I swear that I will have you back and not let you get away. In the morning, I discover that you're still in touch with her."

O God, who created us in this way, are there still other prices to be paid? Isn't all the pain I paid all my life enough? Is tormenting humans part of the law of the universe, an element in the golden construction game the day the world was born? Who enjoys it? And why did you let us lick the wounds which erupt every day with new life?

Reasons (Nahid)

I am driven by a desire to end this relationship and to consider what happened the last thing we have together. After the revolt came the calm. I told him about it on the phone, describing it as the calm of despair or the calm of realizing failure.

I didn't ask myself about the next moment. I felt a strange kind of freedom: the day is long and all the hours are mine. For the first time since I've known him, the time belongs to me without thinking where he is now, what he is doing, and whether he will call me.

I planned to enjoy the time as I liked. I went to work and sat longer than usual with my female co-workers. We used to meet on this day every week. I used to run as I finished routine procedures for the schedule of the week. I answered requests then usually ran away before anybody caught up with me. Today, I enjoyed sitting at a table with the girls around me, laughing and asking me to spend more time with them. On the way home I discovered something strange: I haven't known girls, I mean women, at all. I haven't lived, like all women, in the company of my peers; I didn't know the little secrets and I didn't get close to any woman's body. Omar imagines that my experience with men is a simple one, but he doesn't know that my knowledge of women is similar. My discovery today of that specificity among them encouraged me to realize this beautiful sensation of staying together, without men, relaxed and acting naturally, aware of the absence of peering eyes and calculations. I had strongly resented gatherings of women only because they reminded me of mandatory segregation which I totally rejected. I smiled when I remembered a woman friend who tried to tickle my belly one time and how I escaped, laughing, and how all the girls lay on the floor laughing mirthfully while I was too shy to reach out my hand or to touch them for fear of infringing on their privacy.

A few days later, I was lying down in his arms, having actually forgotten what the quarrel had been about, telling him eloquently why I loved him and no one else. We agreed that each of us would tell the other ten reasons for this choice, on condition that they not be reasons that we had mentioned together earlier. We discovered as we talked, that our reasons, which we enjoyed relating, go back to a phase before we really knew each other, before we declared our love and before each of us had come to know the other profoundly. This put us in a merry mood as we had to know the reasons for continuing this love and why we arouse each other's desire so much.

I said, "I loved your flexible outlook on the world, your ability to understand, that marvelous thing that made you gloss over human foibles and small details, to go directly to the profound and the authentic. I realized that from the first moment. Therefore I didn't need you to give me a complete explanation of anything. Your signals reached me right away, and with time, I became more certain that my assessment was correct."

Omar replied, "Your ability to grasp what I want and your attempts to adapt to what I've offered you, even though it was unfamiliar to your life in the past. You didn't make your previous experience a burden on our life. You picked up all I wanted and responded to it. True, admittedly, I dreamt of a wilder woman to go along with my madness but you, at least, didn't object to my wildness and went along with it."

"Inside me there is a wildness whose extent you haven't discovered. Perhaps it hasn't yet had a chance to erupt. We are at its threshold now, for I had to rein it in, in the past, in order to live in an atmosphere that would have trampled me if it had found out the real me. I kept it for you to explode."

"There's a big gap between theory and behavior, and I am afraid you haven't been able to bridge it."

"These are layers that I put on for protection. I don't need them anymore."

"I feel free as I deal with your body, completely free to do, to feel, and to express. I realize, for the first time, the meaning of a woman's movements, because she is my woman. I also understand her voice, which arouses my manhood, even though I heard similar expressions in different experiences with women, but they didn't have the same effect on me. I love you in your moment of madness when you are different and uncalculating."

"I've never been calculating."

"Do I dare to say that I made you as I imagined what my woman should be like, that I formed you just as I liked?"

"Yes, I came to you a virgin and you exploded in me all that I had desired before without knowing what it was. My responsiveness with you is the peak of our melding without domineering. To the contrary, it is complementary. I loved your being different from all those I knew."

"You are mine by love alone. The connection between the body and love was never achieved by any of the other women I have known, and none would accept it because it would limit their freedom. But you truly desired it."

"There's a gentleness and sensitivity about you that only those who have come profoundly close to you can perceive. That surprises me, despite your gruff features and attitudes. Are you aware of it?"

"I know that you've found it out because you've come closer to me than anyone else. Therefore, I love your understanding me with the least words and without a need to explain."

"I like the clarity with which you deal with life. You know exactly what you want. I might not like some of the things you do, I might have differences of opinion with you, but I respect the fact that you don't do anything unless you are thoroughly convinced of it. I love what you write; I contemplate every word, every character, the softness sometimes, the roughness at other times. I look for the secret of the splendid art mixed with you. I do not view it as separate from you. Your love is what made me myself for the first time."

"It's you who wanted to reconcile with yourself. You gave it the opportunity for fulfillment."

"I couldn't have found fulfillment without you. You restored me to my original instinctive nature, to my real desires."

"I love your softness, there are no sharp edges about you. Sometimes that makes me mad, but it doesn't take me long to appreciate it again."

"Our physical compatibility restored in me the desire to live, to enjoy."

"You are full of that desire, even without me. And perhaps that was one of the reasons I first noticed you."

"I like your persistence in staying with me, even though you are prone to boredom."

"Your patience and forbearance, your waiting for me, the room you give me; thousands of little details that I list but which are endless. Wait, I love your work also."

Landmines (Omar)

The circumstances of her job, which begins at 6:30 in the morning, force Nahid to stay close to the dig sites to facilitate matters and supervise the work, then stay with the team at the guest house in the evening to discuss what has been accomplished and prepare for the following day's work. That time, in most cases, is the time we meet. She ends her evening meeting quickly then comes to our house in Maadi. When a discovery is made though, excitement, joy, and desire take over and she follows every development closely, for at such times the inspector shoulders the major responsibilities. I love her devotion to her work even though it sometimes takes her away from me. But Nahid is Nahid, with her preoccupations, her mummies, her great kings, and the mysteries of the ancestors, as she takes delight in relating.

I am too busy for her these days. I've been following the U.N. task force on landmines which has come to Egypt on a fact finding mission. They are here to meet with inhabitants of regions where landmines had been deployed since World War II to try to come up with suggestions for a solution to this problem. There are landmines all over the Western

Desert, an area extending more than five hundred kilometers, in addition to the whole of Sinai and around the Suez Canal—approximately twenty-two million landmines. That means that Egypt alone has more than one fifth of all the landmines deployed in the whole world. Thousands of Egyptians have already lost their lives or limbs in accidents, not to speak of the thousands upon thousands of acres that are lost to agriculture or grazing.

The problem is not just the presence of the landmines but the absence of clear and precise maps of the landmine locations that have shifted with time and natural phenomena. Some locations still have warning arrows that the British forces had placed, but in many places there are no warnings at all.

Many conferences are being held in various parts of the world, some of which are calling for reparations to countries harmed by other countries deploying landmines on their soil, but to no avail. It all depends, of course, on the ability of injured countries to demand their rights. It's enough to mention the reparations that Israel got because of the crimes the Nazis committed against the Jews.

I attended two conferences in Ottawa in 1996 and 1997 on banning the production and use of antipersonnel landmines. Members who attended the second conference approved the resolutions banning the production, use, storage, and transportation of landmines. They represented a hundred and two countries.

The Egyptian delegation did not sign that resolution. The major mine producing countries also did not sign. As a result, the efforts of the international community to help in the locating of landmines by sending search teams to small countries including Afghanistan, Cambodia, Vietnam, Mozambique, Senegal, and Yemen among others, were stalled. As for why Egypt didn't sign the treaty, the reasons were quite logical and very important: Israel is not a party to the Nuclear Non-Proliferation Treaty, has refused to sign it, and refuses inspections. The second reason is that the Middle East problem is one of the hot spots in the world and landmines represent one of the cheap solutions to protect Egypt's extensive borders with Israel, which fights all its neighboring countries.

As for the reasons the major powers, the USA and Russia, have not signed the treaty, it is because they are producers of landmines and they themselves use them in various parts of the world. The USA, for instance, cannot dismantle the landmines it deployed between South and North Korea to protect its military deployed there, as they are in various parts of the world. Thirty-seven countries have not yet signed the treaty.

I went to Mersa Matruh with the UN mission headed by Mary Fowler and I remembered the Canadian, Mrs. Forster, who chaired the Ottawa conference in 1996 and was bossy and very biased against Egypt during her one-sided visit, as opposed to Mary Fowler, who met with the inhabitants and saw firsthand the suffering of the Bedouins in Mersa Matruh and Dabaa. She saw the impact of the explosions on victims' bodies. One of the researchers told us that the number of casualties amounted to ten percent of the population in the region and that they didn't receive any compensation from the countries that had maimed them for life. We experienced with them the state of terror that they lived through and we hoped we could solve the problem. But how, when we are facing this international injustice visited upon us by countries that created the problem in the first place?

I remembered an accident that I had followed around 1990 in Hurghada, which one morning was rocked by the explosion of a landmine that killed one child and maimed another for life. When an investigation began, it was discovered that a local teacher had learned how to handle landmines and explosives, trained the two children to enter minefields to obtain explosives, and then extracted dynamite from them to sell to fishermen and quarry operators. His greed resulted in tragedy for the two children.

I came back in a very bad psychological state.

I wrote my story for the paper and sent it by fax, then called Nahid and told her to cancel all her appointments and wait for me at our house. I didn't want to go to work or home for two days at least. I found her waiting for me. She took me in her arms and didn't talk much; she let me do the talking.

Then I suddenly remembered that, before arriving at our house, I had stopped at the newspaper to deliver some documents to a colleague and found Salma suddenly in front of me, walking flirtatiously up the stairs. Nahid laughed saying, "Of course flirtatiously."

"She's become so skinny and that glow that she used to radiate only two years ago has disappeared and is now replaced by an inner sadness that she is trying to hide with makeup, expensive clothes, and artificial merriment," I said.

"I found out that she's living with your friend, Husam. I hope she has found true love with him. Do you still remember her? Did she leave part of herself behind in you? I think you can answer me more freely now that years have passed since the end of that story," Nahid said.

"By talking to you I got rid of all traces of that relationship. I knew that as long as I didn't tell you, it would persist inside me, even though I had put a full stop to it some time earlier. It was easy to tell you, but I saw its effect on you with every sentence and every detail, which impacted my continuing. At the time, I resisted the desire to be brief, or to finish the whole story, no matter what consequences might ensue, as long as I had taken the first step. So I glossed over some details which at the time I figured you couldn't handle. But I told them to you later on—these were details of the sexual act itself. The question here is, why did I agree to tell you in the first place? I wanted to test you; I wanted to know how far my woman, who wanted the whole truth, would go and whether she could actually handle the whole truth.

"I know the schizophrenia among intellectuals: the dichotomy between the willful and declared on the one hand, and actual behavior on the other. There is a clear gap or obvious contradiction. I wanted to know more about you and see how you'd behave in the face of the difficult situation that I'd lay out before you: would knowledge, candor, and clarity be the supreme values or would you react in the conventional way?

"The result was a dual one: you took both stands: the emotional reaction dominated by personal pain had the upper hand sometimes, and at other times, knowledge did. They were not totally balanced but they were both present. I say that now because it is behind us. But at the time, my impression was different and your immediate reaction made me wonder if I had made a mistake in telling you. Of course the reaction did not come right away, nor was it over with quickly. It took some time and was interspersed with lack of confidence about some of the details related. There was also a bit of cross-examination on the facts and words describing some of the details and a search for contradictions or gaps or holding back information: 'Why do you say such and such when you said something else before?' The reactions took longer than I expected.

"That means that you were not convinced of getting over the crisis with me and the effects of that crisis on me, but thought of getting over it by yourself, or in other words, just pacifying me and totally eliminating my pain. What I asked of you was that we be our actual truth, that we get over the results of our mistakes together, bearing them together until the crisis has safely passed. Didn't you ever reconsider your attitude and visualize the situation had you been in my place?

"We've gotten over it with the least possible losses because the act had been over and the talk was about the past, not a present whose consequences you were suffering from."

"But you didn't tell me at the beginning that you had ended your relationship with her," Nahid said.

"I was ending what I considered moral debts, which is quite different from the continuation of the relationship itself. Moral debts can only be repaid at the end of the relationship. With you, there were no debts, material or moral, but with a woman with whom I have ended a relationship, there are debts that have to be repaid because she has become an other, a stranger. And as long as I have been telling you the story, the relationship has been over," I tried to explain.

"You mean on a psychological level, not an actual one, for your telephone contacts continued and I continued to have suspicions about the possibility of the two of you getting together, which by the way I never found out about," Nahid persisted.

"I never met her after my return from London. As for the second factor in getting over the crisis," I went on, "it was that you, even if you had cried and screamed or said nasty things during your reactions, you did that while in my arms, not from the outside. The future of the relationship would have changed if your reactions had erupted while you were away from me. More importantly, your outraged reaction did not take a long time, which would have prolonged the tension and made the situation unbearable; therefore, it was easy to overcome the crisis."

"I've asked you repeatedly to tell me about the warmth that you experience with a woman you care about and appreciate, the warmth that I believe you are totally entitled to enjoy, because life is not a fixed line, otherwise we would dry up and ossify. Talking in this case will spare us the risk of getting this warmth distorted, will enable us to see its true measure, a moment of happiness in connecting with another that we need when the world turns and gives us pain. Getting close to another, a stranger, might be a wiser cure, preventing the authentic spring with your lover from drying up. Talking in this case will deprive it of the illusory pleasure of theft, and the joy of sin, so it can be uncovered at once rather than taking it down to the dangerous dark depths. It makes me happy when you defend talking about the idea that you fought long and hard for. Talking means that our thoughts no longer belong to just one of us but that they are part of both of us, of the melding of us," Nahid said.

It was midnight. I let Nahid go without me, alone, to her house, in the hope that she would be back in the morning. When I saw her off, I truly felt like an orphan. I needed her warmth. When can I live a normal life, one that is not waiting for the landmine of chance to destroy it when we are found out? For even though Nahid has not been a wife for many years, at least to society she is still his wife.

Betrayal (Mustafa)

"If she is cheating on me, can I forgive her?" Mustafa wondered as he seethed with anger, his emotions taking him hither and yon—he wanted to stay alone in the house while his daughter stood at the door ready to go out with him, stylishly attired and preened. He looked at her for a long time. She is the young Nahid that he once loved, with her bubbling gaiety and her urgent requests that compel others to comply at once. He asked her to wait until he got ready and pondered how to answer the agonizing question, "I usually cannot forgive those who deliberately deceive me. I ignore them; I sometimes forget but I don't forgive. Today I became certain that there was a man in her life. I haven't pinpointed him yet, but I know that she is planning on divorce and on marrying another. Pure coincidence led to the discovery of the betrayal.

"She didn't tell me when she was coming back from Paris. She said, 'I'll call you when I confirm the reservation.' Then we suddenly found her at home after we returned at the end of the day. We became occupied with her many stories about the trip and Paris which she loves and the gifts she brought us. A few days later, I took her passport to buy a few things that Maha wanted from the duty free shop. She said, 'The two of you can go and I'll try to catch up with you.' I opened the passport and found the arrival stamp indicating that she had come back two days earlier than she had. I did my best to rearrange the events to correct the date in my memory, to no avail. The day she returned was unforgettable: it was our wedding anniversary, and I was wondering whether she would bother to come back and celebrate it with me. When I entered the house, having given up on her return, I found her waiting for me with a cake and we had a little party.

"I looked repeatedly at the date stamped on the passport but the result was the same: Nahid disappeared for two days in Egypt. Where was she? And why the secrecy when all her life she has been able to go anywhere with no need to ask for anyone's permission? A man. There is a man in her life.

"I couldn't fight my desire to cry, but I didn't shed a single tear. I want to run away from everything; from confronting her, from confronting myself and the questions. I refuse to see her and I refuse to stay away from her. I want to interrogate her and I want her to come to me on her own to tell me the truth and I want her to have a reasonable explanation for what she did. I don't want to believe that she's cheating on me, that she has another, secret life. Come, Nahid, get us out of this situation. I know that you won't lie when I ask you, but is it my right to ask you? Yes. I don't know.

"After years of separation we have turned into residents of a boarding house who share meals and sleep under the same roof, then each goes their separate ways, without obligations to the other. We have this secret divorce syndrome. It would have been best if we had parted company. But no, we haven't agreed to that, for she is still my wife and she has no right to sully my name. So it's a matter of name then? Yes, for the scandal, if there were to be one, wouldn't be hers alone; it would ruin me and the children. So, why does she put herself in such a situation? Is it now time for me to choose between continuing the relationship as it is now, with the possibility that there is another man in her life, and divorce, wrecking the home and creating eternal separation? And what would I tell the family, which looks upon us as the ideal couple of all time? How would I face my daughter's and my son's questions? Maha is about to get married, and Nahid has caved in to her choice of a partner, even though she hasn't finished school yet. All she could do was convince her to postpone the wedding until she got her college degree. Yusif has been admitted to the University of Alexandria and will leave home at the beginning of the school year. The house no longer has a family; we are at a crossroads and each of us is on the verge of entering a new world. So where am I in all of this?"

Silence (Nahid)

Silence before our bodies propel us to each other's embrace, only to be followed by more silence. I contemplated him as he sat there abstracted; the fire of longing had not cooled down, nor had my desire to squeeze him so tightly that I became part of him diminished, nor had my hunger to fight fiercely to go through all material barriers to occupy his interior as I wanted been shaken. I want to hear directly the sighs of his heart burning with love and smash all the restraints that he sometimes wears like a suit to protect against the uncovering of his inability to bear being away from me, so that *I* will express my longing for him. And yet, I restrained myself from throwing myself onto his chest, waiting for him to say a word but he hasn't said anything.

We began to go around in the orbit of time without either of us expressing their real desire for the other, for no reason. I was simmering madly on the point of screaming: "Why don't you admit that you need me?" And I refused to say it to him as I used to, since I noticed that he had taken a step backward that vexed me and raised all kinds of suspicion in me: Is he bored of me? I waited until our bodies pushed us to meld in such a way that all apprehensions were swept away only to find ourselves, once we subsided, again facing the silence. Whatever happened to us? Omar said, "I treat my frayed nerves with a medication that sets up a transparent wall between me and the world. It makes me lethargic. Do you understand now?"

"I've been screaming helplessly for days, repeating how much I need you, but you fall silent. Why have we entered this strange maze?" I asked.

"The accumulation of the effect of the double life we are leading, my mind on the alert all the time to remember which role to play at a given moment, with you or with her? My constant awareness of anything coming from me, even during sleep. I am afraid to pronounce your name or call it out at a time when I am not fully awake. I don't, unlike others, go through phases of my senses awakening; I am catapulted into sudden wakefulness. My nerves cannot take it anymore. I fear for myself when I see friends around me fall like the dry leaves of autumn. But autumn leaves fall on time, when their juices dry up gradually and their lives come to a timely end, while we wither all of a sudden without warning: Majda Hasanayn, Arwa Salih, Sanaa al-Masri are all gone now. I've come to fear what our insides hide from us. There are no manifestations showing what is happening, what is gnawing at us. I was in need of a tranquilizer after I saw the muscles of the left side of my face shake and the tips of my lips quiver before I spoke. The doctor had prescribed it for me some time ago and allowed me to refill it if I needed it," Omar explained.

"Let's go to a doctor. You are exhausted, you don't eat regularly, and you work hard day and night. You need rest before you think of tranquilizers. How many times did we arrange for a trip together that never happened?"

"Nahid, you are relishing this double life. I've told you several times that the exception cannot become the rule. So when will you make up your mind? When will you end the situation that has us living on the brink, with tense nerves all the time? How can you trust the future so easily?"

"I am not used to trusting it. I know I am just playing for time until my daughter's wedding. I know how complex things are for her and I want her to get her independence from a home that seems solid to her at least. I am not worried about the others, as you might think. She is all I have sacrificed for, so why don't I complete this sacrifice now that I am so close to doing my duty by her. Afraid? Yes, I am afraid. I don't deny it, perhaps because I realize how much my two children will suffer."

"They're no longer children."

"Perhaps I am content with what life has given us. That's quite possible. There's more to it than a mother wanting to do her duty. I am afraid of not being able to help you complete your project, at least now. I am supporting you without any direct obligations: you see me when you can take time off from your work. You come totally devoted to me, your desire your only reason for being with me, not interests or social form or even children. I don't understand how you can totally forget the problem that Sharif will face. I know you are capable of being decisive and you can stay apart from them and take care of them. But I am thinking in another way: you now, like all busy fathers, come at the end of the day to his son, who finds an excuse for his father's not spending more time with him, secure during the phase of growing up, even if that sense of security is false. I fear for Sharif just as I fear for my children. If society permits divorce for me so it can be official and does not recognize separation alone as an entitlement to see another man, the situation is not as complex for you. At least it makes it possible for you to take another wife."

"You know that it would be impossible for Maggie to accept my marriage to you and keep her as a wife, even if that were my legal right. You also know very well that she would not even consider a discussion of the matter. The divorce is supposed to take place before she knows of my commitment to you because it would be hurtful."

"I only meant to open up another possibility for you, to tell you that I accept it or, more precisely, I think a lot of a secret marriage that would keep alive the passion that we have now. I don't know if its public nature is the reason, but I, at least, know that habit will fade away, so you could keep all the pluses of this phase of our relationship and be rid of all its problems. Even though I believe that daily familiarity breeds another kind of love. Day and night I dream of love continuing the way I want."

"I now think that you are running away from confronting the situation with ideas that I sometimes feel are diabolical. We have spent years and years of our lives to reach a solution, to no avail."

Apartment

Peace and a joyous atmosphere reigned in the car carrying the family back from Alexandria. Laughter rang out as the car raced with the other cars in the caravan carrying the families that used to spend their summer vacation together. They sang more boisterously and gleefully than they had on their way to the summer resort. There they filled the cabins where separate rooms were designated for boys and girls. They stayed up all night and got nice tans and fully enjoyed the carefree life. Mustafa had such a feeling of rest and intimacy that he almost believed that he and Nahid were intimate friends rather than a married couple. He felt reconciled to their situation, despite his desire to fulfill his body's needs.

They opened the gate of the villa, took down the suitcases, not quite yet believing that they'd go back to their pre-vacation routines the following day. They agreed to maintain the spirit and gaiety of the vacation and spend as much time as possible together. The phone rang. Mustafa, who answered it, heard a voice saying, "This is Felicity Real Estate. I would like to tell you that Mrs. Nahid's request is now available and the landlords have agreed to her conditions."

"She's busy right now. Any more details you want me to tell her?"

"The apartment, sir, is quite a gem, the likes of which would not be easy to find. It's quite large and the price is reasonable; it overlooks a big garden and Mrs. Nahid herself inspected it, and we won't disagree about the changes she wanted made. The landlords are good people and they felt comfortable dealing with her and are willing to make any accommodations."

"She'll contact you right away, God willing. Bye."

For whom is the apartment? Is it for a friend? But he said she had gone and inspected it and asked for changes before buying it! Is she thinking of Yusif's marriage? But it's too early; he is only seventeen. Where did she get the money? Why hasn't she told me? Who are you, Nahid? Who is the woman who lives with me? Was the peace we enjoyed throughout the vacation a false one? Were we living an illusion?

I was right when I talked with the broker and didn't call for her. Should I tell her what I've found out? Or tell her to call him without any comment and await her reaction? Or just let her carry on without knowing that I've found out?

The threads are gathering now: departure without a return date; sleeping over at the guest house with the French mission all the time; trying to buy an apartment. So you're planning to leave. That will never happen. You're not going to get out of here that easily. You have deceived me so thoroughly all this time and let me maintain a defeated love to raise your children as you wanted. And now you're planning to innocently get out of it all and leave me suspecting the presence of another man in your life, without any clues. You're a devil. I have let a devil play games with me and that must never be.

Pursuit

I am pursued by journalists from respectable papers and others from scandal sheets. They know I work at night and they call at 3:00 a.m.

"Ustaz Omar, what do you think of the article in the newspaper *al-Sha'b* with the headline 'Who Will Make a Pledge for Death with Me?' and the incitement to kill authors? Are we turning into another Algeria that is killing its intellectuals and writers and everyone with an opposing point of view? How do you write in such an atmosphere? Will internal self-censorship, become stricter after incidents triggered by *A Banquet for Seaweed*? What do you think of al-Azhar's acting as a censor of literary works? And what's your opinion of Shaykh al-Azhar's articles on creativity published in *al-Ahram* newspaper? The rector of al-Azhar

University told the students that the novel was 'infidel' and asked them to stay calm, then disappeared. Did the rector, Dr. Ahmad Omar Hashim, contribute to inciting the demonstrations? Do you think that the State is involved in the *al-Sha'b* newspaper affair or was the issue of the *Banquet* author, Haydar Haydar, a convenient circumstance exploited by all sides: The Labor party to gain publicity before the election and proving its strength in the Egyptian street; the government to deal a blow to the Labor party which dared to play in dangerous zones? There's an opinion that says that the government will hit both sides: the Labor party by closing down its paper, and the intellectuals by tightening censorship. Do you know that the Supreme Council of Culture has changed the published program of its Cinema Club and cancelled the screening of some films that dealt with some topics with great freedom after the hubbub over the *Banquet*? What do you think of the news that the Government Publishing House has set up an outside vetting committee whose work begins after internal vetting committees have given their permission to publish? Did you also know that the Ministry of Culture is re-reading the creative works of specific writers that *it* has already published? What do you think of the suspension of *al-Sha'b* newspaper's publication? Why didn't the Journalists Union take a stricter stand vis-à-vis the transgressions of *al-Sha'b*, which explicitly called for killing some authors who are them-selves journalists and members of the union? Is the reason that the union has fallen in the hands of certain currents after the last elections? Why did the union renege on its offer to host the intellectuals' convention to discuss the issue? Do you know what is meant by 'the nation's constants' and who determines them? Cliques dominate literary and cultural life in Egypt now. What do you think? Is what's happening now a result of the corruption of cultural life?"

"There was an initiative to reprint the novel, but the author Haydar Haydar refused. The call for blood bore fruit at al-Azhar University: the people against the people. The season for profits began early after they turned religion into zealous anthems. The inciters are defeated politicians and limelight seekers and political parties without ideas. The report of the academic panel of the Ministry of Culture: '*A Banquet for Seaweed* is a work of resistance that supports religion. It is the author of the inciting article who's insulted the Quran and not the novel. Those with their own agendas deliberately ignored the responses of the other characters to that one character they considered crazy.' What Haydar Haydar has written has nothing to do with creative freedom. Begging your pardon, I disagree with you."

"What do you think of *al-Sha'b* newspaper's headlines: 'The Conspiracy Turns into a Scandal'; 'God is Great: al-Azhar Condemns the Infidel Novel and Those Who Published It'; 'Shaykh al-Azhar: The Novel Despises Religion and Is Blasphemous Against the Deity, the Messenger, the Holy Quran and Morality'; 'The Conspiracy to Strike Us Is Uncovered, The Police Support the Thugs'; 'Are you Going to Strike al-Azhar after the Labor Party? Are you Going to Strike the Whole Nation'; 'Shukri: I Will Go on a Hunger Strike If They Carry Out Their Threats Against the Party and the Paper'; 'Sayf al-Islam: The Labor Party Battle Is an Honorable Battle against Corruption, Zionists and Blasphemy'; 'State Security Bans Conference of Creative Writers and Intellectuals Called for by Labor Party'; 'A Campaign to Collect a Million Signatures: *Fellow citizens, express your anger with something stronger than irritation. Write to the president, ask him to punish those responsible for publishing books that are offensive to Islam and what we hold sacred. Don't forget to sign your letter and include your name, occupation, and, if you like, your telephone number.*'"

"Shaykh al-Azhar was asked, 'Are we watching the funeral of Egyptian culture?' And the Grand Shaykh said, 'The judiciary will settle the dispute between al-Azhar and the writers. The inciters must be punished.' Thugs and traffickers in religion are inflaming the coming elections. The farce continues. Poets are accused of being infidels and heretics. Is it a coincidence that the terrorist group Gama'a Islamiyya, which deems political parties and their members infidels, is denouncing the suspension of the Labor Party as a banquet for the People's Assembly elections?"

The questions and newspaper headlines besiege me as I am about to finish my novel, thinking that I had killed the internal censor and have written it exactly as I wanted to. I am besieged by an oppressive society in which I cannot be what I want to be: I cannot marry the woman I love, I cannot let my son be taken by a wife who might take him to her country never to become Egyptian again. Problems in the newspapers are besieging those that have talent. I look at the institutions and wonder at all the corruption—have the really qualified and efficient made it to the top at any organization? I smile as I look at the bill for the computer installment while reading about members of the People's Assembly who default on unsecured loans in millions and millions of pounds. I go back to the infernal circle of the corruption of cultural life in Egypt, the battles for travel opportunities and making life miserable for authors. I ask myself, "How can I publish such a novel in this atmosphere? Should I re-read it and delete anything that might arouse 'suspicions'?" I refuse to change and I refuse to write. I wander around aimlessly—I cannot even go on reading or meeting friends. Boredom is the champion of my day. I suffer imaginary diseases and events just follow in succession. I remember how Egypt used to absorb all fanatics in its civilization and reshape them and turn them into non-fanatic Egyptian citizens. I bet on the seven-thousand-year civilization and decide to publish the novel as is. Doubts sting me: will the publisher accept what I write now? I answer optimistically: even if I don't find a publisher in Egypt, I'll find one in Beirut or Morocco. It will stay in a drawer until it is published. I will not change my style, and give in to the dark.

The Truth (Omar)

I feel especially refreshed: this is a day that deserves celebrating. Nahid welcomes me with arms longing for embracing. She tells me,

"It's time, Omar. I need to rest. I am tired of this double life. I hide from you many of the pains I suffer with Mustafa. I am torn under the pressures of the balancing act. I find myself a stranger in the midst of my family and my lifelong friends. I no longer speak with them because I won't tell the truth and I am used to telling things straight. I've learned to be silent with them if we meet by chance. You know how my time is divided between the demands of the two lives I am leading now. Let's see how I should ask for divorce and try to figure out what problems we'll face until it happens. You think Mustafa will reject my request?"

I am at a loss what to say. I tell her, "You know him better than I do. If you insist on your request, you'll get it." I've never before felt the strength of her will as I see it today. She was calm, not happy, but not suffering as she was every time we broached the subject before. I knew she was thinking of her daughter and her son as children who needed care. We didn't talk about her daughter's wedding or her son settling down at college. She said optimistically, "It is time to think of Nahid's comfort! To be truthful with her, for she deserves it."

I was not boisterous despite the delight inside. It's a form of caution to which I've been accustomed all my life. I don't like to expect much from life and suffer when it doesn't happen. I leave a little room for the vicissitudes of time. I embraced her and kept hugging her for a long time without words. We needed silence and a deep understanding of our journey which has taken all these years and that we have taken at a slow pace, without either of us doing anything to obstruct the other's life or push him to act rashly. Maybe we've exhausted a not inconsiderable part of our lives and maybe I have been against the whole idea, but I couldn't just snatch her out of her world so easily. I'd fallen in love with a mother and I had to pay the price for our late meeting. She didn't know that I considered her words to be merely a wish or a dream, a hope, and that I left their actualization to fate. The ecstasy that I had brought to her was closer to good news.

I had decided to finish my novel in favor of truthfulness with self. I wrote a draft of the idea then left the house optimistically, even though, inside, I did not expect a great change in my life, for I have gotten used to its difficulty and trained myself to face new surprises. Nahid changed my ability to bear with Maggie by absorbing my anger. After I meet her, I come back with feelings of resentment washed away.

I opened the door. There was a faint light coming from my study. In the quiet I went in to put down my papers and begin the journey which I like to go on alone in the dark of the night, with myself, recalling my day. I had not yet come out of Nahid; her fragrance was still on my fingers and my body was oozing happiness. My eyes were struck seeing Maggie lying in a heap on a corner of the couch, under the little lamp. In front of her was a black package that I couldn't make sense of.

I was assailed by the smell of smoke as I uttered a greeting. Maggie smokes a lot these days. She didn't raise her head, which was between her knees. I got close to her and stroked her hair. She raised two blood-shot eyes to my face and an aging complexion furrowed with severe pain. I pressed the lamp button before asking her about the harrowing event written all over her face. I was shocked to see the notebook of the novel totally burned, nothing left except the spiral wire attached to the burned covers.

Modern Arabic Literature
from the American University in Cairo Press

Betool Khedairi *Absent*
Ibrahim al-Koni *Anubis*
Naguib Mahfouz *Adrift on the Nile* • *Akhenaten, Dweller in Truth*
Arabian Nights and Days • *Autumn Quail*
The Beggar • *The Beginning and the End* • *The Cairo Trilogy: Palace*
Walk, Palace of Desire, Sugar Street
Children of the Alley • *The Day the Leader Was Killed*
The Dreams • *Echoes of an Autobiography*
The Harafish • *The Journey of Ibn Fattouma* • *Khufu's Wisdom*
Life's Wisdom • *Midaq Alley* • *Miramar* • *Naguib Mahfouz at Sidi Gaber*
Respected Sir • *Rhadopis of Nubia*
The Search • *The Seventh Heaven* • *Thebes at War*
The Thief and the Dogs • *The Time and the Place*
Wedding Song • *Voices from the Other World*
Mohamed Makhzangi *Memories of a Meltdown*
Alia Mamdouh *Naphtalene* • *The Loved Ones*
Selim Matar *The Woman of the Flask*
Ibrahim al-Mazini *Ten Again and Other Stories*
Ahlam Mosteghanemi *Chaos of the Senses* • *Memory in the Flesh*
Buthaina Al Nasiri *Final Night*
Haggag Hassan Oddoul *Nights of Musk*
Abd al-Hakim Qasim *Rites of Assent*
Somaya Ramadan *Leaves of Narcissus*
Lenin El-Ramly *In Plain Arabic*
Ghada Samman *The Night of the First Billion*
Rafik Schami *Damascus Nights*
Khairy Shalaby *The Lodging House*
Miral al-Tahawy *The Tent* • *Blue Aubergine*
Bahaa Taher *Love in Exile*
Fuad al-Takarli *The Long Way Back*
Latifa al-Zayyat *The Open Door*